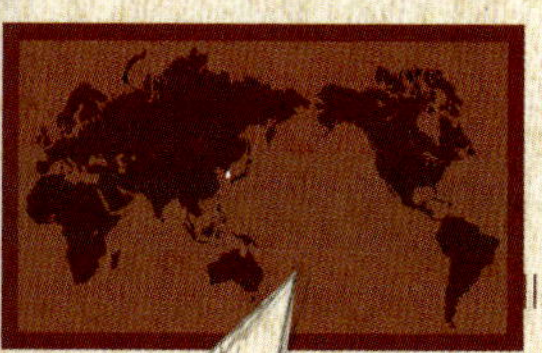

THE ORIGINAL CLASS DESIGNS OF OVERSEAS SERVERS

KOREA

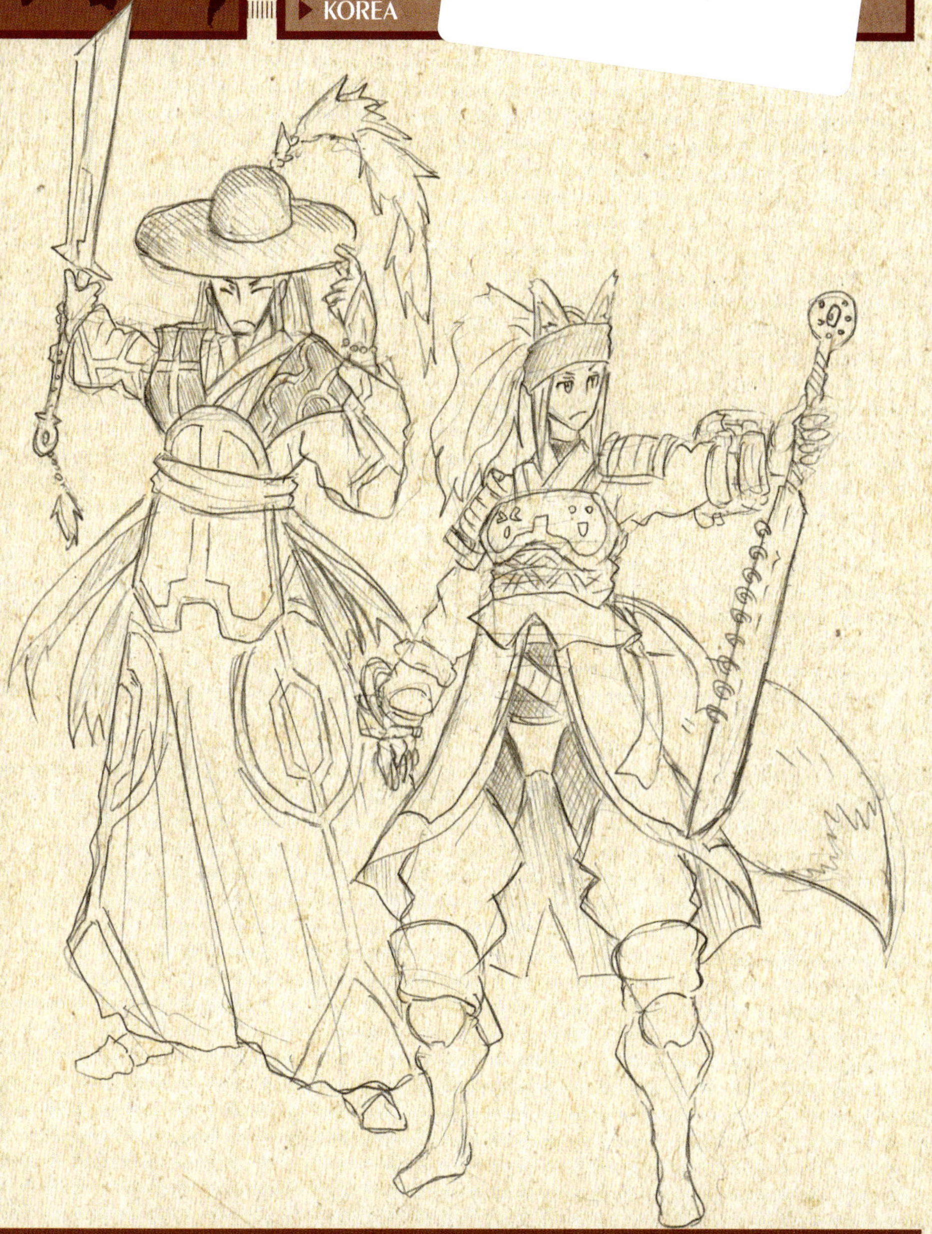

HWARANG

▼Comment from Mamare

This is the Warrior class for the Korean server. Ishihira has captured their coolness and a vaguely familiar nostalgia really clearly!

KOREA

TAOMANCER

【RACES】

♂ DWARF

♀ HALF ALV

▼Comment from Mamare

Since dwarfs are a short race, their silhouettes tend to all look about the same, so this is a great invention! Very cool!

THE ORIGINAL CLASS DESIGNS OF THE OVERSEAS SERVERS

CHINA

DAOSHI

[RACES]

♂ RITIAN

♀ FELINOID

▼Comment from Mamare

Their treasure items (the magic items they're holding) are swords, talismans, and incense burners, like something out of a Chinese fantasy story. Cute!

CHINA

YOUXIA

【RACES】
♂ ELF
♀ FELINOID

▼Comment from Mamare

The director made sure to keep the atmosphere of traditional martial arts and their practitioners. The tall wooden clogs were his idea, too. Members of this class are very gallant.

LOG HORIZON ANIME DIRECTOR

THE ORIGINAL CLASS DESIGNS OF THE OVERSEAS SERVERS

OVERSEAS SERVERS ORIGINAL CLASS DESIGNS

There are thirteen servers in *Elder Tales*. In response to a fervent appeal from Mamare Touno, the author of the books, director Shinji Ishihira of the *Log Horizon* anime has specially contributed concept sketches for the original classes on each server!!!

More details on page 234!

Director Ishihira says...

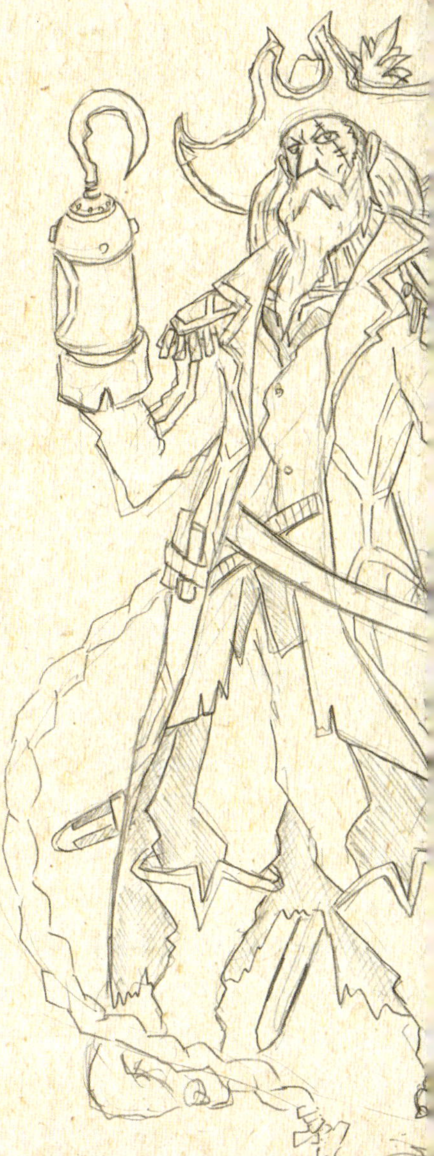

Not only do I get to be in the privileged position of anime director, but they're also putting my drawings in the original book! I'm deeply moved. These were meant to show the distinguishing characteristics of each server, and I got to draw from a perspective of things I'd want to see or play. My favorite is the medicine man! Actually, I'd like to put these in the anime someday, too...

PIRATE

[RACES]
♂ HUMAN
♀ WOLF-FANG

CAPOERISTA

[RACES]

♂ FELINOID

♀ HALF ALV

▼ Comment from Mamare

They're cheerful, they're dynamic, a
use that leg blade for amplifying ki

Adventurer, you whose weight is borne by your winged soul! The mystical world of Theldesia is home to dragons and giants, magical beasts, and demihumans. Fragrant green winds blow across this new yet ancient land that opens before you like a blank page. Fill it with your life.

LOG HORIZON

9 GO EAST, KANAMI!

MAMARE TOUNO ILLUSTRATION BY KAZUHIRO HARA

YEN ON
NEW YORK

CONTENTS

HAKUTAKU

A white horse that speaks human languages.

ELIAS

An Ancient who boasts peerless combat power. Having been born to a human and a member of the fairy race, he bears the deep sadness of being a "forbidden child." The most famous hero in *Elder Tales*.

KANAMI

Former leader of the Debauchery Tea Party. Has the spine to say what she feels without hesitation. She's also serious about and fully invested in everything and has a cheerful charisma that pulls in the people around her before they know what's happening.

COPPÉLIA

Unemotional and inexpressive with a modest, devoted personality. During battle, she uses shields in both hands and disposes of enemies pragmatically.

LEONARDO

An American from New York. He wears a costume based on a frog ninja from American comics, but although his outfit is bizarre, he's a skilled player who was high in the national rankings.

CHAPTER. 1

TRAVELING COMPANION

▶ NAME: LEONARDO

▶ LEVEL: 90

▶ RACE: HUMAN

▶ CLASS: ASSASSIN

▶ HP: 9601

▶ MP: 9451

▶ ITEM 1:

[NINJA TWIN FLAMES]

FANTASY-CLASS FLAME-ATTRIBUTE TWIN SWORDS WITH EXCELLENT ATTACK SPEED AND FORCE. THEY BEAR THE INSCRIPTION "NINJA TWIN FLAME" ON THEIR BLADES IN CHINESE CHARACTERS. TO GET THEM, YOU MUST FIND FIVE NINJA MASTERS WHO ARE LURKING ALL OVER THE COUNTRY AND DEFEAT THEM IN DUELS. IT TOOK HIM A YEAR.

▶ ITEM 2:

[HIDDEN TOAD]

A GREEN SUIT USED FOR DISGUISE. ITS DESIGN IS BASED ON A FROG. IT REDUCES THE INCREMENTAL INCREASE OF AGGRO AND BOOSTS MOVEMENT SPEED NEAR WATER. ITS PERFORMANCE, DEFENSE INCLUDED, ISN'T BAD, BUT—POSSIBLY BECAUSE IT'S EYE-CATCHINGLY BIZARRE—THERE AREN'T MANY PEOPLE WHO USE IT.

▶ ITEM 3:

[PIZZALION BOX]

AN ITEM CREATED ON THE NORTH AMERICAN SERVER IN COLLABORATION WITH LITTLE NINJA, A PIZZA CHAIN. IT'S A MAGIC BAG THAT LOOKS LIKE A TAKE-OUT PIZZA BOX. IT DOESN'T HOLD MUCH, BUT IT WAS A POPULAR ITEM THAT WAS SEEN ALL OVER TOWN DURING EVENTS LIKE SNOWFELL.

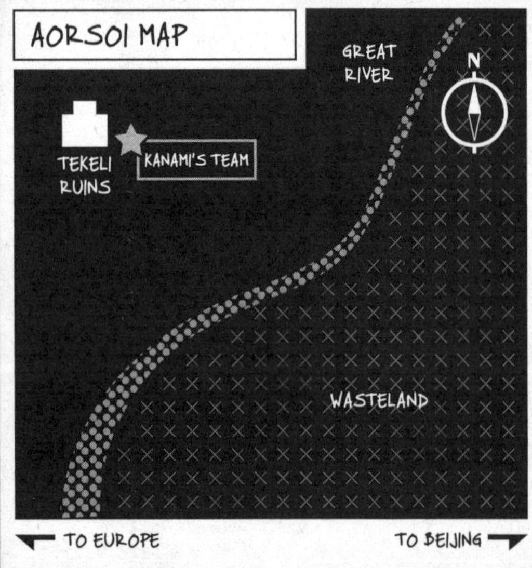
AORSOI MAP
GREAT RIVER
N
TEKELI RUINS
KANAMI'S TEAM
WASTELAND
TO EUROPE
TO BEIJING

▶1

The vast space was filled with the fragrance of greenery.

Calling it a botanic garden would only be natural. Although it was indoors, there were areas with exposed soil, now occupied by planted trees from southern countries. Sweet-smelling flowers bloomed riotously in pots, providing a brightly colored feast for the eyes. The air was hot and humid, making the place seem tropical—but truthfully, the space was a bathhouse.

Although the space was fifty meters square, its interior sight lines were cleverly obstructed by vegetation, making it look even larger than it was. At its center stood a warm-water bath made of marble. Judging by its size, *pool* seemed to be a more apt term for it, but this thing—which even had a sandy shore that resembled a gradual, shallow beach—was just another bath. White steam rose from the hot water within, and the vapor that left the water's surface filled the space with warmth.

A lovely girl with crimson hair was sitting on the marble edge.

The girl was lightly splashing the water around with her ankles as though she was taking a footbath. After a little while, seeming to tire of this, she twisted around, leaving the enormous bath behind her. Although the space was illuminated, the steam made the air vague and misty, and as she walked through it in her white dress, the girl was an unearthly sight. She was petite, and although there was arrogance in the way she walked, she exuded a kind of elegance. The most striking things about her were her pomegranate-colored hair and eyes, each with a translucent luster.

She strolled along as if she was used to this place, and after a long detour, she emerged in an area that mimicked a white, sandy beach. It was on the opposite side of the bath from the spot where she'd been warming her feet a moment before. Large trees that looked like palms grew there, and an elegant sun lounger had been set up in their shade. A large glass of tropical tea, garnished with a hibiscus flower and sweaty with condensation, sat on a little table beside it. It was a picture-perfect vacation scene.

With her chest still puffed up, the girl raised a slim, bare foot, then brought it down squarely on the young man who was lying stretched out on the deck chair. The movement was casual, but her toes burrowed right into the space between his ribs. The guy bounded up as if he were spring-loaded, then fell back gracelessly, yelling unintelligibly: "*Fook, oogk*, d'ouch!"

Mirthlessly, the girl twisted her toes two or three times, then flicked the youth's ridiculous eye mask out of place. He used them habitually in this conservatory, indulging his laziness.

"Owwww. That hurt, Gar-gar!"

"Don't yowl. Shut up."

"Did I do something? I didn't, did I?"

"You sleep far too much."

"I wasn't sleeping. I was working, using Soul Possession."

"You were sleeping."

"……"

"There, you see? You looked away."

Stretching out her slender fingers, the girl gently stroked the young man's T-shirt-clad side (right where she'd just dug her toes in) and broke a rib.

It made a light sound as it went, and it was the perfect thing to divert her mood.

The adorable sensation pleased the girl.

* * *

"*Gugh, agh.* Ow! Seriously, that hurts!!"

"Don't get flustered, boy."

Her companion was down on all fours, writhing in pain, and the girl took over his place in the comfortable sailcloth lounge chair.

"You do this every time, Gar-gar. Why are you like that?"

"No Adventurer worthy of the name should whinge so. Even young dragons are slightly more moderate in their remorse."

"I'm not whining, I'm protesting injustice. Yeesh."

With a brief gesture, the young man summoned a *kikimora* and had it cast a recovery spell upon his rib.

The Adventurer's name was KR.

A former member of the Debauchery Tea Party, he was now the lowest-ranked member of the Ten-Seat Council that governed Plant Hwyaden, currently the largest guild in Yamato. On the Council, whose reign was based out of Minami, he had the byname "Transforming Jester," and he was a master Summoner.

"You're as clever as usual."

"Don't underestimate Summoners."

Summoner was one of the magic attack classes. In the MMORPG *Elder Tales*, their main role was to inflict damage on targets using magic. Sorcerers, the leading magic attack class, personified that role: They were pure attackers who controlled enormous elemental energy and sowed death far and wide. As another magic attack class, Summoners could do similar things, but they were a bit of a hybrid class. So, while their attack skills were typically far below the experts', they were able to cleverly handle everything, including material attacks, defense, recovery, and support.

The *kikimora* the young man named KR had summoned was a magical beast, and it could chant recovery spells. Summoners were a highly adaptable class in part because they could "summon" a servant with abilities the caster didn't personally have.

"I'm neither underestimating you nor complimenting you," the young woman said.

"For a servant, you're pretty cold, Gar-gar."

"Treat me like a servant, and I'll bite you down to the bone next time."

"Maaan..."

KR, who'd regained his health through magical recovery, swung his arms around in circles and sighed.

The girl, looking prim, used the straw to take a sip of her tropical tea.

Her lashes threw shadows into her jewellike eyes, and KR gazed at them with a feeling that vaguely resembled heartburn. The girl certainly looked like an incredible beauty, but this wasn't her true form. He couldn't let himself be fooled.

"And? How was it?" she demanded.

"How was what?"

"You were using Soul Possession to reconnoiter, were you not?"

"Oh. Yeah. It looks like the steel train's on its way back."

"Oho. The thing that stinks of iron."

Mizufa Trude of Plant Hwyaden's Ten-Seat Council, "the General Who Dominated the East": The train in question was a military apparatus that had been earmarked for the special unit she commanded and its ongoing mission.

So that train is returning, is it? the girl thought. She had never been at all interested in human society, but lately, that tendency was beginning to change. After forming a relationship with this young man and observing human society through him, she'd seen that it held mingled joys and sorrows, in its own way.

Most of all, there were individuals with too much internal fire to scoff at. Even though her partner, KR, was nothing short of tragic as far as mental capacity was concerned, this was true of him as well.

Yamato, this Far Eastern island country, was small compared to her birthplace, the Northern Ridge Rus. The Holy Empire of Westlande, which was managing to govern only half of tiny Yamato, could be considered an insignificant organization as well. However, the Ten-Seat Council that controlled it was full of interesting individuals who truly could not be mocked.

These outsiders, the Adventurers, seemed powerful even to her, but the Ten-Seat Council wasn't made up entirely of Adventurers. Mizufa, "the General Who Dominated the East," and Jared Gan, "the Great Wizard of Miral Lake," were People of the Earth, and they looked quite self-seeking. The People of the Earth were nothing to sneeze at, either.

"They're probably planning to pick a fight with Eastal," KR noted.

"That's the East's organization of self-government, is it not?"

"That's the one. They've got a partnership with Akiba."

"Isn't it unwise to make war with the Adventurers? The difference in combat strength is far too great."

"Westlande may think Plant Hwyaden will save them if they start a war with Akiba. Actually, they're probably planning to drag us into it under cover of the confusion."

"Relying on others, hmm? That's how inconsequential people think."

"They're small-timers, but y'know, they're just really... Sometimes, low-down small-timers are tougher to deal with than heroes."

The girl folded her arms and considered this. *Hmm.*

Her partner was an idiot, but he occasionally spoke like a sage.

"Profound words. I'll take my reward."

When she gouged at his side with the nails of her white toes, KR stuck out his hands and arched backward, shouting, "*Ow!* Seriously, I can't believe you! Gar-gar, you fiend!"

Still, on hearing those words, several things had clicked for her.

"Is that why you told that departing Samurai of the matter on the continent?" she asked.

"What was that about, again?"

"It was the one who calls himself Kazuhiko."

"Oh. Yeah."

KR looked away, his response short.

He hadn't given her much of a reaction, but she didn't think it was because he wasn't interested. This young man was shyer than he looked, and he had a habit of hiding his emotions at times like these.

"That's not the only reason," he admitted. "Kazuhiko's always been way too serious... In a different way from Shiroe. If he'd kept that up, he would've burned out."

"Compassion for an old companion, hmm?"

"...I probably wanted to tell somebody about it. It's too big for one person to keep to himself. If I got too psyched up and my chest exploded, we'd have massive trouble. If my heart stopped, my entrails being eaten would be the least of my worries."

"Keh-keh-keh-keh."

The girl's smile indicated her agreement.

Their adventure on the continent had been quite thrilling.

There had been a battle for the sky the likes of which even she, in her long life, hadn't often seen.

The protection of dragons, the blood of the fairies, the principle of transmigration, the skills of the great ones: That place had held all four of the grand powers that governed this world. The woman whom they'd supported, Kanami, had certainly had the look of a hero. Those imposing forces had swirled around her, and yet they hadn't seemed to affect her at all. She hadn't even been aware that she was receiving support.

"Where are they now, I wonder?"

As she asked the question, the dragon girl's eyes narrowed softly into a smile.

She'd last seen them in the distant land of Aorsoi, beyond a wasteland, in a place that even she couldn't easily reach. She'd never spoken with them, but through KR's Dragon's Eye, she knew the band of travelers well. Remembering the woman's group was quite pleasant.

"I dunno. They're probably headed our way, though."

Seeming to give up on the deck chair, KR sat down on the white tiles and—without permission—leaned back against her knees. She was on the verge of rebuking him for his insolence, but in deference to the sage words he had once again produced, she decided to lend him her noble legs for a few moments.

"Kanami will come here, aiming for the sun."

"Undoubtedly."

"That guy, too."

"You think well of that man, do you?"

KR shrugged his shoulders: Of course he did. Kanami was special-made. She smashed everything to pieces and let in a fresh new wind. However, it was hard for her to show her humanity there. In that sense, she was too far from human.

The corners of KR's mouth rose, fearlessly. He was remembering the reunion and adventure in faraway Aorsoi. Elias, Coppélia, Leonardo, and Kanami. The journey of KR's former friend to Yamato, and the slight assistance he'd been able to give her…

This oncoming tale of adventure might belong to Kanami.

But at the same time, it had one other protagonist, too:

The level-90 Assassin and hero. KR's friend Leonardo.

It belonged to the man cloaked in the strong, dry Aorsoi winds.

▸2

The vast sky was high.

Infinitely high.

And the sunlight within it was obstinately strong, shining white and bright.

However, as a result, even though it was still full daytime, the color of that sky was a dark blue that was nearer to indigo than the shade generally termed "sky blue." It was a hue that seemed to hint at what lay beyond the atmosphere.

At the far edge of this landscape was a range of hazy, perfectly ordinary gray mountains. This was nothing remarkable; these peaks could be seen from anywhere within the surrounding two hundred kilometers.

The sunlight was intense, but the wind held a knifelike chill. Considering the altitude, that was only to be expected.

This place was under the jurisdiction of the Chinese server.

It was the southeastern portion of a vast region known as Kazakhstan in the real world.

It was an ancient town called Tekeli.

In the world of *Elder Tales*, this area was called Aorsoi. That was the name of the region, not of a country.

This vast inland area was surrounded by deserts, including the Skull Desert and the Desert of Red Sands. Yet even the areas that weren't desert were nothing but arid, desolate wasteland. There were very few plants that grew thickly enough to provide a place to hide; the greenery that seemed to cling to the ground only covered the gray-brown earth here and there. This was a transitional region between a steppe and a plateau, and although it was impossible to tell just by looking, since the scenery was similar for as far as the eye could see, the altitude was quite high.

Even in summer, the hottest temperature was only a bit above twenty degrees Celsius.

Now, four months after the Catastrophe, when night came, temperatures quickly fell below ten degrees.

There was a reason "Aorsoi" was the name of a region, rather than a country: Very few people were in this immense area.

China's economic development might be remarkable, but that only meant the wealthy class had grown—the majority of it in a few of the bay areas—and reality was still harsh elsewhere. In any case, real-world western China, Kazakhstan, and the rest of Central Asia were most definitely not densely populated.

Elder Tales had been designed with the intention of having players play on the servers of their native lands, and so an area's player population was directly linked to the number of Adventurers in that region. In other words, the emptiness of the Aorsoi region was linked to Kazakhstan's dearth of *Elder Tales* players.

MMOs were a type of free-market service, and the amount of resources that would be directed toward development reflected the number of users.

Kanan Internet Corporation, which ran the Chinese server, had naturally concentrated its development resources on the coastal areas at the eastern edge of the continent, where it had the most users. As stages for fantastic adventures, the Great Wall and the areas around Beijing had also received elaborate designs.

Meanwhile, Aorsoi had few native users (and they weren't picky), so it was an undeveloped area that still held only sparse, scattered dungeons and quests.

However, even in a region like this one, the basic terrain was a faithful re-creation of the real world. In the first place, the basic topography in every area of *Elder Tales* was real-world topography, gathered from laser measurements taken by drones and satellite photos.

The intent of this idea had been to reduce development personnel expenses, but the realistic topographic data and the ease with which it captured user sympathies had made it one of the distinguishing features that had boosted *Elder Tales*' reputation.

In Aorsoi, the weather emulator and the Half-Gaia Project—in which real-world Earth was reproduced with its distances halved—had re-created the sights of Central Asia, which had remained unchanged since antiquity: arid land, cold wind, and a sky that was far too blue.

This beautiful scenery signaled an unforgiving natural environment, and in the post-Catastrophe world, its fangs barred Adventurers' way with a realism that surpassed reality.

"Jesus," Leonardo muttered. He was lying limply in the center of the ruined town of Tekeli.

This town was his prison.

Leonardo, who had come to this town through a chain of events, had learned that it had a temple. Temples were game-related buildings that functioned as resurrection points, and there was one in every player town.

Adventurers who died in *Elder Tales* were revived at the last temple they'd visited. Even in this world, which had gone mad following the Catastrophe, that hadn't changed.

Temples were composed of the resurrection point—meaning the temple itself—and a wider "detection area." In most cases, detection areas were the same size as the town that held the temple. In other words, the moment anyone entered the town, they were treated as if they'd visited the temple and "registered." Afterward, if that Adventurer died, they were revived at the temple where they'd been registered.

Raid zones and high-difficulty dungeons were equipped with these mechanisms as well. In other words, those entire zones were detection areas, and if you died in them, you revived at the resurrection point at the dungeon's entrance.

The temple in the ruins of Tekeli was no exception, and its detection area was the entire ruined town.

At first, Leonardo had been psyched that this temple existed.

After all, due to those certain circumstances, he'd been traveling through Central Asia, and this temple was a welcome save point. Journeys in this region were merciless and harsh. If he'd died, he would have had to restart his journey from a far-distant place.

He'd even thought of this temple—which stood right smack in the middle of the wilderness, all by itself—as a divine favor.

However, the reality was quite different.

"Dammit… I can't do a blasted thing like this."

Moving sluggishly, Leonardo looked toward the outskirts of town. There was something like a heat mirage there, undulating slowly.

A Daylight Shade.

It was a level-52 spirit monster.

When Leonardo had entered the town and climbed the bell tower at its center, he'd accidentally touched a water mirror. That had probably been the trigger: An event had begun.

At this point, guessing was all he could do, but it had to be a raid event for level-50 players. The ruins had been surrounded by countless Daylight Shades.

Leonardo was level 90.

Bragging aside, as an Assassin, he was top-notch. In close combat with two swords, he was near the top of the national rankings. He was a true New Yorker who lived on Avenue ABC, and as an über-geek who enjoyed Shake Shack burgers every week in Madison Square Park, he'd devoted all his enthusiasm to *Elder Tales*.

…Put bluntly, he was a hopeless American fanboy, but his enthusiasm was the real thing. Battle after battle. Junk food and more junk food. Of course, that wasn't all. He also had those constant companions to online games: trivial gossip and squabbles and cheap melodrama, bragging nonsense stories, the limitless competition to acquire rare items, and a few really important connections.

Since he was that sort of guy, level-52 monsters weren't enough to scare him. Not if there were only five or six of them, at any rate. Even if there had been thirty of them, at the worst, he probably would've been able to charge through them.

However, the situation surrounding the ruins of Tekeli was different. Even at a low estimate, there were several thousand Daylight

Shades encircling this town. Under the circumstances, no one person, not even a level-90 player, could escape.

He hadn't known that at the outset, of course.

Leonardo had gotten the information by firing himself up to get out or die, plotting his escape, then losing, dying, and finally resurrecting. The town was completely sealed on all four sides.

The situation couldn't have been worse.

Ordinarily, no matter how hairy things got, when a player resurrected, they were sent to a temple in a safe location. Moreover, even without dying, they could get back by using Call of Home.

However, the ruins had apparently been registered as both a resurrection and a return point for Leonardo.

As things stood, neither dying nor using Call of Home would get him out of here.

"...I'm hungry. I want sushi..."

Sushi was one of Leonardo's favorite foods, and he wanted it so badly he couldn't stand it.

He missed Tasuda in Midtown and Ushiwaka in SoHo. He was partial to tuna with a generous dose of wasabi. No, he wouldn't ask for that much. At this point, he'd even settle for a sketchy East Village California roll. That was how much he missed it.

In this world, after the Catastrophe, hunger felt like actual, physical pain. Nonetheless, Leonardo was short on information, and he didn't know whether starving to death was possible here. He hadn't seen or heard of prolonged hunger lowering anyone's hit points and leading to death.

He still had some rations in his magic bag, but it seemed likely he'd get to run a personal experiment on starving to death in the not-so-distant future.

"If this were the North American server, at least..."

If this had been the North American server, Leonardo would have had friends and acquaintances here. His (lucky) friends who'd avoided getting caught up in the Catastrophe were probably still sitting pretty back in the real world, but still, Leonardo was a severe online game junkie, and he had a lot of acquaintances who were as unhinged as he was.

However, the telechat function couldn't be used across server boundaries.

His friend list had still worked after the Catastrophe, but now it was just a dark gray block, without a single lit-up name. That was only natural: Most of his friends were on the North American server, and this was the Chinese server.

"Holy shit… I can't deal with this, man."

Things had been complete chaos on the North American server, as if somebody had thrown open the gates of hell. Fleeing the panic, thinking he'd find a place to lie low for a while, he'd jumped into a Fairy Ring…and now, Leonardo thought, he was paying for it.

He had more than five years of *Elder Tales* experience, and no matter how little he wanted to, he knew: With the amount of combat power he had personally, he couldn't get through the surrounding Daylight Shades. That said, he had no way of calling for help, and he didn't have a prayer of getting out of the situation by leveling up or getting an item.

He'd long ago abandoned the hope that somebody would pass by.

In the first place, he'd found these ruins by accident. They'd been all on their own, unmarked, in the middle of an immense wasteland, as if they were a prank somebody had pulled.

Now that he thought about it, he probably should have suspected at that point that there was some sort of quest or event.

This was checkmate.

His luck had run out.

In the center of Aorsoi's—Kazakhstan's—blue, blue wilderness, Leonardo had stumbled into a situation where his only hope of salvation was calling the game master.

Of course, in this world, the GM gods didn't exist.

▶3

"Hey. You. If you sleep out here, you'll mess up your stomach."

All of this was why, when he heard those words, he thought it was some kind of joke.

Plus she had a dynamite figure—something just short of a fantasy.

A black-haired woman stood above him.

In what had become an almost unconscious habit, Leonardo checked her status.

Her name was… It looked like "Kanami."

Her class was Monk. Level 90.

She had Asian features, and her hair was pulled back into a thick braid. Her eyes brimmed with curiosity, and her lips seemed vaguely amused; they made her look young, and he couldn't immediately figure out her age. After all, people said Asians tended to look younger for their ages than Westerners like himself. Her equipment was light, as you'd expect in a game world, and her risqué outfit showcased her feminine charms with abandon.

In DC, she might have gotten hauled in and admonished, but for the San Fran coast, she was probably still in the permissible range. When his thoughts had gone that far, Leonardo shook his head. That stuff was common sense from back on Earth.

At any rate, she was a cute beauty with a great figure. All the women in this world were beautiful, but this girl also had an energetic, musical voice, and just from the few words she'd spoken, he sensed a charm that was more than skin-deep.

"Hey!"

Leonardo had been planning to introduce himself, but he yelled involuntarily.

He'd intended to tell her about the temple but had realized he was too late.

The temple's detection area covered the entire ruined town.

That meant this woman had already fallen into its clutches.

"What?"

"Uh, nothing. Sorry for yelling. I'm Leonardo. I'm an Adventurer from the North American server."

"Hmm. I'm Kanami."

Saying this, the woman shook Leonardo's hand, and he got to his feet.

Once their eyes were on roughly the same level, he realized that Kanami was about 170 centimeters tall—taller than Leonardo. He didn't have much confidence in his height, and this sort of thing never made him happy.

* * *

"You came here from the North American server to take a nap? You're pretty awesome."

"Uh, no. That wasn't it…but… Come to think of it, how did you get into these ruins?" Leonardo asked.

"Hmm? I just walked in."

Reflexively, he glanced at the distant end of the broad avenue.

His eyesight had been enhanced through high-level correction, and he could make out a slight, wavering warp in the landscape of the boundary region on the outskirts of town. His expectations had been betrayed.

In short, those Daylight Shades didn't attack anyone who came in from the outside. They trapped Adventurers inside, then annihilated them.

Apparently, it was that kind of event.

"I want you to listen to what I'm about to say without getting too bummed out, or panicking, or taking it out on me."

"Hmm?"

Braid swinging, Kanami turned her large black eyes on Leonardo. Having those mysterious Eastern eyes gazing at him disconcerted the man, but meeting this colleague had been a minor miracle, and he didn't want to shock her, so he chose his words carefully as he went on.

"Umm, see, from what I can tell, these ruins are currently caught up in an event."

"An event?"

"Yeah. A raid event, at that."

"Ooooh!"

Kanami's eyes sparkled in obvious delight.

Leonardo didn't think it was anything to be happy about, and he lowered his voice and continued.

"The situation's hopeless. There's a temple in this town. In other words, the moment you stepped in here, um, Miz Kanami, you also got…"

"Registered?"

"Yeah. And obviously…"

"We can't get away by resurrecting or using the Call of Home spell?"

"Right. You catch on fast. That's a huge help."

"Okay, great! I got it! I'm all fired up!!"

Kanami's naïve response bewildered Leonardo.

Did the woman really understand?

It looked as if she was just getting excited over the word *raid.*

Was it possible she was a newbie?

In *Elder Tales*, leveling up wasn't that hard. Quests were as abundant as an enormous Manchu Han Imperial Feast and generously distributed across all level demographics, so if you chased after them, your level would practically rise on its own.

The game itself boasted a long history, and that meant the difference between veteran players and new players was a serious problem. That difference was particularly noticeable in levels, and it was an element that kept gamers from playing together. Things such as the Coach System had been added with that in mind, but the quickest way to solve the fundamental problem was to eliminate the level difference between players.

To that end, the *Elder Tales* administrators had set a policy of helping new players to level up.

In other words, even for newbies, it wasn't very difficult to grow to level 90, the maximum level. Ordinary players could reach level 90 in less than a hundred hours.

On the other hand, it wasn't easy to get a complete set of equipment suitable for a level-90 player. It took ages to improve all your special skills to esoteric-class and to acquire a full array of treasure-class items.

Kanami's equipment was nothing for a level-90 player to be embarrassed about, but unlike Leonardo's, its specs weren't hard-core. From the look of her gear, Kanami probably hadn't been playing for very long.

"Do you really get it? This town is surrounded, and we're probably not gonna be able to get away."

"Huh? Why not?"

Kanami asked the question as if the idea completely mystified her. As she tilted her head, the word *blank* suited her expression perfectly.

"Well, I mean, it's a raid… Oh! I see. You're Chinese?"

Catching on, Leonardo felt relieved.

He was from the North American server, and he couldn't contact his friends, but if Kanami was from the Chinese server, it was very likely that she'd be able to get in touch with hers. The post-Catastrophe world was filled with chaos and malice, so there was no telling whether any of her friends would come to a place this remote to rescue her, but even so, it was much better than not being able to contact them at all.

If this was level-50 full raid content, meant for twenty-four players, then ten level-90 Adventurers with ordinary equipment would probably be able to break through it. Even Leonardo thought that, if there'd been five or six of him, they'd at least have managed to run away.

"What are you talking about? I'm Japanese. I live in Rome. On the Western European server!"

However, Kanami's words shattered Leonardo's hopes. The automatic translation system was too good, and because it translated everything perfectly, he'd completely failed to notice.

"Then..."

"Never mind. Why are you wearing that?"

Leonardo shook his head a few times before answering Kanami's question.

"No skin off your nose, is it? It's a hobby."

As a matter of fact, he was very used to hearing that question.

"What is it?"

"A frog."

For that reason, Leonardo was able to answer even rude questions with the slickest attitude imaginable: *What are you dressed as? A frog. What does it stand for? It stands for a frog. Why is it wearing a red mask that only hides the area around its eyes? Because it's a ninja.*

Why a frog? Why a ninja?

Don't be ridiculous.

Because it's cooler that way. Obviously.

"Wow, you... You're fantastic! Fantastic!"

However, although ordinary people were usually completely disgusted by his responses, Kanami's reaction was different.

“That’s part of the costume headgear series, isn’t it?! It’s less a frog than a *fuhrahhg*, huh!!”

He looked funny dressed as a comic book character, possibly even absurd, but as Kanami took several more good looks at him, smiling brightly, she seemed delighted. Getting laughed at this much should have made him feel insulted, but although Leonardo was taken aback, he felt no anger.

This was probably because, as Kanami grinned, there was absolutely no derision or contempt in what she said. The sense that she was simply intrigued and entertained came through loud and clear. For that reason, although Leonardo’s twin swords had routed many PKs and insolent individuals he didn’t like, for once, they kept their silence.

“What I look like shouldn’t be a problem.”

“Well, but I mean— It’s just awesome!”

“Lemme alone.”

“C’mon, c’mon! Pose with your sword! Show me, show me!”

“I’ll fillet you.”

“S-so cooool! That’s super-cute!! I want to pet you!”

Laughing brightly, Kanami hugged him. On top of Leonardo’s leather armor—which he’d coordinated in green—and his exclusive Assassin’s tunic, he found a soft body that smelled like young grass clinging to him.

“Uh, a little modesty?! Control yourself, would you?!”

“Wow! You’re kinda great!”

“*What’s* ‘great’?!”

“Come with us!”

Huh?

“We’re headed for Japan. It’s a long way, you know? We’re getting pretty bored. So, listen, want to come with? Besides, if you nap in a place like this, you’ll just mess up your tum-tum.”

Why Japan?

Wait, no, I wasn’t napping.

Never mind that, didn’t she get the part about not being able to get out of here?

That’s not it.

Leonardo’s thoughts were on the verge of overloading, and he pulled them together.

Us. This lovely girl, who was probably about the same age as Leonardo, had just said *us.*

"You've got friends here?!"

"Yep. Oh, right. Since you're coming with us, I'll introduce you."

In the end, Leonardo's objection—*No, hold it, I didn't say I'd go with you yet*—disappeared without so much as a murmur.

Although it probably wasn't because they'd heard what Kanami said, a man and woman had come over the rubble of the ruins, and the man at least was so famous that even Leonardo recognized him.

"Mistress Kanami. I see you've found a survivor. Hmm… Your appearance is quite bizarre, but you look like a seasoned Adventurer. I'm glad to make your acquaintance."

This young man, whose lips were curved up in a charming smile, and who was so handsome it made you want to crack a joke on reflex, was Elias Hackblade.

"Elias Hackblade…"

"Ah. You know me? My thanks, Sir Adventurer."

Elias didn't seem to have any qualms about Leonardo's cosplay gear. He smiled good-naturedly and held out his hand for a handshake.

Elias Hackblade.

He was one of the handful of people who were globally famous in the world of *Elder Tales.*

He was a hero affiliated with the Knights of the Red Branch, one of the thirteen global chivalric orders that were said to keep the peace around the world. He was a Blademancer and a Blue-Blood Ancient.

Ancients were one of the game elements that had existed since this world was just an MMO known as *Elder Tales*. Most of the NPCs—in other words, the game characters who weren't players and who filled supporting roles—were known as People of the Earth.

Townspeople and nobles, victims and Adventurer clients: In most cases, all of these were People of the Earth.

In this world, People of the Earth were designed to be "less" than Adventurers in a variety of ways.

By doing battle again and again, Adventurers grew rapidly, and their levels rose. Ultimately, they gained vast combat abilities and were able to fight dragons or giants.

Even if they were lethally wounded, instead of dying completely, they returned to the temple and were resurrected, so it was possible to consider them immortal.

However, this wasn't true for the People of the Earth.

An overwhelming majority of them had levels in the single digits, and if they died, they didn't revive. After all, you didn't need levels or combat abilities for "game functions," such as working at the bank or running an inn.

In addition, since this was a game, the protagonists of the adventure had to be the players—the Adventurers. The idea of journeying in another world that was swarming with villagers who were stronger than the players was enough to give anybody chills.

The People of the Earth were weak because they had been designed that way, due to a variety of interconnected elements like these. However, from the perspective of the game's story, when it came to building drama or constructing quests, it would be inconvenient if all NPCs had zero combat ability.

Of course, if the NPCs stole the Adventurers' part of the action, they'd be stealing the thunder. However, sometimes people wanted scenes where NPCs and Adventurers fought shoulder to shoulder.

It was probably these circumstances that had given rise to the beings known as Ancients.

In short, Ancients were exceptional NPCs.

They had high combat abilities, and not only were they the Adventurers' equals, they occasionally surpassed them. They appeared in a variety of quests; sometimes they saved Adventurers, and sometimes they asked Adventurers for help.

As in all RPGs, in *Elder Tales*, the scale of adventures expanded, growing from trivial, low-level quests to high-level conspiracies involving nations or whole regions.

On low-level adventures, the best you could hope for was guarding a village or hamlet from wolves or goblins. While they were on adventures like those, no Adventurer would ever get the chance to interact with an Ancient.

However, as Adventurers' levels rose and they began to face invading evils that shook entire nations, these beings appeared within the background lore to introduce new quests.

Most—or rather, nearly all—of the Ancients were affiliated with one of the thirteen global chivalric orders. These thirteen orders were organizations made up of Ancients, and there was one per server. Their role was not to intervene in national or regional power struggles but to protect the world of *Elder Tales* from evil overall.

For example, on the North American server where Leonardo had spent many years adventuring, there was a brigade called the Wen Keepers. They helped out with the sort of quests that led to raids and acted as the backbone of such stories.

A high-level Adventurer would hear from the Wen Keepers that a member of their brigade had vanished while away on an investigation. In searching for the missing knight, the Adventurer would close in on the mystery of a terrifying ancient secret concerning the Sedona Ruins… That was how it usually went.

Naturally, there were far fewer Ancients than there were People of the Earth. However, since there were many chances to meet them on high-level adventures, it was possible for some Ancients to become famous among the Adventurers.

Elias Hackblade was, without a doubt, the greatest hero and most famous person in the world of *Elder Tales.*

He was an invincible hero raised by the fairy tribe and had been taught fairy sword techniques; there was an introductory article on the official site that said so. Elias Hackblade actually appeared on the package art of the version of *Elder Tales* that was sold in stores.

He had chestnut hair and eyes, and he wore a pure white, armored coat with indigo accent lines. His weapon was Crystal Stream, an enormous two-handed sword, and he used the absolutely invincible sword technique Fairy Arts… He was a hero so cool, and so typical, that it made you wonder what middle schooler had dreamed him up.

▸4

"And so, Eli-Eli..."

"I wish you wouldn't call me Eli-Eli, Mistress."

"But Eli-Eli sounds cuter!"

As Leonardo stood there, dumbfounded, Kanami and Elias fell into conversation. Elias was an Ancient. He wasn't an Adventurer. Not only that, he was an NPC. In other words, he wasn't even human.

Since that was the case, why was this woman talking to him as if they were on really good terms?

Or, no, even before that, why was Elias even here?

The Knights of the Red Branch, the order he was affiliated with, was supposed to be attached to the Northern European server.

Of course, Elias was one of the most famous of the many Ancients. His fame was equal to that of Ling Tianfeng, the "White Wing Princess."

That was why Leonardo, who was a resident of the North American server, not one of the European servers, had recognized Elias on sight. Even so, Ancients didn't often leave the servers they were responsible for. Unless there was a special worldwide event, it wasn't even possible, and more than anything, in the current *Elder Tales*, there were no administrators to plan those events.

A low, calm chime rang in Leonardo's stunned brain. It was a system sound, and when he checked, there was an open window inviting him to a party. Thinking it was probably from the group in front of him, Leonardo accepted without really looking it over.

When a party was formed, a mental list of the members' names appeared. From that screen, Leonardo learned the name of the slight girl who had invited him.

The girl's name was Coppélia.

She'd appeared with Elias a short while ago, but she'd seemed quiet and plain, and the shock of Elias had made him nearly forget about her.

The girl was small, only about 140 centimeters, and she was dressed in a Victorian maid outfit. She was apparently a Cleric. Of course, her level was 90.

She came closer, looked up at Leonardo, delicately pinched up her skirt, and performed a graceful curtsey.

"Coppélia is called Coppélia. It is good to meet you. Coppélia looks forward to working together. Do you wish to be healed?"

"Oh, uh, I'm Leonardo. Nice to meet you. No, I'm good. No healing necessary."

There was something odd and doll-like about the girl. As he looked down at her, Leonardo thought that, although her responses were a bit strange, she seemed like the most decent member of the group.

Now that he'd registered with the party, he knew that there were only four people in Kanami's group. The breakdown consisted of himself—who'd just been press-ganged in—the black-haired beauty Kanami, the girl Coppélia who was standing here with him, and Elias.

Kanami was a level-90 Monk.

Coppélia was a level-90 Cleric.

He got that much. It made sense. Three people would make for a small group, but Monks were evasive tanks that kept enemies in check on the front line, while Clerics were in charge of healing. Then there was Leonardo, an Assassin who single-mindedly pared down the enemy's numbers. The balance wasn't bad at all. It was a simple party, built from the bare essentials.

However, Elias was part of it, too, and what was he?

A level-100 Blademancer.

The landscape in front of Leonardo seemed to roll and undulate, and it felt like he was losing his grip on the situation.

In the first place, how could an NPC and a party team up at all?

Even the "Blademancer" part was a mystery. In *Elder Tales*, there were twelve main classes to choose from: three Warrior classes, three Weapon Attack classes, three Recovery classes, and three Magic Attack classes. An off-the-wall option like Blademancer certainly wasn't one of them. The same went for level 100. The maximum level limit for Adventurers was 90. That hadn't changed since the expansion pack that was added two years ago.

Having a level so high it surpassed the limits of those around you and a unique main class that no other player could acquire? That was the sort of stuff you only ran into in anime.

Everything about this seemed to mock what Leonardo knew to be common sense.

"Your heart rate is exhibiting irregularities. Do you wish to be healed?"

"No, it's fine. Am I the one who's weird here?"

"Coppélia did not notice an abnormal status icon."

"That's not what I meant… So, uh, you've been traveling for a while?" Leonardo quickly asked.

"Master picked up Coppélia in Via de Fleurs."

Registering the presence of automatic translation from the slight time lag after her lips moved, Leonardo let his thoughts run for a little. He was pretty sure that "Whatever-Fleurs" was Paris. That meant that Kanami and Elias had come from the Northern European server and cut across Europe before reaching Central Asia. They might have been serious about making for Japan.

However, at that point, his thoughts were forcibly interrupted.

There was a loud sound of something being crushed, and Leonardo realized that Kanami and Elias had disappeared while his mind was elsewhere.

"Combat has been initiated. Coppélia intends to secure an appropriate distance for healing. Please forgive her withdrawal from this conversation."

"No, you're fine. I'm going, too!"

Leonardo broke into a run, racing through the arid streets with the girl.

They didn't even have to look. The ruins of Tekeli didn't have many buildings to block the view; the cold highland wind and the intense sunlight had easily eroded the ancient brick. Only a sparse few of the ruins' remaining walls and pillars were as tall as Leonardo, which made it easy to pinpoint the scene of the fight.

Near the point where one of the wide avenues that divided the town into quarters went eastward toward an exit, a violent thunderclap echoed. It was electroshock magic. The horde of heat mirages, enough of them to warp the landscape, was probably Daylight Shades.

From the look of the distortion, there were definitely several dozen of them gathered in that one area.

Elias, who was still a few hundred meters away, raised a transparent two-handed sword over his head, then began fearlessly slashing his way to the center of the host of monsters.

What are they doing?!

A river of cold sweat ran down his back.

Elias was fine. Leonardo didn't know the details of that special Blademancer class of his or his true level-100 skills, and so, although it was a faint hope, it was possible that he'd be able to rout countless Daylight Shades by himself.

However, Kanami—who'd dived into the melee on Elias's heels—could never do it. Any attempt would be utterly suicidal.

This was clear from the fact that Leonardo, who was also level 90, had been slaughtered in under five minutes.

"Tactical distance secured. Initiating combat support. Chanting: Sanctuary, Shield Pact."

If things were like this, there was no help for it.

He'd just have to die again.

Leonardo steeled himself. Coppélia, who was running next to him, seemed to have entered the spellcasting range. She'd begun to cast support spells on her companions. She hadn't attacked directly, but using support spells was a solid backup action— In other words, she'd joined the fight.

The Daylight Shades were bound to notice, and they would set their sights on her.

Since Elias and Kanami were fighting on the front line, things were all right at this point, but if those two fell, the demons would mark the slight girl as their next prey. When that happened, it was as clear as day that the Frenchwoman would lose her life.

Ultimately, she'd practically signed a delayed-action death certificate. This was true for all the members of the party, aside from Leonardo.

And if that was the case, he needed to dive into the jaws of death, too.

Of course he thought it was stupid, but that was what made him a geek: doing stupid stuff like that. Leonardo was a genuine New Yorker, and he had his pride. It wasn't like anybody would ever understand it, but frog ninjas were, by definition, allies of justice.

How could he just stand here staring at some woman's tail?

"Rraaaaaargh!"

With a howl as if he were squeezing the air out of his lungs, Leonardo charged at the horde of monsters, which rippled like a heat mirage. He used his reinforced physical abilities to flip, running right over his opponents' heads. It was Mobility Attack. In most cases, this would put him in a monster's blind spot.

I ain't holding nothin' back!

For his first attack, Leonardo chose the biggest lethal move he had.

A warrior's reason for existing was to draw the enemy's attention, erasing their companions' presence from their minds. The role of a healer was to keep their companions recovered, preventing their deaths. And magic users had to control the battle, keeping unforeseen situations from coming up until the fighting was over.

Then what did Assassins, a weapon attack class, do?

The role of Weapon Attack classes could be summarized as "destroy the enemy." Among them, Assassins in particular were designed with abilities geared toward eliminating enemies.

The greatest of these techniques, Assassinate, inflicted close to ten thousand in damage instantaneously, just as Leonardo had predicted. In addition, as an incidental effect that targeted enemies more than ten levels below him, it caused instant death.

A dry, high-pitched sound like a fired blank echoed through the area.

Along with the noise, which sounded almost comical, a single Daylight Shade burst, its existence ending.

"Aha! You're finally here, huh, Croakanardo?!"

"Lay off the rude nicknames, all right?"

"In that case, let's begin in earnest. —Come, Crystal Stream! Fairy blood within me! Lend me strength so that I may slay the enemies before me!"

You think you're in an anime or something? Leonardo snarked silently, but he didn't have the leeway to actually mutter it aloud. Having destroyed a monster in the blink of an eye, he surveyed his surroundings carefully. There was still a ton of enemies left. He could actually see several dozen right now, and he knew from previous experience that, if the party took their time, the ones who were currently surrounding the town would gather here.

He had to cut down the enemy's numbers without losing his cool, and he had to work at maximum efficiency. Elias's body was wrapped in a torrent of shining purple and pale blue light. When he took a closer look, that protection seemed to have been cast on Kanami, Coppélia, and himself as well.

Thanks to that effect, which seemed to reinforce their defenses, they were currently managing to hold the battle line. However, even if these were level-50 monsters, with this many of them, they absolutely couldn't underestimate the pressure.

If they were able to whittle down the enemy's numbers this way, fine.

That said, if the speed with which their opponents summoned backup and increased their ranks was faster than Leonardo could cut them down, the balance would crumble easily. When that happened, Coppélia's recovery spells wouldn't make it in time, and the front line would gradually crumble. They'd push themselves, and as a result, they'd be wiped out.

In the end, this fight was a battle to reduce numbers.

Leonardo bit his lip.

In which case, as an Assassin, he held the key to the battle.

▶5

The Daylight Shades welled up from the ground like mist.

As their name suggested, they looked just like heat mirages.

"Hiyah!"

Leonardo swung the fantasy-class twin swords that were his pride and joy.

Assassins weren't as good at fighting with two swords as Swashbucklers, and the ones they wielded were exclusive equipment that had unique modeling and effects. The effect of this particular item added additional flame damage to all of Leonardo's attacks. The blanket term for this type of incidental effect was "process activated ability," or "proc," and it was often seen in highly realistic magic items.

Leaving tracks from those flames in the air, Leonardo raced through the enemy horde.

Assassins were a class that specialized in attacking, and they were the most lethal of the twelve main classes. However, in order to inflict maximum damage, they had to clear several conditions.

For example, the enemy's attention had to be focused elsewhere.

In this case, the vanguards were Kanami and Elias. Relying on that shining, pale blue effect, they were managing to completely draw the monsters' attention. Some of this might have been due to their personalities: Elias stood grandly in the very center of the Daylight Shades, and Kanami gave cheerful yells and swung her arms and legs around. Both had the intensity to attract attention.

The second condition was that attacks had to be made from the enemy's blind spot. This was done by circling around behind its back and attacking from an angle it'd failed to check. Fortunately, Assassins had plenty of skills designed to make this happen.

If you were concentrating on creating party dynamics that were true to the basics, these two conditions weren't at all difficult to achieve. The formation in which the vanguard Warrior classes attracted the enemy while the Assassins circled around behind it and dealt damage was basic practical knowledge in *Elder Tales.*

However, Assassins had great offensive power. If he inflicted too much damage, the monsters would probably decide that Leonardo, who was behind them, was more of a threat than the warriors in front of them, and they'd switch their target. If that happened, Leonardo would be on the receiving end, and not only would he take damage, he wouldn't be able to put his vaunted attack power to work.

In addition, once monsters took massive damage from the rear, even if they didn't shift their attention to Leonardo, they'd still pay more attention to their surroundings for a little while. In other words, it would get harder to attack them from their blind spots.

To prevent losses like these, Leonardo dashed across the battlefield.

By moving, he increased the number of enemies he could attack.

Among those expanded alternatives, he focused on finishing off monsters that had less health and destroyed the ones that'd gotten absorbed in attacking the vanguard and had left themselves open.

This continuously moving attack was the answer Leonardo the Assassin had come up with after the Catastrophe.

Leonardo's combat was top-class, and no true game junkie could have been ashamed of it. However, the one that was clearly abnormal, even from Leonardo's perspective, was Elias.

Though, of course, Elias was an Ancient. He wasn't an Adventurer.

It was probably a mistake for Leonardo to use his common sense to decide whether he was normal or abnormal. Still, reflection on his error did nothing to calm his need to perform.

"Go forth and conquer!! Crystal Stream!! Spirits of clear water, transform yourselves into a ten-thousand-foot blade and shine! Aqua Thousand Rain!!"

Responding to Elias's shout, a magic circle came together around him, and a semimaterial water spirit appeared from it. It was a Lady of the Lake with flowing hair. No sooner had she extended her slim fingers than, with a piercing yell, Elias swung his crystalline magic sword.

A water-attribute aura sprang from the sword tip, changing countless water droplets into needles that mowed down the Daylight Shades.

It was powerful enough that the spawns would stay low for a little while, and more than anything, its range was broad: probably about 120 degrees in front, with a distance of ten meters. It was a nonstandard attack skill.

If that had been a Sorcerer's attack, it probably wouldn't have startled Leonardo. Sorcerer's attacks were on par with Assassins', and they were ranged attack experts. That meant it was only natural for their spells to be powerful.

However, Elias wasn't a Sorcerer. In spite of that, he was fighting as a vanguard whose defense was at least as good as Kanami's, if not better—like a Warrior. In addition, the pale blue spell that had been cast to protect everyone in the party was performing as well as a healer's.

Leonardo was forced to admit that the guy had the advantages of every class that existed.

Frankly, he was so strong it seemed fake.

What the hell is he?!

Even as he inwardly shouted in amazement, Leonardo took out one enemy, then another. Assassin attacks concentrated their damage on individuals. Elias's range attacks were highly effective, but Leonardo flattered himself that he wasn't losing to the other guy where damage per second was concerned.

Leonardo captured the back of a Daylight Shade that Elias had sent flying, freezing it temporarily, then swung his twin swords with the speed of a swallow in flight.

Assassinate was a lethal skill, and its recast time was three hundred seconds. He wouldn't be able to use it for a while. However, when a top-class Assassin hit an enemy from behind with a well-aimed attack, the critical rate was over 50 percent. He compensated for Assassinate, accumulating damage.

"Finish them off, if you would, Adventurer Leonardo!"

"I told you, he's Croakanardo!"

Kanami's cheerful voice made Leonardo's head hurt. *Gimme a break.*

"I am unable to kill the enemy with my sword technique, Fairy Arts!"

Elias began saying something that didn't make much sense.

"I have been marked by the fairy tribe, and the curse of Fairy Eye runs through the Mana Circuits within me."

At first, Elias's words made Leonardo think that the translation function had gone haywire, but when he saw that his expression was completely serious, he was sure: This guy was what they'd call a "background info fiend" in Japan—somebody with severe delusions. With a louder voice, Elias kept saying the sort of words that made Leonardo's spine crawl.

"Due to the curse of Fairy Eye, I am unable to finish off monsters!"

"Huh?"

At that confession, even Leonardo stopped and turned back.

"And so, if you would, finish them off!"

"Umm, Croakanardo? He's saying, well, you know. Elias is an Ancient, so he can't drop monsters' HP to zero."

That's nuts!! For a moment, Leonardo was stunned, but then he reconsidered. Maybe there was no help for that. Come to think of it, Ancients were NPCs. Their duty was to support players' game experiences and to make things more interesting. There wouldn't be any point in grandstanding all on their own.

That was probably why Elias had been saddled with the restriction of being unable to finish off monsters.

Leonardo didn't know whether this restriction was true for all Ancients or whether it was specific to Elias, but from what the Ancient had said, he thought it might be the latter. After all, Elias had been given detailed background information—it was "due to the curse of Fairy Eye"—in order to rationalize the restriction. It made Leonardo's head ache, but it was self-reported. He couldn't deny it.

Either way, it didn't change Leonardo's job.

Bending low to evade a gust of hot wind coming at him from the side, Leonardo swung the straight sword in his right hand, crouching even lower. He slashed through the enemy without feeling much resistance.

Then he moved, seeming to slide. He attacked.

It didn't matter whether the other fell to Leonardo's attack or survived it. He kept moving, continuing to attack blind spots.

Having killed one Daylight Shade, Leonardo shot a glance at Kanami. His expression looked as if he'd just chomped down on something bitter.

Elias was one thing. He was an Ancient and a Blademancer, a special class that wasn't available to Adventurers. Even if Leonardo couldn't be satisfied in the face of those ridiculous abilities, in terms of the system, there was room to think it at least made sense.

However, Kanami was another matter.

She was a proper Adventurer, and her class was Monk, something Leonardo was used to seeing. Her level was 90, too, the same as his own.

She didn't seem to be using any equipment that was particularly rare or high-class. At the very least, it didn't look as if she had any powerful items like Ninja Twin Flames, the fantasy-class Assassin twin blades, or Siolo's Darkwalker Belt, a fantasy-class accessory.

The weapons she'd equipped to both hands were probably Giant-Killer Gauntlets, a level-89 production-class item.

Her equipment wasn't shabby, and she seemed to have put careful thought into its selection, but it couldn't compare to a high-ranker's. All of it seemed to have been pulled together somehow or another within the limits of her budget.

"Yahoo! *Thwok, pow, kabooom!*"

Kanami paid out punches, putting her back into them.

She stepped in farther, thrusting out her left fist, then her right, and landed a body blow using her elbow and shoulder. To round out the magnificent combo, she leapt into the air as if gravity had vanished, then, extending a single leg like a stake, nailed a Daylight Shade to the ground with a kick.

The Daylight Shade flickered palely, then disappeared.

Kanami's attack power was simply abnormal.

Leonardo had a lot of experience in *Elder Tales*, and he could tell. It was true that, as Warriors, Monks had high offensive abilities. They were the type that linked small blows together to accumulate damage, and an astonishing number of moves went into their combos and serial attacks. However, even if that was true, the amount of damage was still only "high for a Warrior."

The role of the Warrior classes was to draw the enemy's attacks on the front line and hold them there. In other words, the class was characterized by the ability to keep the enemy in place and the ability to survive.

Compared to Guardians, Monks' ability to reduce damage with armor or shields was extremely low. In exchange, they were a type of Warrior who supported the front line with high evasion rates and abundant HP. They had several abilities that were suited to independent movement; in combination with their relatively high attack power, this made the class a favorite of veteran gamers and one that was well suited to solo play.

However, there was no way they could have attack power that rivaled

Assassins', the attack specialists. In the balance structure of the *Elder Tales* game, that was a natural rule.

That isn't even...

How could her results be possible? Leonardo checked again and again.

At this point, in the world after the Catastrophe, damage dealt to monsters wasn't visible. However, you could get a rough idea of attack power by seeing how many seconds it took to defeat the same monster.

In terms of the total, Kanami was putting down Daylight Shades in about the same amount of time as Leonardo, or even less.

Of course, if he used Assassinate, Leonardo could kill monsters instantly. That only worked once every few minutes, though, and it only took out one enemy. For a while now, Kanami had been steadily inflicting the sort of damage that Leonardo could manage only with Assassinate.

What's going on here? This doesn't make any sense!

Leonardo felt himself slipping toward panic.

Was Kanami what you'd call a *youkai*? She was still cheerfully flattening enemies, but all of a sudden, Leonardo felt as if she'd turned into a creepy monster.

"Ah!"

Abruptly, seeming to rise high on her toes, Kanami looked at the far edge of the battlefield.

"A space has opened up in the battlefield."

It was Coppélia who'd spoken. She'd come right up behind Leonardo before he noticed her. Coppélia was a healer. She wasn't like that joker Ancient or the enigmatic Asian battle maniac. Leonardo scanned their surroundings warily, but possibly because of Elias's range attacks and the fact that Leonardo and Kanami had both taken out every monster they could get their hands on, the Daylight Shades were hanging back. They seemed to be watching for openings.

Just then, a white horse ran up gallantly, and Kanami grabbed its mane. Stretching out her left arm, she pulled Coppélia up.

"Let's go! The more we punch these guys, the more of 'em show up, and it's kinda boring!"

Kanami had taken a gourd-shaped canteen out of her bag, and she tipped her head back and took a swallow of water.

"Wait!! What's the meaning of this?! Are the two of us traveling on foot?!"

Elias had almost screamed. Leonardo was in full agreement, and he nodded several times, but the only response Kanami gave them was a brilliant smile. The blue, blue sky was behind her.

"Let's go! To the East!"

Thus began the journey of the quartet and its horse.

▶6

The wind that blew across the wasteland was already so cold that it felt like a wintery blast.

Yet for this wilderness, the word *night* didn't mean "saturated in darkness." It meant the silence was filled with a clarity that had lost the inelegance of light.

The blue of the universe stayed as it was, seeming to lie on the earth, whose colors had dimmed into shadow. If you looked up, its expanse bled into a sky filled with hundreds of millions of stars.

This was night on the Aorsoi plateau.

The distant mountains showed their dark shapes only subtly, as holes in the starry sky.

Leonardo and the others were illuminated by an orange, crackling campfire.

Leonardo had started the fire, and a tin kettle that Coppélia had taken out of her bag was hanging over it.

The hissing puffs of steam that escaped the kettle were scattered by the cold highland wind, vanishing almost instantly.

Having found a windbreak, Elias and Kanami had pitched the party's tent and regrouped with the rest of the party. Kanami had wrapped herself in a thick mantle of rough cloth.

Adventurer bodies were sturdy, but the night chill was probably hard for her to take. Because she wore an outfit that showed off her midriff, that was only to be expected.

Carefully, Coppélia poured a black liquid into four battered tin cups that she'd also taken out of her bag. It was coffee, with plenty of honey.

"And? What do we do?"

Leonardo's mouth was set in a dissatisfied line. As he asked the group his question, he shrugged into a thick tunic he'd pulled out of his bag.

"What do you mean, 'what do we do?'"

"I mean, what're we going to do now?"

"I told you already. We're going to Japan."

Kanami answered Leonardo, sounding casual.

"Did you know you need to cross an ocean to get to Japan?"

As a geek, Leonardo knew more about Japan than the average North American. Japan was a weird, cool country that was right next to the east side of China, at the very end of the world.

Leonardo didn't know exactly where they were, but he did know it was somewhere in the central northwest of the Eurasian continent. In general terms, they were probably somewhere above and to the right of places like Iran and Iraq.

Travel from here to Japan? Not only that, but do it without Fairy Rings? That didn't even sound sane.

"Nah, it'll be fine. Right?"

Kanami turned to Elias. Elias nodded, wearing a magnanimous expression. It wasn't clear whether he really understood or not.

"If we swim real hard, we'll get across."

Kanami said something ridiculous. She was holding her coffee in both hands.

Flustered by her new companion's reproachful gaze, she elaborated:

"I mean, I moved to the EU a little while back, and they've got these old grandpas and grandmas who swim across the Dover Channel. That's the ocean, you know? The Channel. It's not much different from the gap between Japan and Taiwan. It'll work."

Was that right? It sounded fishy to Leonardo, but he couldn't flat-out deny it. When he searched through his fuzzy knowledge, it did seem as though Japan was pretty close to China's bulge, but would things really go that well? In any case, he was pretty sure the people who made the Dover crossing were refugees, but not saying that was what discretion was all about. Since the "vital fall," things were pretty much the same everywhere.

"Anyway, with the Half-Gaia Project, distances in this world are halved. On top of that, we've got Adventurer physical abilities. There's no way it won't work!"

When she put it that way, Leonardo started to feel like maybe she was right.

He didn't notice that, beside him, Coppélia was quietly shaking her head.

"…Well, uh, say the crossing-to-Japan thing is fine. What are we going to do until we get there? We're right smack in the middle of Eurasia, y'know. If the earth is about forty thousand kilometers around, this is a quarter of that—ten thousand kilometers. With Half-Gaia, that's five thousand kilometers."

"If we go five hundred kilometers an hour, then in ten hours we'll be—"

"What the heck kind of traveler can do that?! We'd generate sonic booms!"

Leonardo sighed, and Coppélia spoke to him, quietly.

"According to Coppélia's calculations, if we travel fifty kilometers per day, we will arrive in one hundred days. It will be all right. There is a good possibility that we will arrive within half a year."

Come to think of it, she was right.

He'd had a really bad time in the ruins of Tekeli, but three of their four members were level 90. The remaining member was Elias, and he was a definite irregular. Assuming they were just moving along, and this was just a journey through the wilderness, unless they got pulled into some kind of event, he couldn't say it would be all that dangerous.

It would have been one thing if they had a time limit, but if they were just traveling, they'd probably get there "someday."

However, with that said…

The mere idea of a journey that would take half a year, more or less, was a weird thing for a modern-day human to have.

"Why do you want to go to Japan that badly? You said you were Japanese, right, Kanami? Is that why you want to get back there?"

"Well, I'm not saying that's not part of it."

Wrapped up in her thick mantle, Kanami gazed at Leonardo across the campfire with a smile that wasn't at all feminine.

"Don't you know? Keh-heh-heh."

There was no point in asking him that. Today was the first time Leonardo had ever seen her. There was no way he could know about her circumstances.

When Leonardo shook his head silently, Kanami began to speak softly.

"This incident… There has to be some sort of cause, right? I want to know what it is."

Kanami's words were as frank as a child's.

Those innocent words struck Leonardo square in the chest.

In that case, Leonardo wanted to say it, too: *So do I. I want to know.* He couldn't, though. He'd lived through every day until this one that way, unable to say it.

Leonardo's hometown in *Elder Tales* had been Big Apple. This town, which had been modeled on real-world New York City, held his birthplace, his neighborhood, and his pride.

In Central Park, the flowers were beautiful all year round. If you left the park's south side, there was the brick and terra cotta Carnegie Hall. In Big Apple, instead of being a concert hall, it was a place that sold shish kebabs and tacos, but it was the perfect place for Leonardo and the other denizens of downtown to gather.

If you kept going south on Seventh Avenue, you emerged in Times Square, the messiest, nastiest intersection in the world. Even in crowds like these, true New Yorkers didn't lose their cool. They had their own destinations firmly in mind, so they were able to keep walking at maximum efficiency, without paying attention to anybody else. The only people who stared up at the skyscrapers with their mouths half-open were yokels visiting from the country.

They headed, android-like, for the Chrysler Building or the Diamond District or the United Nations Building, but in *Elder Tales*, all of these were ruins and had been turned into the strongholds of the guilds that haunted Big Apple.

FAO Schwarz, Trinity Church, Radio City Music Hall. Each of these was used as the headquarters for a renowned major guild, and their crumbling yet still magnificent shapes stood proudly against the blue skies of this other world.

Simply put, New York was the best city anywhere.

That was true both on Earth and here in the world of *Elder Tales.* New York was a megacity overflowing with neighborly love and a power like upturned chaos, and it was Leonardo's home.

However, the Catastrophe had changed everything.

After that nightmarish day, half the guilds had been forced to disband, and half of what remained had morphed into organized crime groups dominated by tyrannical monsters.

Guilds didn't have personalities. After all, they were just names—mere systems. And so, in the midst of that confusion, when everyone had abandoned themselves to grief, the guilds that had adopted vicious goals were stronger.

If they permitted stealing from fellow Adventurers—or from People of the Earth, who were easier to exploit—they generated profit. Power structures grew up around that profit, and as long as they created organizations that used violence to subjugate those below them, those guilds managed to keep existing.

Meanwhile, the neutral guilds that most players belonged to had been weak. When it came to surviving in this world, individualism and fairness couldn't serve as goals. At heart, individualism was nothing but personal benefit, and fairness was a guideline for distributing profit. Morality that wasn't backed by any major authority didn't even last a week.

Guilds that proclaimed fairness and solidarity among their participants, but in fact did nothing except try to force responsibility onto one another, fell in a single night. The players got paranoid and jumpy, and they slipped away without saying a word.

It was true that most players weren't going to resort to violence, but in the same way, they had no intention of doing anything for anyone else. In other words, in this world, rather than suppressing conflict, individualism was useful only as a way to turn a blind eye.

To players like these, guilds had probably been nothing more than places that were convenient to use. It was simply that, since *Elder Tales* had been a game, the problem hadn't been visible until now.

Some guilds had been peaceful and had adopted upright principles. However, even guilds like those restricted which players they would accept. Many players had been in shock over the Catastrophe, and their hands had been full just trying to protect their own safety and interests.

In essence, guilds were mutual aid organizations. But no guilds in Big Apple had been hospitable enough to support players who had zero intentions of aiding one another.

...Well, I mean, there was rioting.

After the 6.01 food riots and the subsequent public lynchings, Big Apple had become completely bloodthirsty. Leonardo had spent a long time hiding in the sewers, and the few companions he could really trust also left the city, one after another.

In the space of a few blinks, his beloved Big Apple had turned into a city of rejection and violence, populated by individualists with dull eyes.

Leonardo had finally made the decision to leave his hometown as well and had gone on a journey in search of a hiding place where he could lie low for a while. If he was leaving Big Apple anyway, he didn't care how far he went. That said, jumping into a Fairy Ring that sent him to the opposite side of the globe had been a huge miscalculation...

"The cause of the Catastrophe... I can't even begin to guess what that was," Leonardo muttered, remembering his hometown.

If there was a cause, of course he wanted to know what it was. After all, if it was something understandable, he thought the people in his hometown probably wouldn't have panicked so badly and lost all common sense.

However, as simple as the question was, he hadn't been able to ask it. His instincts had told him that asking would mean getting involved with the mysteries of this world. He'd unconsciously shrunk down, thinking it would be too presumptuous for a regular citizen like himself to put that question into words.

As a result, Leonardo gazed at Kanami's frankness, feeling dazzled.

"I don't have many ideas about what would have caused a mess like this. I don't know whether it's the direct cause or not, but *Homesteading the Noosphere* strikes me as fishy."

Elias nodded once, agreeing with Kanami. From the looks of it, the two had already discussed this.

That could be it, Leonardo admitted.

However, at the same time, it was nonsense.

The incident had happened on the third of May. The expansion pack had been scheduled to unlock on *May 4*.

In *Elder Tales*, expansion content was downloaded little by little, even during play, using the bandwidth available during the game: the "leeway" in the transmission speed. The *Homesteading the Noosphere* expansion pack had already been dormant on players' computers around the world, but it was supposed to be unlocked on the day after that incident.

In other words, that data was still asleep.

True, it was odd that the date and time had been so close. However, since the data was still dormant, there was no way to test it. Since they'd been assimilated into the world of *Elder Tales*, they had no way to directly examine the data on their computers.

"Well… Yeah, true, the expansion pack seems suspicious. I know the Catastrophe hit right before *Homesteading the Noosphere* came through. There could be some connection. Still, even if there is, so what? …The fact of the matter is, the expansion pack hasn't been implemented. In this world, there's no way to examine something that hasn't been installed, is there?"

Kanami was the one to answer Leonardo:

"That's why we're going to Japan!"

"Why? I don't get it."

"Japan is an eastern country."

"Huh…?"

"It's fourteen hours ahead of New York. In other words, the Japanese server is the only server in the world where *Homesteading the Noosphere* was implemented, and that's where we're going. If we do, at the very least, I think we'll probably find some sort of clue."

▸7

Fourteen hours. That was the time difference.

In regions that were farther east than New York, May 4 would have already arrived.

Right: the introduction date for *Homesteading the Noosphere* was May 4. Once his thoughts had taken him that far, Leonardo yelled in astonishment:

"The expansion pack's been implemented in Japan?!"

"Yes, it has."

The indistinct male voice startled Leonardo again.

When he looked at Elias, the other man shook his head as if he was startled, too. True, it probably hadn't been him. Elias had a deep, carrying, "handsome guy" voice that suited his slender build and mild face. Even his voice had been designed for the female fans.

It wasn't a mumbly voice like this one.

When Leonardo shot a tentative glance at Coppélia, she gazed back at him blankly with dark ultramarine eyes like polished turquoise. No matter how he thought about it, it couldn't have been her.

"Kanami. This is a serious conversation. Quit with the weird voices."

"And why exactly would I be talking like my nose was all plugged up, Croakanardo?"

"I'm not Croakanardo. I'm Leonardo."

"Right, respect the original work."

"You said it, pal. This frog suit is a hero's… Who was that?!"

Leonardo had heard the low voice again, and when he looked over in the direction it came from, he saw a white horse.

"Oh. It's the horse from earlier."

The fact that a horse had spoken was strange to begin with, but Kanami's easygoing tone made his surprise shrivel up as if she'd dashed cold water over it. It felt pointless to pay attention to her every single time.

"It's *your* horse, Kanami. Right?"

"No, it isn't. Didn't you have it waiting to use in your escape, Croakanardo?"

"Nope."

Even as he answered, Leonardo somehow managed to keep from retorting, *You mean you got right onto a horse you thought somebody else had waiting and made that somebody run beside it?!*

In any case, the sort of horses and other mounts that could be summoned with items were meant to be used as transportation. It took a set amount of time to summon them, and it really wasn't something you wanted to do in the midst of battle.

Most midlevel Adventurers owned whistles that summoned horses. As a hard-core gamer, Leonardo even had a kelpie summoning pipe that he'd won in a raid, but this white horse wasn't his style.

"And why is a white horse talking, anyway?"

"He is not a white horse. He is a hakutaku. From what Coppélia knows, they are traditional sacred beasts in China, believed to understand human language and have detailed knowledge of everything under the sun. In *Elder Tales*, they are classified as mystical beasts."

"Bingo!"

"Ah. So you can talk because you understand human speech. I see. And you fell in love with me and came to save me—"

"Wrong!"

At that word from the white horse—the mystical beast hakutaku—Kanami looked put out.

The horse continued, "And anyway, why should a mystical beast have to waltz into the middle of a battle like that and rescue a girl Monk? I'm under no obligation to do any such thing. I've got no motive for it."

"Are you sure?" she retorted. "If I saw one of those, I'd dive right in. They look like fun."

It was Leonardo's turn to scowl at Kanami. When he glanced to the side, Elias also looked tired. Apparently, he didn't welcome everything about Kanami's personality, either.

"Hmm. Well, I don't have any horsey friends…," she added.

"You turned into a Monk, Kanami," the magical beast noted. "It's been two years since we last met. It looks like your entire account is different. How's life in England treating you? Is eel pie lethally nasty?"

"Boy, is it ever. Seriously, England's brutal about stuff like that.

Whoever said the only delicious thing in England is breakfast hit the nail right on the head. I've gotten really into doing my own cooking over the past two years. But if you want to know why the food's bad, I think the water quality in England is iffy to begin with… And, um, who are you, Mr. Horse?"

"KR. Long time no see."

"Huuuuh?!"

Kanami's loud yell was sucked into the highland night, where the only other thing that howled was the wind. Elias, who'd been serenaded with that scream at point-blank range, twisted his expression—which was usually handsome—into a grimace like a Buddhist ascetic and muttered, "If he's a friend, introduce us."

In spite of himself, Leonardo laughed quietly. *You're wrecking your looks, buddy.*

"Um, KR is…"

"I'll tell 'em myself. If I let Kanami handle this, she'll turn it into a cheap play instead of an introduction."

"You're a meanie, KR."

Apparently, Kanami and this mystical beast were old friends.

"I'm KR. You can't tell from the name, but I'm Japanese. I was friends with Kanami here back when she lived in Japan. Up until two years ago, she acted as the leader of a certain play group and flustered the bejeebers out of us."

"She sounds like kind of a pain."

Her excellent hearing seemed to have caught Leonardo's murmured verbal jab.

"Oh, who cares? It was fun, and they were all good kids."

"Well, Kanami was the leader of that play group, and I was one of the members."

"I see, I see. So you helped Kanami out on a daily basis, KR."

"No, I thought it was funny, and I went along with her and made the messes worse."

Would you listen to this horse?!

The creature that looked like a white horse had come closer to the fire; it made a low whuffling noise, then lowered its long neck and nuzzled up to Coppélia. There was a third eye in its forehead, and its hind legs were covered in luxurious fur. It was a fantastic animal that only resembled a white horse.

"Hey! KR! Quit harassing her!"

"I'm not harassing her. We're communicating. Besides, I want some water, too. You could have a little consideration, you know."

The words had been directed at Kanami, but Leonardo took his canteen out of his magic bag, hesitated a little, then poured it into a basin. The mystical beast who'd called himself KR thanked him and began to drink.

"Still, in that case, you're an Adventurer, Sir KR? That shape…"

"Maybe the Catastrophe turned everyone on the Japanese server into animals, and now the place looks like a safari park?!"

Kanami looked terribly happy, as if stars were about to start falling from her eyes, but Leonardo thought, *Yeah, right. There's no way.*

He was starting to understand this Kanami woman.

In exchange for holding in the comeback, he directed a question at KR.

"So, KR, you're a…Summoner?"

"Correct. Hey, Kanami, did you notice? We've got somebody clever here."

"Hmm! Croakanardo is clever? Cute on top of being clever?! Bweh-heh-heh! I got myself a bargain."

Leonardo glared at Kanami reproachfully, but it didn't seem to get through to her at all. In the first place, KR had been saying "You're dumb, Kanami" in a roundabout way, but even the sarcasm seemed to have gone over her head.

"Can Summoners take animal shapes? I'd heard that type of sorcery was a secret technique of the fairy tribe, but—"

"Nah, that's not it. This is probably Soul Possession."

KR gave a low whinny, as if agreeing with Leonardo's comment.

"Exactly. It's Soul Possession. In other words, this hakutaku is a mystical beast I summoned myself."

"So what's this 'Soul Possession' business?" Kanami sounded puzzled, so Leonardo began to explain.

"Uh, well… Soul Possession is a Summoner special skill. I don't know much about it, either, but when this was *Elder Tales*, I'm pretty sure it was a spell that let you swap control with a summoned pet."

In *Elder Tales*, being able to call servant entities wasn't a particularly rare gimmick. Naturally, Summoners were the top authorities when it came to this skill, but if you weren't picky about variations or abilities, almost all the Recovery and Magic Attack classes could summon beings of some sort.

A typical example was Bug Light, an area-illuminating spell that all Recovery classes learned. Strictly speaking, it was a summoning spell: It called upon mystical fireflies that gave off a faint light.

The world was believed to hold several thousand diverse varieties of special summoning skills, including types that were item activated. Even Leonardo, who was a veteran player, didn't have a clear idea of the whole picture.

There was also a way to classify those countless summoning techniques by whether they could be controlled.

For example, once the previously mentioned Bug Light was summoned, all it did was float near the caster, illuminating the area, until it was released or the effect time ran out. It wasn't possible to control it, and it wasn't likely to be put to practical use.

On the other hand, some summoned creatures were completely controllable.

One example was the Summoner's servant. A summoned mystical beast—a Salamander, for example—was able to take orders to attack, defend, or move from its caster. In other words, it could be controlled by the caster's orders.

In the *Elder Tales* game, this element of control had been handled by giving orders to summoned creatures.

However, there hadn't been many order types. Attack, defend, prioritize recovery, move, follow me, stay there, and guard the area—that was about all of them. Even if, hypothetically, the summoned creature had had lots of special attack skills, the decision of which skill to use had been left to the creature's AI, and the AI's capabilities certainly hadn't been high.

That was what the situation had been like. However, Summoners'

Soul Possession spell had allowed them to control a summoned creature in its entirety.

When a player used Soul Possession, their control screen changed to the perspective of the mystical beast that had been targeted by the spell. The ability values that were displayed belonged to the beast, and it became possible to select its special skills using icons, the same way the player had done as an Adventurer.

Of course, most mystical beasts didn't have them, but it was even possible to display equipment and item screens and to speak using the beast's mouth.

As the skill's name indicated, you possessed a mystical beast. The spell had some interesting special characteristics, but it also had a big disadvantage: The body of the one who'd conducted the possession—in other words, the Summoner's own body—could now be controlled with simple orders, like a summoned creature, by the possessed mystical beast.

In short, you could say it was a spell that took a caster and a summoned creature and switched their control methods.

Generally speaking, the Adventurer-Summoner had all sorts of special skills that were far more adaptable than the summoned creature's handful of skills. In addition, when you compared the servant mystical beast and its summoner, the Adventurer, it was clear which one was more important.

On top of that, Soul Possession took a long time to cast and a long time to release. If a sudden crisis came up, the Adventurer couldn't return to their body quickly.

As a result, during the days of *Elder Tales*, the Soul Possession spell had been treated as a special skill that was "interesting enough, but mostly just a joke."

"Oho. Oho!"

After listening to Leonardo's explanation, Kanami nodded. The nodding seemed to be because she was convinced, not because she was sleepy, so Leonardo deemed it a win. He couldn't take responsibility for the question of how much she'd actually understood, but at this point, as long as she didn't yank the conversation around, he wasn't going to sweat the small stuff. To a certain extent, good code masters let their audiences' reactions slide.

"In other words, you haven't turned into a horsey, KR."

"Of course not."

"So is this white, silky horse a Thoroughbred fraud?!"

"What are you talking about, Kanami? Are you maybe—no, are you actually an idiot?"

"Eh-heh-heh-hehhh."

"Why are you acting all moonstruck? It's creepy."

"Well, I ran into an old friend, and I'm pretty happy about it."

Watching the two joke around with each other—*Is that right? It certainly is, yes indeed*—Leonardo shrugged.

In the first place, Thoroughbred racehorses were considered living works of art. The velvety coat was noble, and it wasn't as if he didn't understand the urge to touch it… But the way Kanami moved her hands toward KR was creepy, abnormal, and just wrong.

"Then where are you, Mr. KR?"

Coppélia had been silent up until now, but when her sweet voice spoke, KR answered.

"In Japan. Of course. We didn't think about it when this was a game, but apparently distance doesn't affect how this special skill works."

"Whoa, hold it, is your actual body okay? Soul Possession is a gag spell that leaves you unprotected, remember?!"

"Never fear. I'm on vacation in a guarded house that's hidden deep in the woods and very hard to find. That said, I haven't actually been back there in over two months."

"I see… So that's how you're using it."

Now that he thought about it, it was an excellent idea.

Since *Elder Tales* was a game, movement had been restricted to the control screen. However, after the Catastrophe, they'd probably gained more freedom. KR had doubtless made clever use of that to get his own hideaway and guard. It was possible that KR's friends were taking care of his actual body for him.

After all, as long as you resolved the problem of your own body, Soul Possession was a special skill with a wide range of applications.

"Well, never mind about me. It's true that *Homesteading the Noosphere* has already been implemented on the Japanese server."

"Are you sure?"

"Positive. As proof, several Adventurers on that server have already hit level 91."

Level 91.

That was definite proof.

For close to two years now, the level maximum in *Elder Tales* had been 90, but there had been an announcement that it would be increased with the new expansion pack, *Homesteading the Noosphere.*

"So are there new dungeons? New quests or monsters, new items? Or actually, are there any hints about how to clear up this mess?"

After he'd practically yelled those questions, Leonardo was surprised by the sharpness in his own voice. *Am I really this starved for information? Do I think the situation is unfair?*

It was enough to make him aware of these things all over again.

"I'll only answer the stuff I can answer, but… That's right— Mind if I call you Leonardo?"

"That's fine. Call me whatever you want. And? How're things?"

As Kanami, Elias, and Coppélia watched, Leonardo stood up and walked over to the white mystical beast. In the wilderness night, below a sky of twinkling stars, the orange campfire snapped loudly.

"I possessed this mystical beast and crossed to the continent in order to gather information. I figured that Specs or the Captain or somebody would pick up on anything in-country, even if I did nothing; that's why I prioritized the areas overseas. I hit shore on the Korean server, circled around from the Chinese server to the Russian server, then headed south and back to the Chinese server. I went all over the place in two months."

"…"

"The world's in horrible shape. Seriously wasted. Of course, every place has people who are trying to maintain order. However, I found out there are also lots of people who aren't doing that. Even in areas where the Adventurers aren't plotting something heinous, they're working desperately just to survive. The Adventurers have abandoned most People of the Earth. They think the world is on a fast track to destruction and walk around looking gray."

"——!"

"I've heard rumors—lots of 'em. Right now, though, I know nothing about new quests or dungeons. It's all vague. Nobody knows anything specific. What little intel there is melts into delusions and vanishes. There aren't any bulletin boards that discuss solutions, and there aren't any wikis. Adventurers are astoundingly hopeless. Over these two months, I learned that real well. It may be half-sized, but the world is big. I didn't think we'd be this useless without the Web. To put it bluntly, right now, Adventurers are just blockheads. Without information support, modern people are good for absolutely nothing."

CHAPTER. 2

VILLAGE OF THEK

▶ NAME: KANAMI

▶ LEVEL: 90

▶ RACE: HUMAN

▶ CLASS: MONK

▶ HP: 15163

▶ MP: 4615

▶ ITEM 1:

[GIANT-KILLER GAUNTLETS]

PRODUCTION-CLASS WEAPONS MADE WITH A TON OF MATERIALS ACQUIRED ON QUESTS. AS THEIR NAME INDICATES, THEY'RE HIGHLY EFFECTIVE AGAINST GIANTS. SINCE THE WEAPONS ALSO HAVE GOOD BASIC PERFORMANCE, THEY'VE REMAINED POPULAR EVER SINCE THE PRODUCTION RECIPE WAS IMPLEMENTED.

▶ ITEM 2:

[ORCHID MANTIS BATTLE COSTUME]

SECRET-CLASS CLOTH ARMOR SAID TO HAVE BEEN CUSTOM-MADE BY THE KING OF THE FAIRIES FOR A TOMBOY FAIRY PRINCESS WHO WANTED TO BECOME A MONK. ITS MAIN COLORS ARE WHITE AND LIGHT PINK, BUT CONTRARY TO ITS SHOWY APPEARANCE, IT WAS DESIGNED WITH AN EMPHASIS ON OFFENSIVE PERFORMANCE.

▶ ITEM 3:

[TAMAHAGANE SKILLET]

A STEEL FRYING PAN MADE BY A FAMOUS SWORDSMITH IN A MISCHIEVOUS MOMENT. EVEN WITHOUT GREASING THIS ITEM, FOOD WON'T SCORCH OR STICK TO IT, AND IF YOU TAKE GOOD CARE OF IT, IT WILL LAST A LIFETIME. IT'S VERY HEAVY AND MAKES A GOOD WEAPON IF YOU SWING IT AROUND. THE PERFECT TRAVELING COMPANION FOR CHEFS.

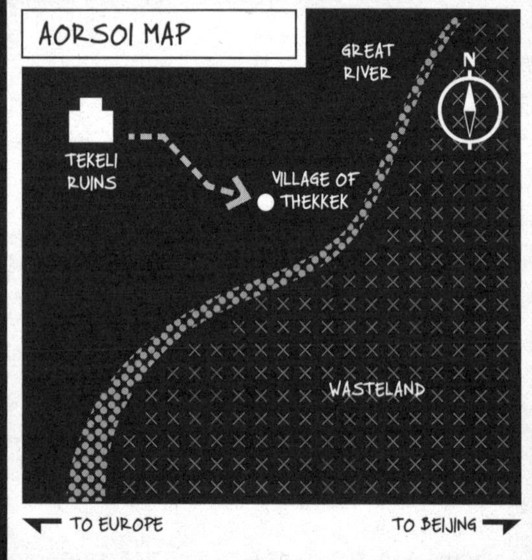
AORSOI MAP
GREAT RIVER
N
TEKELI RUINS
VILLAGE OF THEKKEK
WASTELAND
TO EUROPE
TO BEIJING

▸1

The journey was going smoothly.

Having escaped the ruins of Tekeli, Leonardo and the others were traveling through the land of Aorsoi. Their destination was the place where the land ended: the Far East. Japan.

However, they couldn't just go blindly east.

It was easy to lump it all together as "wilderness," but midwestern Eured was full of ups and downs. The land itself was a plateau, but there were several hundred mountains running across that high-altitude wasteland.

Of course, metaphorically speaking, those mountains were no more than wrinkles in the handkerchief of the earth. Compared to the vastness of Eured, they couldn't have been that tall.

Even so, for the four people and lone horse who moved over the earth as if clinging to it, this wasn't true. The mountains that appeared one after another like screens boasted heights of several thousand meters each.

Because the land was far too vast, their senses had been numbed, and it had seemed as though they could climb over them easily. With nothing to block it, the sky was just that wide.

To the north was one of the highest mountainous regions in the world, the Tian Shan Mountains. In *Elder Tales*, this area was called Tian Mai, and it was known as a place where species of dragon-type monsters lived and where no human had yet set foot.

Many new players found it surprising, but in *Elder Tales*, which utilized the Half-Gaia Project, unexplored regions weren't all that rare.

Even if there was a twelvefold difference in the rate at which time passed, and even if the size of the earth had been halved, this land was vast. In addition, compared to the population of Earth, there were only so many players in *Elder Tales*. It might be a super-class MMO with a twenty-year history, but the population of all the servers put together was only seventy million.

The idea of exploring the whole world was a dream within a dream.

What had regular game play been like in *Elder Tales*?

Ordinarily, players would form parties with the members they planned to play with that day in the player town they used as their home base. Alternatively, if they were playing alone, they'd go shopping and make other preparations. Then, using the Fairy Rings, they'd travel to their destination dungeon or field zone. Once they reached their target zone, they'd adventure or do battle. That had been the general flow.

As long as they played that way, places that weren't near the Fairy Ring network naturally ended up as unexplored territory. There was really no help for this, and conversely, precisely because that was how things were, it was possible to romanticize the exploration of primitive areas and the implementation of new content.

The introduction of an expansion pack typically meant that appealing fields, towns, and dungeons were designed for a previously unexplored place, monsters and treasure were distributed across it, a story was established within it in the form of quests, and Adventurers were guided there using the Fairy Rings.

The projects were a bit like planned community developments executed on a global scale.

But the region of Aorsoi had low population density. In other words, there weren't many players, and it wasn't very profitable. If other areas grew overcrowded, the developers would probably start paying attention to it, but at present there was only arid wasteland rolling away on all sides.

Four people rode through that wasteland on horseback.

Leonardo, Elias, and Coppélia each handled warhorses they'd summoned, while Kanami was on the hakutaku that KR was controlling with Soul Possession.

The morning sun shone down brightly and impartially over the group and the wide world.

It was easy to call it a wasteland, but its appearance wasn't monotonous. The ground under their feet was crumbling, dull gray sandstone, but from the sheer, roughly five-hundred-meter cliff on their left, they could see a great S-shaped, winding river far below.

The river was probably more than five hundred meters wide. Although the land couldn't have been drier, deep forests of vivid conifers lined the path the river had carved on both sides.

The green of those forests and the blue of the sky's reflection in the river were so brilliant that it almost hurt to look at them.

The party was traveling roughly south across a plateau that looked down over the expansive river. There were a couple of reasons for this: Crossing the mountains would have been difficult, and if they were going east, they couldn't do it very efficiently without finding a road they could traverse on horseback.

In addition, as long as they kept going south along the great river, if they happened to run out of food, they thought they could probably hunt some sort of game. When they asked what Kanami had chosen as her production class, they found out she had selected Chef. If push came to shove, they'd be able to count on her.

"If we keep going south, there's a village."

"You sure know a lot, KR."

The Adventurer who was possessing the three-eyed hakutaku, a mystical beast that looked like a white horse, spoke to Kanami, who was on said beast's back. However, from the volume of his voice, it was clear that he'd been addressing their surrounding companions as well.

This Kanami woman had a sort of natural leadership, or possibly a cheerful charisma, that pulled everyone around her in with her. She was willful, but there wasn't even a hint of the deviousness that would have tried to force that will onto others, or of the greed that would have used her willfulness to satisfy her own desires. Her personality wouldn't have gone over well with everybody, but you couldn't hate her.

That said, acknowledging her charisma and respecting her were apparently two different things.

KR, who claimed to be her old friend, acknowledged Kanami's leadership, but he didn't seem to be relying on her sense of geography or surroundings in the slightest. They were crossing the wasteland on what were his very nearly arbitrary decisions.

For her part, Kanami seemed to generously accept this; she saw no problem with it. Looking at that relationship made it seem she was, if nothing else, made of impressive stuff.

"A village, you said?"

"Yes, well… It really could have been a town."

"What do you mean, Sir KR?"

At Elias's question, KR fell silent and kept moving forward. It seemed more as if he was thinking about how to answer him than as if he was ignoring him.

That was probably only to be expected.

Elias and Kanami seemed pretty close. He'd heard that they'd already been traveling together when Coppélia had joined them. Still, Elias was an Ancient. He wasn't a human from Earth. It was hard to decide whether it was all right to explain parts of the *Elder Tales* game situation to him or whether those were still secret.

Since the time they'd made camp the other day, Leonardo and the others had been talking about the expansion pack, and Elias seemed to see it as ritual magic so enormous it affected the world itself. That understanding was correct, in a way—it did influence the world—but it missed the mark with regard to the fact that a game development company on Earth, somewhere outside this world, had created the place.

Leonardo sighed. *It was program code that created this world, not magic.*

Central Eured, the area around Aorsoi, hadn't yet been sufficiently developed as game content. The topography had been automatically created from satellite photos and laser measurements, and the plants and rocks were program-generated fractal objects.

In the same way, the "village" they were headed for was bound to be a featureless place that had been generated automatically by an "automatic village creation program" based on random numbers.

* * *

On real-world Earth, villages were built based on the locations of rivers and the type of terrain. Then the villages were linked by roads, and if conditions were good, they would grow into towns and cities.

Although the world of *Elder Tales* had been designed based on Earth, even if it had a fictional history, it hadn't actually gone through progressive development. This meant that, where there was a town of a certain size in the real world, the designers created a residential area, using this method to simulate the growth of villages in a general way.

For major cities, the game designers were involved from the very beginning, and they modeled them to be unique residential areas bursting with distinctive features. In particular, the cities where the game began—the ones known as "player towns"—had been given elaborate buildings and scenery, and many People of the Earth and facilities had been placed there.

Midsized cities were mostly places for People of the Earth to live. However, for those occasions when Adventurers visited, they had several shops and People of the Earth who'd been given special conversation data in order to move quests forward.

That said, smaller villages were created by the automatic village creation program.

Leonardo was just a player, and the only development system–related knowledge he had came from interviews on game information sites. However, according to what he remembered, once they determined the location, size, and population of a town, they just distributed wooden houses in ways that corresponded to the actual terrain, had some appropriate People of the Earth move in, and decorated the nearby scenery with farm fields and similar things. In other words, the automatic village creation program was a design support program that created villages that "felt legit," even if they had no distinguishing features.

"Ordinarily, in terms of the traffic on the nearby river and roads and the scale of commerce, it wouldn't be weird for the place to be a city or a town, but at this point, it's just a village… That's what he meant, Elias," Leonardo said.

Over the past few days, Leonardo had built amicable relationships with the members of the party. Kanami didn't have a fussy personality, and Coppélia was quiet and reserved about everything—a likeable young woman.

As a hero who'd been born to a fairy and a human, Elias was somehow incredibly difficult to comment on, but his personality itself was uncomplicated, and he was easy to get along with. If you kept an eye out for the delusions of grandeur that crept in sometimes (and he actually did have magic he could use, so you couldn't unconditionally call them "delusions"), he wasn't a bad traveling companion.

"Coppélia has detected a shape that appears to be the village up ahead."

As she sat sidesaddle, dexterously controlling her horse, the small figure in the maid uniform pointed out a spot far ahead of them.

They could see the smoke from several cookfires rising like white threads into the transparent, glassy blue sky.

Even if the village had been automatically generated, they'd probably be able to replenish their supplies and get food to tide them over for a while. On top of that, if they asked, they might be able to learn about the state of traffic in the vicinity and find out how well the highways were maintained.

As things stood, they didn't even know if they'd have to cross a desert in order to go east. Easygoing Kanami aside, the entire party was in agreement that they needed more information.

"Yes, that's it. That's Thekkek, the village I was looking for."

So spoke KR in a laid-back manner.

▶2

Thekkek was a featureless People of the Earth village.

That was only to be expected. If something randomly generated by a program had character, it would be a problem. This "ordinariness" that generically matched the terrain was exactly what had been intended.

It was probable that each server and region had a list of general data and registered models. The houses in the dusty village were made of sun-dried bricks and gnarled wood, and they really did look as if they'd been built in the wilderness by a nomadic people.

The well at the entrance was built from neatly assembled dark gray rock—the only structure in the village that was. In the early-autumn sunlight, the broad-leaved tree that stood at its edge cast a deep black shadow.

There seemed to be about thirty houses.

Most of the villagers were inside, in neighboring narrow fields, or on their way back from the wilderness while following astonishingly large flocks of sheep. It was a small village, tiny enough to take in with one look around. Its entire population could have lived within one city block in New York. That seemed to be the entirety of this bubble that floated on the wasteland.

As Leonardo's party traveled down the road that ran through the center of town, the People of the Earth moved out of their way. They seemed wary, but not afraid. Leonardo thought it was likely, even if they hadn't had any direct contact with Adventurers, they'd at least heard rumors of them.

Up until he'd arrived at the Tekeli Ruins and encountered that hideous trap, Leonardo had traveled across the vastness of Aorsoi by himself. Due to his experiences in Big Apple, he'd avoided groups of other Adventurers, but he'd stopped at a few People of the Earth villages for necessities like food and oil.

Judging by that experience, the reactions of the People of the Earth in this village were par for the course.

"Say! Is there a place that sells food around here?"

Kanami, who was up ahead of Leonardo, cheerfully chatted up a local man, middle-aged and wearing a square cap on his head. He looked taken aback at being addressed, but after thinking for a little while, he answered her.

"There's no place where you can buy cooked meals. We're a tiny village, see. If you're after travel rations, though, I think you could get some at Yagudo's place."

"Yagudo?"

"The village chief."

From that brief exchange, they learned that this village had no independent shops.

You couldn't expect much else from a town whose population wasn't even three hundred; peddlers provided all the commercial goods they needed from the outside world. Leonardo had stopped by villages about this size before, and they'd all been similar.

"I see. Thanks!"

Saying that there was no need to thank him, the middle-aged villager returned to his house.

The People of the Earth around them also went back to their own jobs in twos and threes, tending the fields or drawing water. The Adventurers had probably struck them as unusual, but they seemed satisfied upon learning that the strangers were in the midst of a journey and had only stopped to replenish their supplies.

All villages are the same, Leonardo thought.

Though, he preferred this sort of awareness. The People of the Earth here were much better than the ones in Big Apple. Back there, all he'd seen in their faces had been despair and emptiness. In that case, the wary expressions in this village were far better. They were the sort of thing you often saw in wilderness villages, and if Leonardo had been in their shoes, he probably would have felt the same way.

Come to think of it, I've been traveling through Aorsoi all this time, but…

"Hey, Kanami? Elias? Where did you come from?" he wondered aloud. "Have you been traveling on horseback the whole way?"

"Yep," Kanami replied immediately. "Well, though I guess we've been together since Ulster."

"What's Ulster?"

"Britain."

"So you went to England, too? But then what was the Via de Fleurs business?"

"We ran into Coppélia near Paris. Before that, I circled around Europe. There were lots of things I wanted to know."

Kanami's answer sounded a bit absentminded; she'd gotten down from the hakutaku and was rummaging through her magic bag. Maybe Elias noticed; he'd also dismounted and was stroking his horse's neck, but he helped her out:

"Lady Kanami and I met on the outskirts of Londinium."

"Oh, really?"

Leonardo dismounted from his horse as well.

Traditionally, this area was populated by nomads. The People of the Earth—even the children—were skilled at horseback riding. However, he thought staying on his horse in the center of the village might be a breach of etiquette.

Coppélia was hesitating, and he gave her a hand.

She was unexpectedly heavy. It was apparently due to her armor, which looked like a maid outfit at first glance.

That said, Leonardo's arms were stronger now that he was an Adventurer, and the weight wasn't much of a burden. In this world, he wasn't an IT worker–geek who holed up in his house and took in maintenance work for servers and e-commerce sites. He was an unbeatable ninja hero.

"You said you went around Europe. So, uh…how are things there?" Leonardo asked.

When he thought about North America—his home—hesitation came through his voice. It wasn't clear whether or not Elias had noticed it; the Ancient sighed heavily and gazed into the distance.

He was looking at the western sky.

"'Europe,' hmm? The word isn't familiar to me, but the western parts of Eured are as I expect you imagine them to be, Sir Leonardo."

As he continued, Elias took his horse's bit and began to walk.

"The coastal areas of Liderutz and the Land of Seven Queens have been sealed off."

"Sealed?"

"Independent cities. Perhaps 'city-states' would be a better term. Both keep groups of Adventurers as if they were knight brigades and are protecting themselves and guarding against other cities."

"Is there a war on or something?"

"No, not in so many words. However, the world is unforgiving. If left undisturbed, the monsters' numbers grow, and they begin attacking people. Royals and aristocrats have chosen to fortify the cities in which they live and barricade themselves inside them. A few good rulers are working to defend their territories and maintain peace and order, but most small towns and villages, those with no defensive walls or soldiers, are being abandoned."

"What do you mean?"

"Exactly what I've said. Even if monsters attack, no help comes. At the very least, the lords' soldiers don't go to save them."

"Why not? Even though it's their own territory?"

"They claim that, if their main stronghold were to be attacked while they were off providing aid, more of their citizens would suffer."

Elias's face twisted in disgust.

"In order to protect themselves from monsters, they gather Adventurers and keep them close. However, you see, if a city has assembled Adventurers, the surrounding cities begin to fear invasion. And so, in defense, they must form contracts of their own with Adventurer guilds and set them to work defending their own cities. It's an arms race."

The sight rose vividly in Leonardo's mind.

It was the sort of thing that seemed terribly likely to happen in this chaotic world.

"In the Land of Seven Queens and the Military Nation of Galient, the unions of People of the Earth have become mere figureheads. The venerable Ulster Knights Sword Alliance has fallen apart. The fortified cities are competing to see which of them can contract with the strongest, most celebrated Adventurer guilds. Cities that have successfully hired powerful Adventurer guilds advertise how safe they are, strengthening their influence over nearby farmers and traders. Because the church's forces are also cozying up to the Adventurers, contract deposits are going through the roof."

By "powerful Adventurer guilds," he probably meant the sort of major guilds that took part in raids. Guilds of that size could put together legion raids, which were combat units composed of ninety-six members.

In *Elder Tales*, that was probably the strongest military unit in existence. Of course, the People of the Earth could put together armies larger than that, but each Adventurer had outstanding combat abilities, plus they were able to communicate using the telechat function. A unit of ninety-six Adventurers would have higher combat potential than several thousand People of the Earth.

"However, the money for those contract deposits is taken from the populace. In their attempts to cope with the Catastrophe, the nobles and lords have set heavy taxes everywhere and ruined public finance. It's terrible—riots are breaking out. There are also some lords who want to pay Adventurers for their contracts in rights and interests, and in material goods."

"Material goods…?"

"Please don't ask. I don't even want to say it. Although I don't think much of the people who accept such things, either."

"Even so."

Hearing a murmuring voice, Leonardo turned.

It was Coppélia.

She went on, gripping her horse's reins, her face expressionless.

"Coppélia says that life in the urban areas is safer than it is in the wilderness or in remote regions. The danger of life in a farming village is one thousand five hundred percent greater than it was in the previous year. This is due to the influence of patrolling Adventurers and uncleared quests."

Leonardo and Elias had fallen speechless. Coppélia continued.

"Poison Ghouls appeared in Romalnes. Death that resembles a contagious illness is spreading through the People of the Earth who reside in that region. Coppélia subjugated fifty-six hundred and twenty-nine Poison Ghouls in the salt-sown land of Romalnes, and yet the situation did not change."

"Why so many? All by yourself?"

"When Lady Kanami and I passed by," Elias added, "Lady Coppélia was fighting alone."

"……"

Coppélia nodded as if that was nothing.

Her pure white maid's headdress wavered over her indigo bobbed hair. Did her struggle mean nothing to her? Still wearing no expression in particular, the girl impassively went on:

"On the green plain where Coppélia was fighting, there was a village very similar to this one. It was a commonplace village, the sort one can find anywhere. Commonplace villagers lived in it, four hundred fifty-nine of them. Conveniently for Adventurers, it had a Blacksmith who was able to repair weapons. It also had a grocer. Both were People of the Earth, and there was nothing particularly noteworthy about them, age and gender included."

Leonardo listened closely to Coppélia's voice.

"To Coppélia, that village was a very convenient base. Coppélia had been patrolling in order to hunt targets in the area, and she often returned to that village to have her equipment repaired, and occasionally to replenish items. On Coppélia's seventh visit to that village, the village had acquired another resident. A young Person of the Earth child with no real distinguishing characteristics had joined it. The villagers requested a blessing from Coppélia. They seemed to anticipate that, as a Cleric, Coppélia would have beneficent abilities of some sort. Coppélia did not know how to give a blessing."

It was a strangely moving story.

"Coppélia asked, 'Do you wish to be healed?' The villagers did not seem to understand. Coppélia used a level-85 Symbol of Sun. Because the villagers were ignorant, they seemed to believe that its effect was a miracle. They thanked Coppélia effusively. Coppélia learned to ask others what they wanted. It was useful knowledge."

Coppélia gazed into the distance as if remembering something.

However, to Leonardo, it didn't look as if she'd found what she was searching for.

"On Coppélia's ninth visit to the village, the village's population was zero. There were several dozen Poison Ghouls still in the village. Coppélia eliminated the targets, then went to the plain and continued to do battle. There were many targets, and Coppélia had no shortage of opponents. Her weapons broke, and the lack of a base where they could be repaired was inconvenient, but the results of her hunt were favorable. Even when her armor was destroyed and she lost her shields, Coppélia obeyed her orders perfectly. If she had not encountered

Master, no doubt Coppélia would still be carrying out her previous orders."

Leonardo couldn't tell how the young woman felt as she told her story. She was only giving a report in a matter-of-fact way.

"Coppélia, you're—"

Just as Leonardo started to speak to her, although he didn't know what he should say, there was a loud crash, and a cloud of dust went up far ahead. It was beyond the house of the village chief that had been pointed out to them. There were screams in the clamor.

"Elias!"

"Yes, Sir Leonardo. Kanami's gone. *Tch!* So she's charged in again, has she?!"

Leonardo and Elias sprinted straight for the uproar.

▶3

Thekkek was a small village that had been built in the wilderness.

Naturally, its main street wasn't even two kilometers long. Elias and Leonardo, who had Adventurer leg strength on their side, reached the site of the dust cloud in the blink of an eye.

"Hold it, time out!!"

Kanami had been blown in Leonardo's direction. For a moment he considered ducking, but no matter how mouthy she was, Kanami was a girl, so he thought better of it and caught her. However, she was moving as though she'd been hit by a dump truck, and after catching her under his arm, Leonardo immediately tossed her aside.

"What do you think you're doing, Croakanardo?!"

"You're fine. I killed your momentum, so it's not like you got hurt."

Raising his blades, Leonardo glared at the building up ahead, which was something between a shed and a stable. He couldn't provide a more specific guess than that because the building was already broken so badly that it was practically a ruin.

Some enormously strong being had gone on a rampage, snapping pillars, bursting through walls, and sending Kanami flying.

Next to him, Leonardo saw Elias level his transparent two-handed sword. His expression was tense, too.

"Lady Kanami, what's over there?" he demanded.

"It looked like a little boy, maybe?"

"What?"

"It looked like a little boy."

That was as far as the answer went.

With a roar, the shed collapsed in front of them. Something came flying out of the cloud of dust and crashed right into Elias. The People of the Earth, who'd dashed out of their houses to see what all the noise was about and were hanging back at a distance, screamed.

The thing that Elias had blocked with his sword was a lone boy.

His clothes and height were unremarkable, no different from the other children in this village. However, his expression was warped with insanity. With his teeth and hands, he'd stopped Elias's sword as he crouched in a beast-like stance.

Elias had frozen up in astonishment. Taking advantage of the opening, the boy intentionally lost his balance, then flew into the swordsman's chest with the speed of a black gale.

Their brief crossing opened a big tear in the pure white coat Elias wore.

Elias belonged to the renowned Knights of the Red Branch, and the lustrous garment was practically his trademark. At first glance, the cloth looked smooth, but it had outstanding resistance to blades, and its defense was higher than mediocre metal armor.

However, the boy had ripped that coat easily. He licked his long, overgrown nails.

Through the slit cloth on Elias's chest, a faint wound was visible.

"Eli-Eli, you okay?"

"I'm fine, Lady Kanami. More importantly, that boy is—"

Without giving them time to talk, the boy leapt at Elias again. He moved with the speed of a wild animal, bending low. It wasn't the stance of a bipedal being; it belonged to a quadrupedal beast. The black shadow shifted through mesmerizing changes in course, as if he were gripping the ruined ground with his feet, and launched himself at Elias from an unexpected direction.

"No!!"

At Kanami's cry, Elias flipped his blade over.

The transparent two-handed sword interrupted its trajectory partway through, then swung down like a giant club. The boy leapt backward, away from the swing, but it hadn't been the sort of attack that would wound him, so he seemed unfazed.

"Croakanardo..."

"I know."

Ignoring the fact that she'd called him by that rude nickname, Leonardo picked up on what Kanami was trying to tell him:

The boy's status.

His name was Sejin. His level was 34.

...And his main class was Gnoll.

It was impossible.

Gnolls were a type of malicious monster. They were a vicious race with doglike heads and small, round ears. They behaved like hyenas, hunting in packs.

They were highly intelligent, and they used leather armor and one-handed weapons. They were a type of monster known as demihumans, and they walked upright as a rule, but when fighting or traveling for long distances, they ran on all fours.

There were many similar monsters in the world of *Elder Tales*. Goblins, orcs, and lizardmen were the famous examples, but bugbears and kobolds existed as well. All of them were formidable enemies who built communities and menaced Adventurers in groups. Gnolls were one of the obstacles encountered by midlevel Adventurers.

Naturally, Leonardo had fought them before and was well acquainted with them. But gnolls did not look like this. They had thick hair all over their bodies, were dappled with sinister spots that were a color somewhere between gray and brown, and had shining yellow eyes, as if the moon had been set in their eye sockets.

They certainly didn't look like People of the Earth, and they couldn't mimic their shapes.

The deciding factor was that the boy's—Sejin's—status column was blinking. The "Gnoll" main class blinked repeatedly, switching with "Settler," and the level flowed back and forth between 34 and 2.

"What's happening here, Sir Leonardo?!"

"Don't take him down!"

Leonardo yelled back, responding to Elias's question.

However, he didn't know what they should do, either.

Level 34 wasn't very strong.

Elias had taken those two attacks simply because he'd been caught off guard and surprised. If he decided to take the boy down, it wouldn't be hard to destroy him.

Elias's quirk might not let him finish the boy off, but he would probably still be able to drive him into immobility.

Leonardo was sure he'd be able to kill him with a few attacks. Now that the dust had cleared, those rapid movements weren't so fast as to be untrackable.

That wasn't the problem.

"What the heck is this kid?"

"You don't know, Croakanardo?"

"No, I don't. Wait, do you know, Kanami?"

"If I knew, I wouldn't be asking! Geez!!"

Leaving the useless Kanami, Leonardo ran toward the boy. Possibly out of feral caution, the boy didn't want Leonardo getting anywhere near him; he leapt back five meters. However, Leonardo's physical abilities had already completely locked onto his movements.

Easily matching his trajectory, Leonardo drew his twin swords in midleap.

"Don't! Leonardo—!"

"Don't be an idiot. He's an enemy. If this keeps up, we'll have victims over here!"

Using the motion of his bending body, Leonardo slashed at the boy's torso with the sword in his left hand. He'd gone for the biggest target, and it had been a straightforward attack. No matter how the boy dodged, it would hit home. The attack wouldn't be lethal, but it had sharp fighting spirit behind it, and it was bound to inflict great damage on Sejin.

"Gishaaaaa!!"

The boy gave a bestial scream. He hadn't avoided Leonardo's sword.

On the contrary: He'd slammed his right palm vertically into its path. Leonardo had no time to brake the motion; the sword bit into the boy's palm, splitting it in two, then cut its way through his arm, his elbow, and even his forearm.

The sword stopped when it reached his shoulder, but the boy was no longer a two-armed creature. He was an animal with two useless cords hanging from his right shoulder like ragged rubber tubes.

"*Gishaa-shaa-shaa-shaa!*"

Bloody spittle bubbled and dripped from his mouth, and his breathing was harsh. It wasn't possible to call him a Person of the Earth anymore.

The throng of villagers gave heartrending screams and averted their eyes.

At this point in time, there was no way to tell whether the boy was from this particular village or an intruder from elsewhere. That was probably all for the best. The sight was so horrible that, if the boy's mother had been here and had recognized him as her son, her heart would have been irreparably wounded.

Make him stop moving...

Leonardo steeled himself.

He hadn't been holding back with that last attack, but he hadn't attacked in earnest, either. With his next attack, he'd overload the boy's motor nerves. It was Paralyze Blow, a paralysis attack. If that didn't stop him, he wouldn't hesitate to use Sweeper.

Having made up his mind, Leonardo wasn't startled by Sejin's surprise attack. He calmly stepped back, then slammed a front kick into his stomach, shoving him away. He even had the leeway to call to Elias, who'd circled around in front of the boy, who had been about to attempt an escape.

"Elias! Toss 'im over here!"

"Understood! Haaaaaah! Arm of the fairy of black night! Night Splash!!"

The boy had been flung into the air like a soccer ball, but using his feral sense of smell, he sniffed out his prey. When he slammed into the earth, he used the rebound and ran, staying very close to the ground. He sprinted, becoming a gust of black wind.

He was heading for Coppélia, who'd finally appeared, pushing her way through the shapes that had gathered at a distance.

When he saw the black shadow making for the unexpressive Coppélia's small, kind figure, Leonardo abandoned all attempt at control. With a speed that must have looked like teleportation to the bystanders, he closed in on the boy's neck.

In the midst of a moment so slow that even sound grew viscous, Leonardo saw a shining blue dead point on that neck. It was the marker for Sweeper, an instant-kill attack. If Sejin's level had been 70, things might have been different, but at 34, it would be unavoidable, a grim reaper's scythe.

"Hah!"

However, without giving an exaggerated yell or calling out the name of the lethal move, Leonardo selected Paralyze Blow. He knew this adversary was an NPC. He also knew he was averting imminent danger here. Even so, when Leonardo thought about lopping that head off, about forcing Coppélia and his traveling companions to see something like that, he felt a terribly visceral, unpleasant sensation that made his face twist.

Fortunately, the boy fell as if he'd been glued to the ground.

His motor nerves had been paralyzed, but he seemed to be trying to force himself to move anyway. His body spasmed over and over, like an insect, and Leonardo swiftly held him down. A muffled groan came from the boy's throat.

Now that he'd restrained him, the boy was pitifully small, just a kid with a dark Aorsoi tan and the thin, sharply planed face unique to the People of the Earth who lived in this region. There was something ominous and gruesome about the fact that a boy like that was lying as paralyzed as a broken machine, a ferocious expression on his face.

"Coppélia..."

"It is all right. Coppélia is aware of the situation."

Kneeling beside the boy, Coppélia chanted a recovery spell.

It wasn't clear what she meant to do by recovering him, but the moment she approached, the boy seemed to change. As if afraid, or maybe agitated, his spasms grew more intense, and although he couldn't speak, his faint, failing breath escaped his throat in gasping wheezes.

"Seven bells, white wings deserving of praise, use pealing fortune to do the will of the Lord—Sacred Cure."

In a quiet, murmuring voice, she healed the boy's paralysis.

The boy's insanity couldn't have been a regular status abnormality; it hadn't been a familiar effect like paralysis. It had to have been something more terrible and mysterious. Yet even so, Leonardo's misgivings aside, the ferocity drained from the boy's face.

As Coppélia observed him calmly, one hand on his forehead, the boy's breathing gradually quieted, growing regular. The bestial aura that had been there a moment before was gone.

"Did you…save him?"

Kanami asked what was on everyone's mind.

Coppélia responded to those words with a nod, then swept a hand through empty space.

Leonardo thought he glimpsed a jet-black shadow that Coppélia's fingers whisked away, but a moment later, all that remained was the cold, clear Aorsoi wind. It was as though nothing had happened at all.

▸4

"*Yi gui*? A plague demon?"

At Kanami's words, Yagudo nodded.

"So…what's that, exactly?"

"No idea. This is the first time I've seen one. I'd heard stories from peddlers, but…"

Yagudo, the village's chief and leader, shook his head several times. His expression was grave, and he looked very tired.

Yagudo's house was built of sun-dried brick. The door and windows were square and open, and the room was fresh and airy. The culture in this village was somewhere between nomadic and settled ranching; half of the buildings that could be called houses were simple things made of sun-dried brick, while the remaining half were tents made from thick cloth.

Some houses had been reinforced with wood or had built-in floors. Yagudo's house also served as the reception room for the whole village, a place where visitors from the outside world were welcomed. As a result, it was twice as big as the houses around it, and it was composed of several square rooms built around a central courtyard.

Leonardo's party was in a large, five-meter-square room in that house, talking with Yagudo about the disturbance that had just occurred.

"What sort of stories have you heard, Sir Yagudo?"

No matter whom he was talking to, Elias was always sociable and polite. In response to the question, Yagudo stroked his goatlike beard two or three times, then began to speak, remembering as he went.

"They say uncanny beings possessed by evil spirits have begun turning up in the Aorsoi wasteland. They call them 'plague demons.'"

"I see."

The view outside the window was gradually turning wine-red. Inside the room, Yagudo's elderly wife had already fed the hearth fire and was boiling water.

"The plague demons appear in the wilderness. They're said to be the survivors of destroyed villages, or lunatics, or possessed by devils. If the flocks are out at pasture, they'll steal sheep. They kill the sheep right there and eat them. Because of the way they look, they're called evil spirits or plague demons."

The chieftain's voice was low and hoarse.

"However, they don't seem to attack villagers. They pass right by people as if they can't even see them. That isn't to say they don't rampage. Some have seen them drunk on blood in the wilderness, as if they've gone mad. I also hear that, when they find an Adventurer, they attack them."

Leonardo gave a small nod.

If the "Gnoll" he'd seen on the status screen had been the truth, then the situation wasn't impossible to explain.

Gnolls really were vicious demihumans, but they didn't attack People of the Earth. This wasn't out of goodwill; it was because they were cunning and cowardly. They knew that, if they attacked a Person of the Earth, the whole group would take steps to defend against them. Those beasts tended to go after their livestock, not the People themselves.

On the other hand, if they saw an Adventurer, they would actively attack them. They knew that People of the Earth would run if they let them go, but they seemed to be aware that Adventurers were "enemies" who had come to drive them away.

If that boy had been a gnoll, it made sense that he'd attacked Kanami and had then attacked the rest of them. To gnolls, People of the Earth were mere insects, not worth attacking.

However, although that might explain why it had attacked Leonardo's group, it didn't explain why it had looked human.

"Sir Yagudo. We hadn't heard of plague demons before. Have there been tales of them in this region for a very long time?"

"No, not at all. It hasn't even been three months since we first heard of them ourselves. They appeared real suddenly," the old man responded to Elias.

"In that case, was that boy, um…"

"Was he a member of this village?"

The answer to Kanami and Coppélia's respective questions was "No."

The boy did have the characteristics of a Person of the Earth from this region, but he apparently hadn't been from this village.

The assailant himself was asleep in a corner of this same large room, wrapped in a blanket. In addition to fixing his abnormal status, the healing spell Coppélia had cast on him had recovered his split right arm, but he still hadn't regained consciousness.

To Leonardo, the boy didn't seem dangerous anymore. Most importantly, his status had stabilized so that his name was always Sejin, his level was 2, and his class was Settler. From the look of his sleeping face, he was no different from any other Person of the Earth boy, to the point where that buggy status seemed nightmarish.

"…That boy…"

"Coppélia guarantees that the boy is normal."

Yagudo continued to examine the boy's face carefully. There was no disgust in his expression, only pity.

"Do you suppose he was taken from some other village and is considered missing there?"

"There's no telling. The boy's boots are very worn, and his clothes are torn and ragged. It looks as if he's traveled quite a long distance. I think he may have been wandering for several months."

At Yagudo's words, Kanami nodded.

From her attitude, Leonardo suspected that Yagudo's guess might have matched some information she held and convinced her of something. However, Elias shrugged, and from the look of his expression, that wasn't the case. In other words, she was just nodding.

They asked Yagudo several detailed questions after that, but he had no more information for them.

When Kanami put her innate charms to work, Yagudo gladly shared his provisions with them. Of course they gave him some gold coins in exchange, but Leonardo and the others were Adventurers, and as far as they were concerned, it wasn't much money. Besides, in a remote village like this, they were just happy that someone had given them provisions at all.

However, after talking it over among themselves, Kanami's group decided to stay in the village for a few days. This was because, according to Chief Yagudo, traveling merchants were due to visit in a few days' time.

After hearing what Kanami had said, Leonardo had started wanting to make for the Japanese server, too. The idea of solving the mystery of the Catastrophe was so ridiculous that it just didn't seem real to him, but the idea of the new patch was appealing. If he leveled his combat skills up past what he currently had, he'd be safer. That would definitely come in handy when it was time for him to return to his home across the world.

That said, the land of Aorsoi was a primitive wasteland. There was no guarantee that what had happened in the ruins wouldn't happen again. It was probably too naïve to think that, even without information, as long as they went in the direction of the rising sun, they'd eventually reach Japan.

In any case, Thekkek was a small village, and the villagers almost never traveled. Naturally, the information they had was limited. The party wanted to buy consumable items, and it was clear that traveling peddlers would have more information about road conditions and similar things. On a journey across this vast continent, that information would be more precious than food.

Leonardo's group had decided that, if traders were coming, getting information would be worth waiting a few days.

When making that decision, the party went out to the stable to discuss it. Naturally, this was so that KR could participate. KR seemed to have good hearing; even from the stable, which was next door, he'd followed what Yagudo had said.

Since they were going to have a discussion, it was convenient that he already knew what was going on, but KR was pretty cross. From what he said, a mare in the same stable had been making eyes at him.

"Check you out, KR! You're so popular."

"Hey, Kanami. 'Popular' is a much finer strawberry quartz charm… And I don't want to hear that from you."

Kanami had pouted over that retort and had been ready to argue further, but they'd ignored her and had their discussion. As a result, they'd finalized their decision to stay in the village for a few days. The fact that Yagudo had offered to provide the group with lodging had been a major factor. Leonardo and Elias were sharing one room, while Kanami and Coppélia shared another.

Naturally, KR would be in the stable, and although he'd complained, Leonardo and Elias had smoothed things over and managed to get him to agree… Although Kanami called it a "love hotel" and was very close to getting kicked by KR for a few moments there.

"Still, what do you suppose that was?"

"……"

At Leonardo's words, his companions fell silent. He hadn't expected to get an answer, though; he'd never seen a status display like that one before. All he could think was that it had been some kind of bug.

"I haven't run into a phenomenon like that before."

"Nothing springs to mind from the oral traditions of the fairy tribe, either."

An unknown bug.

The idea made Leonardo shudder.

Sejin was a Person of the Earth, but could anyone guarantee that bug would occur only in People of the Earth? It was true that Adventurers seemed to be immortal in this world. Even if they fell in battle, they were sent to a temple and resurrected.

However, if they turned into something like that boy… If they ended up as something like that, could they still be called "immortal"?

Say there was a being that was warped that way, then simply did not die. For this world, that being would be a disaster. For the person in question, it would be an endless nightmare, a living hell.

"Is that the sort of 'something' that can be handled by casting an abnormal status recovery spell?"

The question had come from KR, and Coppélia answered it.

"Coppélia has determined that that is not the case. After all, by the time Coppélia chanted the spell in question, the status display had already returned to normal."

"In that case, Leonardo's paralysis attack served to cure the illness."

"I think that idea's off base, too."

Leonardo took a moment to think, putting a hand to his chin. "My weapons are pretty good, but all they do is inflict additional flame damage. The technique I used, Paralyze Blow, doesn't have any special auxiliary effects besides paralysis, either."

"……"

At this, even KR, who tended to talk a little too much, went quiet. This was only natural. Absolutely nobody wanted to end up like that.

If all they had to do was deal with it, the matter was simple.

It was true that demihuman monsters were found across a wide range of levels. However, even if the range was wide, they were gnolls. The highest their levels really got was 70. To Leonardo and the others, they were nothing to be afraid of.

However, unlike combat abilities, there was something about that eerie illness that awoke a primitive terror deep within their hearts.

Wide, staring, lusterless eyes. A mouth from which canine teeth protruded and bloody saliva dripped endlessly. Four limbs, bent and warped, trying to force a human body to move like an animal. All these things were cloaked in a dark, ominous aura.

Even Leonardo didn't want to fight that.

"Well, calm down. Look, it's not like there are a ton of those out there."

"That's probably true. The villagers here said that was the first one they've run into. If there were a lot of them, more people would have seen them. That's only logical."

Kanami had spoken as if trying to smooth things over, and KR picked up where she'd left off.

Even as Leonardo nodded, agreeing with them, he didn't quite feel satisfied. He had a hunch that the incident wouldn't end just like that and that they would wind up getting more deeply involved.

He was right.

▶5

It was true all over this world, but at night in Aorsoi, the sky was particularly clear. Possibly because of the dry air, the sky was high and incredibly transparent, and the stars glittered like crushed white sand.

Unlike the night skies of Midtown, which were polluted with smoke and neon, there was no light from the earth, so even tiny stars that gave off a very faint light shone proudly against the thick cloth of the heavens.

This was night in Thekkek.

Somewhere, an insect sang in a voice like a shaken silver bell.

The sun had been down for two hours. Even though it wasn't yet late enough to call it "night," the village was already quiet. Orange light seeped from the square windows in the sun-baked brick walls, which were fitted only with wooden shutters.

It was about the time when most families had probably finished their evening meals.

Leaving the shed that had been assigned to their group, Leonardo emerged into the cool night wind.

As he stepped out onto the dirt road, a sky full of stars unfolded above him.

Even though it was a September night, a cold wind blew across the plateau.

Yet Leonardo was an Adventurer, so the cold didn't affect him that much. On the contrary, the bracing air was pleasant.

In the midst of that night air, Leonardo walked through the village. He wasn't plotting anything in particular, but his footsteps made almost no sound. This was partly because, since he was an Assassin, the movement was habit for Leonardo, and partly because he didn't want to disturb the still night and its peaceful-looking village.

The settlement didn't have an especially solid defensive wall. The only thing encircling it was a fence meant to keep the sheep together and to prevent animals from getting in. Beyond that, there was a region of cultivated fields. That said, even if they were "cultivated," the soil was rough and dry, and it was enough to make even amateurs worry that it wasn't suitable for farming.

Leonardo climbed up onto a large boulder beside the road that left the village to the south and sat down.

The rock was huge. In terms of height, it was about two meters. It was a funny shape, as if it had been polished all over, softening its edges, and its flat top seemed bigger than a bedroom.

Shepherds apparently used the rock as a lookout post. There was a threadbare cloth spread in the spot that overlooked the upper plains.

Far in the distance, the mountains stood like a folding screen.

He couldn't say where they started or ended. The mountains ran to the edge of what he could see, and they really did look like the wall of the world. While they were eating dinner, elderly Yagudo had told them that the mountains were called Tian Mai. He'd said it meant "the seat of heaven."

In the moonlight, even at night, the snow on the ridgelines glimmered slightly. *I see*, he thought. The sublime atmosphere about them did make them seem like heaven's chair.

The wasteland of Aorsoi spread all the way to the foot of those mountains. There were patches of brush in places, and some things which could safely be called forests, but at this point, all of it slept in the damp night wind.

With the light *crunch* of footsteps on dry earth, Coppélia approached.

Leonardo registered her presence before he could see her. He turned easily and looked down at her small figure from the top of the boulder.

She came up to the big rock with ladylike steps, then looked up at Leonardo.

"Are you acting as a sentry?" she asked.

"Nope," he replied.

This was a People of the Earth village. It wasn't like taking a nap in the depths of a dungeon. He wasn't planning to get careless, but there was probably no need for the sort of wariness that would require a night watchman.

Leonardo simply hadn't been able to sleep this early, so he'd slipped out of his room. He was a true New Yorker, and he loved staying up late.

Besides, he'd needed time to think.

Talking with friends was fun, and he didn't hate cooperating with companions to get jobs done, but if he didn't get some time alone, he got depressed. Leonardo knew being a geek meant having a place like that somewhere in your heart.

"Is that so."

"Yep."

The conversation petered out.

Aorsoi's September night wind slipped past the two of them, caressing them.

They heard the low whinny of a horse and the songs of insects. A cloud covered the moon, then passed by.

Quite a long time had passed, but Coppélia only stood there quietly. She seemed to be gazing at the mountains that towered in the distance, the same ones Leonardo had been looking at a little while ago.

"Want to come up?"

"Yes."

After hearing Coppélia's response, Leonardo stretched out a hand.

She took it, and he pulled her up to the top of the rounded boulder. She brushed the dust away with her fingertips a few times, straightened up properly so that her skirt wouldn't get wrinkled, and sat down.

Leonardo didn't speak to her, and Coppélia didn't pester him with unnecessary words, either. The night was quiet, and the only noises—the low hums of insects and the rustling from the wind—seemed to protect the stillness around the pair.

More time flowed past.

The stars twinkled, and in the distance, they heard the drowsy-sounding bleat of a sheep.

"You're not bored?"

"No, Coppélia is not bored."

Leonardo felt slightly bewildered.

As a geek, he didn't have much experience talking to women. If he'd been doing something game related—in other words, fighting or training to improve his skills, doing some sort of production activity, or pursuing a quest—he would have had something to talk about, but situations like this were outside his area of expertise.

However, on the other hand, he didn't feel uncomfortable.

He was all alone with a girl, a situation in which feeling stressed would have been perfectly understandable, but he was calm, and he didn't feel ill at ease.

"What did you come out here to do, Coppélia?"

"To hunt."

"Hunt?" Leonardo asked.

The term *hunting* wasn't unusual. It was actually pretty common in MMOs. In general, it meant defeating monsters in battle. The narrow definition was taking down single creatures to get trophies, as opposed to defeating quest-specific monsters.

"Yes. Coppélia intended to go to the plains to the south of the village and search for prey."

"Uh, it's night."

"In terms of nocturnal monsters, Coppélia determined that that would be convenient."

"What about sleep?"

"Coppélia does not need much sleep."

Leonardo was a little startled, but he shook it off. She might be telling the truth. Every now and then, there was that sort of player in *Elder Tales*. They typically thought, rather than wasting time, it was better to subjugate even minor monsters and get a little money.

Coppélia hadn't looked like that much of a battle fiend, but experience had taught Leonardo that players' appearances and main classes didn't necessarily match their personalities.

And so the words "Want some company?" came out naturally.

They'd encountered monsters a few times on their way from the Tekeli Ruins to this village, and the average level had been around 20. They'd be no match for level-90 Coppélia, even though she was a Recovery class and low on attack power.

However, if they were emphasizing efficiency, since he was an attack class, Leonardo thought things would go much better if the two of them worked together.

"That will not be necessary. Coppélia's plans have changed."

"They…have, huh?"

"Yes."

Coppélia's answer was matter-of-fact. He couldn't pick up any particular emotion from her tone or expression.

If she said it wasn't necessary, then it probably wasn't. Leonardo promptly gave up on pursuing the matter further. The question of whether a player earned money or just killed time should be up to them. If Coppélia wanted him to keep her company, he would, but he had no intention of being pushy in a misguided attempt to be nice.

Leonardo got to his feet.

Coppélia's eyes followed him, but when he told her, "Don't worry about it," the indigo-haired girl nodded, seeming satisfied.

Leonardo tested the texture of the rock with his toes. It felt massive, heavy, and hard. Reassured that it would be all right to jump around a bit, he slowly leveled his swords.

The technique he activated from the icon that surfaced in his mind was Deadly Dance. He thrust out his left hand sharply. From that stance, with a shrill sound cloaked in cold air, the sword in his right hand flashed. The recast time for this skill was one second. A second later, he visualized selecting the icon again. Once again, he swung his right hand. This attack was sharper than the previous one.

Deadly Dance was a unique skill. When used back-to-back, its power gradually increased. It reached its maximum level on the eighth attack, and at that point, the damage inflicted was roughly three times what it was on the first attack.

The first attack inflicted only as much damage as a normal attack, and because of its stance—with the left hand thrust out and the hips lowered—its damage efficiency was fairly bad. If you planned to stop with one attack, you could inflict damage more effectively by using some other special skill. This attack skill was based on the assumption that you would be attacking several times in a row.

Leonardo repeated this a few times, putting his body through its paces. Over the past few months, he'd grown completely used to the sharp motions, and nothing about them felt strange. However, he sensed that this time would be a breakthrough.

Movements he wasn't used to made his elbows and knees ache sharply.

Now that he had an Adventurer's body, both his physical strength and his stamina had greatly increased. It wasn't just a boost; he felt as if he were a completely different person. After all, this Adventurer body was exactly what Leonardo had dreamed of: the body of a hero.

However, when he put stress on muscles from angles he didn't normally use, apparently heat did build up.

"Healing Light."

Leonardo had been rubbing his elbow, and Coppélia chanted an instant recovery spell for him. Adventurers' sturdy bodies would recover from a problem of that level in about ten minutes, but even so, the healing spell drew the heat away, and it felt good.

"Do you wish to be healed?"

"No, I'll be fine in a few minutes."

In response to Coppélia's words, Leonardo thanked her, stretching as he spoke. As he spread his legs again and lowered his hips into the stance, he asked her a question:

"What do you think about the new patch?"

"Coppélia hears it has been introduced on the Japanese server."

"Um… Okay, so, what do you think about going to that server?"

"As it is Master's wish, it has been assigned a high priority."

The conversation really didn't seem to mesh with Leonardo.

Between Elias and Coppélia, this party was well stocked with mysterious characters. Well, to be accurate, Elias wasn't human, so his eccentricity made sense. Besides, the greatest source of bewilderment was Kanami. It wasn't often that you met somebody that loony. Leonardo thought that, since Kanami was the one who'd brought these members together, they were pretty much bound to be weird.

That said, he was completely overlooking the fact that he'd been included in that selection.

"About that 'Master'..."

"Yes. It refers to Kanami."

According to what he'd heard that afternoon, Kanami had spotted Coppélia fighting on the plain and had made her a companion. Maybe Kanami had saved her life or something, then. Over these past few days, he'd noticed that the attitude Coppélia took toward the woman was different from the one she used with her other companions. It was deferential, almost as if she was an actual maid.

Leonardo was open-minded about the way others chose to play, particularly with regard to how they spoke or dressed. After all, he himself habitually wore a cartoon hero costume, a green hooded mask and suit. During the game, everybody had the right to be a hero or anything they wanted.

For that reason, he had no objections to Coppélia's attitude.

"What sort of person is Kanami?"

"______"

Up until now, Coppélia had answered Leonardo's questions instantly, but for the first time, she looked as if she was thinking. Leonardo stretched, slowly swinging his swords, and waited for her to speak.

Even he didn't know how he could be this calm.

He didn't think he'd really seen a cute adolescent girl since high school, and a memory of having talked companionably with one at this distance wouldn't even have shown up in a recommender system. Even so, right now, he didn't feel any more tension than he did when he was changing out a PC graphics board. He didn't want to scratch up the terminal, so he had to work slowly and carefully, without hurrying—it was that sort of tension. Either that, or it was a mood that resembled consideration for others, which would have been even stranger.

"Master is like first light."
"Huh?"

Coppélia pointed at the eastern sky.

"Right now, beyond that horizon, the sun is racing this way. It has only just set, but tomorrow morning at four thirty-eight, it will begin to pale."

Coppélia's eyes reflected the night sky, where the moon had just risen. They were an endlessly deep blue.

"At night, the sky is dark. Before dawn, it gradually begins to turn deep purple in the east. After purple comes indigo. Then ultramarine. It gradually grows more blue, but there is still no light. However, the blue alone is proof enough, and no one doubts that morning is on its way… That is the sort of person Master is."

Leonardo didn't really understand what she meant, but it was clear that Coppélia recognized Kanami's value.

Storing that lone bit of information in his memory, Leonardo began tracing the movements of Deadly Dance once more.

▶6

There was a band that prowled through the depths of that same night, holding its breath.

It was a scouting party from the guild Lelang Wolf Cavalry.

There were three members. All were highly trained level-90 Adventurers.

"Well?"

"…South, I'd say."

The Swashbuckler, who'd been crawling along the ground in order to investigate, answered briefly, then closed the shutter on his portable hand lantern. The item was built around a Hunan Rainbow Pearl, a magic item that gave off eternal light. It was one of the production unit's recent creations: a piece of handiwork constructed with a mirror to amplify the light and a shutter to cover it.

Having checked the footprints again, the group mounted the Great

Wolves that had been waiting nearby. These creatures, which resembled three-meter-long wolves, were mounts seen on the Chinese server.

Seated on leather saddles, the three scouts raced south over the dark steppe.

Traveling on horseback at night was difficult. The moon was visible, but even so, the bumps and dips of the terrain easily blended into shadow, and one wrong step could break a horse's ankle. In an environment like that, Great Wolves had an overwhelming advantage over horses.

However, they hadn't chosen to ride Great Wolves specifically because they were tracking at night. As a rule, all the members of the Lelang Wolf Cavalry guild rode the enormous mounts as the guild's trademark.

The Wolf Cavalry had originally been based in Dadu, the Chinese server's central city. However, after the Catastrophe, public order in Dadu had deteriorated badly. Three guilds that called themselves the Kings of China had fought one another; each of them had occupied important town facilities to hinder the others, and the city had fallen into chaos.

Zhu Huan, the very prescient leader of the Cavalry, had decided to leave Dadu early on. Their mount situation had also proved fortunate, because they had no trouble traveling long distances: Upon departing, all 480 of them had stuffed their property into bags and cleared out of their guild hall.

After that, they'd gone steadily westward. It had taken them a month to settle down in Shimanaikui. They'd established a guild hall there, and although it had taken them a month to stabilize, the Lelang Wolf Cavalry had found a place where they could rest easy. They were probably one of the luckier guilds on the Chinese server.

At present, the Wolf Cavalry acted as traveling guards.

In the Qing dynasty, this job had been known as *biao shi*, or "bodyguard." They accompanied People of the Earth transport units as security personnel, protecting their cargo, property, and lives from monsters and bandits. On the other hand, if they failed in their mission, they paid their client money in order to fulfill their liability for damages.

By acting as traveling guards, they'd made a business out of one of the game's most familiar quest duties.

Shimanaikui, which was known locally as "the City of Mare's Milk," wasn't small. It had a resident population of about fifteen thousand people, and it was also a regional center of commerce.

It was likely that it had originally flourished as a relay base for merchant caravans: The town's main streets were lined with shops selling dried provisions and curiosities from both East and West, and the city was rather wealthy.

However, since it wasn't a player town, few Adventurers were around. It had a temple—which had been the Lelang Wolf Cavalry's biggest reason for choosing it as a base—but there was no bank. As a result, the guild's members kept most of their property in the guild hall's safe and had the guild protect it.

Because of these restrictions, the Cavalry was more like a family than other guilds, and its horizontal bonds were stronger. The People of the Earth saw this, and it helped generate more confidence in them.

The guild generally sent out single parties in response to requests for guards. These parties consisted of six members: a warrior to act as a vanguard shield, a healer to recover the warrior and manage the party as a whole, and a good balance of magical and physical attack classes.

Depending on the request, the routes caravans took differed, and member selections were adjusted to suit the degree of difficulty. However, when it came to journeying over land-based trade routes, there were almost no threats in this region that six Wolf Cavalry members couldn't drive away.

While on the one hand they worked as guards, on the other, the guild leader Zhu Huan was known for sending many scouts out in all directions.

Adventurers could be excellent scouts if they felt like it. The Weapon Attack classes, such as Assassins and Swashbucklers, had stealthy movement skills, while Magic Attack classes often had lights or special sight for seeing in the dark and could use summoned creatures that were convenient for long-distance reconnaissance.

The fact that all members rode Great Wolves, which were good on wilderness terrain and in the mountains, was also a big plus.

These patrols had begun as a project intended to keep the members from getting rusty during the times when they weren't handling requests, and they'd had the secondary effects of improving public order in the vicinity of Shimanaikui and of bringing lots of information to the Cavalry.

By the time a month had passed after they'd set up shop in their new city, the People of the Earth had acknowledged the Lelang Wolf Cavalry as an important part of the town.

After they'd sprinted for a while, the three mounts caught the scent of water in the darkness.

It was probably a tributary of the Railnorth.

A little while after they'd come up against that tributary, the three of them spotted marks on the riverbank. The grass at the river's edge had been trampled, and it was black and wet.

It wasn't water. It was the blood of an animal.

"That's a lot," the Swashbuckler leader muttered, patting the neck of his wolf, who was whining at the smell of blood. Yet, the blood was already almost dry. Whomever they'd been, the ones who'd left this place had gone quite some time ago. Even so, the party was careful. Instead of using a bright light, they continued to use the shuttered hand lantern.

The group belonged to a specially assembled reconnaissance unit.

The recon unit was a large faction whose objective was to gather information in the southwest. When all its teams were combined, it had more than sixty members. The main unit was slowly moving due west, consolidating information as it went.

While their Cleric opened a telechat to the main unit, the leader explored the area further. Overturned rocks. Muddy soil that had been trampled firm. The unit they'd been chasing seemed to have met up with more of their companions—gnolls—here.

The creature that had been slaughtered had probably been a sheep or a deer, something along those lines. After having a bloody meal here, the group had set off again. The number of gnolls that had crossed the tributary had been more than twenty, less than thirty.

The leader, whose subclass was Tracker, determined this and informed the Cleric. Their report would be shared with the other surveillance teams, which, like this three-man unit, were scattered within a twenty-kilometer radius of the main one.

They were pursuing a gnoll tribe.

The Catastrophe seemed to have had a major influence on monster habitats, alongside everything else. On their journey from Dadu (which was on the eastern coast of the continent) to this area, the Lelang Wolf Cavalry had seen many monster tribes on the move.

The gnoll group might be part of that. About two weeks ago, the Lelang Wolf Cavalry had detected their movements—in connection with the destruction of a few caravans—and had planned and launched a large-scale surveillance operation.

If there were several hundred gnolls, this reconnaissance unit alone would be enough to annihilate them. Even if it was a scouting unit, its members had simply been chosen because of their tracking skills, and their fighting abilities were in no way inferior to those of the guard or combat units.

The Chinese server had a lot of light users, but the Lelang Wolf Cavalry was a hard-line guild, and the majority of its members were level 90.

Even if the gnoll group ended up requiring a raid, the possibility of sending in a specialized subjugation unit was on the table. In that case, the guild leader, Zhu Huan, who was currently on standby in Shimanaikui, would also come to the front.

"——! Right. Understood!"

The young Cleric's attitude had abruptly turned anxious, and tension ran through the group.

"What is it?"

"They've lost contact with Team Four, the unit that went southwest ahead of us."

"Up ahead, huh?"

The Swashbuckler glared into the darkness. Had they run into some kind of trouble? According to their last contact, Team Four should have been a few kilometers west of their group.

"The main unit is requesting confirmation."

They didn't even need to think about it. They were the closest team, so they'd have to investigate. The Swashbuckler leader gave the order, and the three of them mounted again.

Once their masters were on their backs, the Great Wolves raced off into the darkness without waiting for a signal.

In the Lelang Wolf Cavalry, mounts were practically family, and by now they didn't need orders from their riders. Picking up on their masters' tension, they ran at full speed through the dark night without a whimper.

The wind that sliced at their ears was painful. It was still September—practically summer. And yet, the wind that blew down from the high mountains was cold and sharp. Running through it after sundown only made it worse.

The Lelang Wolf Cavalry was used to this sort of mission, and they'd turned the collars of their fur-trimmed jackets up and buried their faces in their mounts' necks. As the beasts between their arms leapt, their temperature was high, and if they buried themselves in their fur, a little cold wouldn't bother them.

Before long, about the time the moon began its descent from the top of the sky, huge pillars came into view, standing black on the horizon.

The distance was so great that the pillars looked small, but when they thought about it, they thought it had to be incredibly tall. Since there was nothing to compare them to, it was difficult to guess with any accuracy, but they seemed to be easily over thirty meters in height.

These things—which towered over all else in a world with no modern structures, not to mention in the middle of a wasteland—had a surreal immensity that made them visible even from the distant horizon.

As they drew nearer, the full extent of their imposing appearance was revealed.

They might have been made of steel; the structure looked like three poles standing together, and it didn't seem to have an interior. This was why they hadn't called them *buildings*—in other words, towers—but *pillars*. They looked as spiky as ancient weapons, and they almost seemed to be menacing their surroundings.

Ruined Colonnade Tonnesgrave.

The recon team leader muttered the name to himself, almost silently.

There were no accurate maps of this region.

To People of the Earth merchants, routes were everything. They didn't need detailed maps of an entire region in order to conduct sales along those routes. In addition, the more seasoned the merchant, the less likely they were to carelessly let their knowledge and experience—their property—leave the confines of their own head.

Adventurers did need maps, and they actually created them, but Aorsoi was a savage land that they hadn't really touched. They didn't have enough information to make maps yet, and at the very least, there were no completed maps.

However, collecting information that would lead to map-making was one of this scout team's regular duties. Due to his Tracker subclass, the Swashbuckler who led the team had patrolled this region many times, and he was well versed in the local rumors. As a result, he immediately understood that what he was seeing was the Ruined Colonnade that appeared in the old people's stories.

"Stop!"

At his words, his two companions instantly halted.

In the hollow up ahead on their right, he'd seen a shadow move slightly.

When he strained his eyes, he could make out some gnolls. Far more than a hundred of them, perhaps over a thousand, were advancing through the hollow in complete silence.

For a moment, the three waited with bated breath upon the backs of their wolves, but it seemed they'd gone unnoticed: By nature, when gnolls discovered Adventurers, they attacked with insane ferocity. That said, as long as they were on these particular mounts, they weren't in that much danger.

This was due to the difference in speed. Even if they got surrounded, they'd probably be able to get away. However, if that happened, it would be hard to continue their reconnaissance, and that was a disadvantage. Needless to say, if possible, they'd prefer not to be spotted.

"Why are there so many of them?"

The young Taomancer spoke to him in a whisper, and he shook his head.

He had no idea.

However, for now, it seemed clear that Team Four had encountered these things and run into trouble. After a little hesitation, the leader signaled the Cleric. It would make things choppy, but for now, they should probably send in a report.

"Tell them exactly what we're seeing and retreat about a hundred meters."

Watching his comrades' Wolves slink backward, their bodies low to the ground, the leader leapt down from his own mount. After lightly tapping his loyal partner's wet nose, he began to crawl forward on his hands and knees.

He wanted to get just a little closer, to see what the gnolls were doing and where they were headed. All else aside, it struck him as very strange that such a large group was advancing without so much as a cough.

Activating a Tracker special skill, he concealed his presence, then moved forward, taking care not to let his shape show on the ridge of the hill.

He approached the gnolls, taking quite a long time.

The hyena-like demihumans, dribbling saliva, seemed to be gazing at the pillars on the horizon as they advanced, their eyes filled with a sort of starving desire. They looked like opium addicts, and there was something eerie about them that froze the man's spine.

His instincts were screaming at him to run.

However, he forced them down and continued his approach. In another ten meters, he'd be close enough to check their statuses.

Even as he dripped with greasy sweat, he went closer, and as he'd expected, the statuses belonged to monsters: regular gnolls and Gnoll War Mages. That wasn't unusual; within races, demihuman monsters were often divided into several classes. Goblin and orc tribes included warrior and priest ranks, for instance.

The gnolls in front of him were Darkmancers, assault troops, and Wolf-Fang Captains, and their levels were mostly between 60 and 70.

He had the information he wanted.

Scouting any longer wouldn't just be useless; it would be dangerous. If it came to fighting a hostile group of this size, they'd need the entire guild, or at the very least, a legion raid force. A three-man scout unit couldn't do a thing.

On that thought, he slowly turned back, intending to tell the others to withdraw.

However, what he saw was a moon as sharp as a grim reaper's scythe—and an enormous Black Dragon descending with that moon at its back.

In the midst of a lukewarm fountain, his vision was dyed monochrome, then immediately cut out.

CHAPTER. 3

DRAGON IN HEAVEN'S

▶ NAME: ELIAS HACKBLADE

▶ LEVEL: 100

▶ RACE: ELF

▶ CLASS: BLADEMANCER

▶ HP: 22110

▶ MP: 22110

▶ ITEM 1:

[CRYSTAL STREAM]

A MAGIC TWO-HANDED SWORD THAT THE WATER-SPIRIT LADIES OF THE LAKE CREATED FOR ELIAS BY TURNING THE WATER OF THEIR LAKE INTO CRYSTAL. THE DIVINE PROTECTION THAT DWELLS WITHIN THE SWORD CONSTANTLY PROTECTS ELIAS, AUTOMATICALLY RECOVERING HIS MP AND BOOSTING THE POWER OF COLD-AIR ATTRIBUTE MAGIC.

▶ ITEM 2:

[ANCIENT WATER-DRAGON SURCOAT]

A SURCOAT OF ELVEN CLOTH WOVEN FROM COLD AIR AND LEATHER MADE FROM THE HIDES OF WATER DRAGONS THAT LIVE IN THE ELVEN OCEAN. IT HAS A MYSTERIOUS, MAGIC PROTECTION THAT SHINES PURE WHITE, GIVING ITS WEARER EXTRAORDINARY DEFENSIVE POWER AND ENDURANCE AGAINST WATER AND COLD. WHEN THE USER PROTECTS OTHERS, THESE EFFECTS INCREASE DRAMATICALLY.

▶ ITEM 3:

[CREST OF THE KNIGHTS OF THE RED BRANCH]

A PALM-SIZED MEDAL THAT HAS THE FACE OF A STAG WITH MAGNIFICENT ANTLERS ENGRAVED ON THE FRONT AND A SWORD-AND-SHIELD DESIGN ON THE BACK. IT'S A MAGIC ITEM THAT BRIGADE MEMBERS PREVIOUSLY USED TO CONTACT EACH OTHER, BUT SINCE THE CATASTROPHE, NO ONE HAS RESPONDED TO ELIAS'S CALLS.

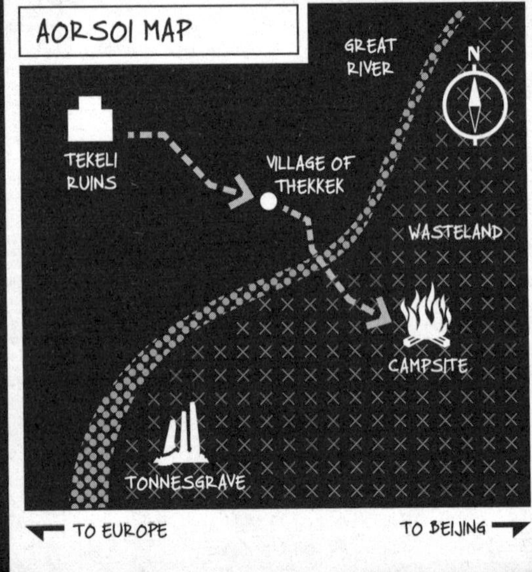
AORSOI MAP
GREAT RIVER
N
TEKELI RUINS
VILLAGE OF THEKKEK
WASTELAND
CAMPSITE
TONNESGRAVE
TO EUROPE
TO BEIJING

▶1

Leonardo woke early the next morning.

Adventurers had high physical abilities, and Leonardo could tell that they affected sleep time as well. Six hours was enough to let him wake up feeling refreshed.

That said, there did seem to be individual differences, and some Adventurers said they got incredibly sleepy, so it might have been a quirk peculiar to himself.

In any case, having woken up, Leonardo changed into clothes that were sturdy, although not made for combat, and left his assigned shed. Elias was still asleep in the bed, which was made of packed straw and was quite comfortable, so he moved quietly, trying not to make noise.

The sun had just risen, and it was glaringly bright.

He cut through the courtyard of Yagudo's house, turned onto the main street, and made for the well. There were several People of the Earth ladies there, and lots of children, too.

Leonardo thought he'd woken early, but apparently, as far as the villagers were concerned, it wasn't *that* early. The place teemed with women having lively conversations as they did chores, and the little kids were energetic.

Thanking the women who'd considerately moved aside to give him room, Leonardo washed his face. As long as its durability hadn't worn down, Adventurer equipment recovered from visible dirt and scratches automatically, but people's moods didn't bounce back so easily. He quickly wiped off his treasured green hood. The cold-water bath was refreshing.

"Hey, mister."

"Mr. Green."

"Why are you green?"

"Why, huh? Why?"

Children had begun to gather around Leonardo like little birds.

Leonardo's mouth bent into a dissatisfied line. *I can't deal with this*, he thought. He wasn't good with kids. They were all immature and rude and temperamental. Would any sane adult ask somebody else, "Why is your face green, huh?" They most certainly would not.

Asking somebody they'd just met would be even further out of the question.

These guys are genuine idiots who don't understand how awesome and cool ninjas are.

"Hmph. This is proof that I'm a hero."

"What's a hero?"

"Can you eat it?"

"Mister, did you eat breakfast already?"

This blows. Leonardo sighed.

Kids couldn't stay on topic for a whole conversation. He'd seen that tendency among certain women, too, but it was more striking in kids. Problems and questions should be resolved one at a time. A little bit here, a little bit there: You couldn't write code or catch software bugs that way. Children were the polar opposite of engineers.

Leonardo hauled up a kid who'd been rolling up his trousers to see if the leg inside was green, too, and flicked him on the forehead.

This was seriously hopeless.

"This head is a tribute to the courage and might of the great frog. As a ninja and a frog, it's the symbol of the bravest hero in the world."

"Um... Did you get that?"

"I didn't get it at all."

"Green! Green frog! *Lu wa!*"

"*Lu wa.* ♪"

They were probably all under ten years old. Some of them seemed to be around five or six. Leonardo, who'd never babysat in his life or lived with a baby, had no way to discern kids' ages. He was just guessing on instinct.

In theory, there had been a time when Leonardo himself was a kid, but he just couldn't believe it.

He didn't want to think that he'd been anything this irrational.

A boy who was built a little bigger, but who still didn't come up to Leonardo's waist, rammed into him from the front. The boy had run up and wrapped his arms around him. Maybe he was trying to wrestle. He pushed at him until his face was bright red, but to an Adventurer, it made less of an impression than an attack from a playful cat. Just the way you'd do to a cat, Leonardo hooked two fingers into the back of the boy's collar and hoisted him up.

A woman who seemed to be the boy's mother, wearing several layers of the tribe's thick, colorful clothes, apologized—*I'm sorry he's disturbed you*—but the boy in question didn't seem to care at all.

"Mr. Green Frog, you're really strong!"

"Heroes have to be."

Leonardo had raised the boy to his own eye level, and he glared at him, trying to intimidate him. Even though the boy's feet were about a meter off the ground, he didn't seem the least bit afraid. He wriggled and twisted in Leonardo's fingers, looking thoroughly entertained.

The next thing Leonardo knew, a girl who was even younger than the boy was trying to shinny up his legs from behind. He really couldn't understand it. Apparently, she'd managed to mistake somebody else's body for playground equipment.

He hoisted the girl up as well.

That made two. He had no idea what their parents were feeding them, but he hardly felt their weight at all. They were like carry-on luggage, just a little heavier than an old-school laptop.

He couldn't tell what was so funny, but the dangling boy and girl were shrieking with laughter. Taking advantage that Leonardo had both hands full, a third assassin appeared.

It was a shy-looking kid with eyes that slanted down at the outside corners.

It was probably a boy, but if the kid who'd tackled Leonardo had been a hunting dog, this one seemed like a pet dog. He looked up at Leonardo with big, apologetic eyes.

"Mr. Green Frog."

"That's Leonardo to you."

"Mr. Green Frog..."

"—Fine. Whatever. You can call me that. Dummy."

The boy's expression clouded, and Leonardo retracted what he'd just said. *Argh, pain in the butt. Irritating. Aggravating.* He considered chucking both these dangling kids at him at once. They'd be a new attack technique: Missile Children.

However, when he imagined the way the kids would shriek and laugh as they flew toward their target, the feeling withered on him instantly. It would be too much of a mockery. Battles were about slipping through the gap between life and death, something more sacred. They weren't the sort of thing you could insult with little kids' laughter.

"Mr. Green Frog. Food..."

Failing to register Leonardo's internal scream, the boy with drooping eyes timidly held out a white lump. The lump was more than thirty centimeters long. It was probably made of baked wheat flour or something similar.

After thinking a little bit, Leonardo accepted it.

This was partly because a few of the women were bowing away so vigorously that it looked as if they'd broken, and he felt sorry for them, and also because he thought spending any more time dealing with the happily frolicking kids around him would only tire him out.

In order to take the thing, he had to free up his hands, so he let the captured boy in his right hand and the girl in his left hand go. They bounded around gleefully, singing some sort of local song that Leonardo didn't know, and ran around the area.

The kids seemed to have decided that getting caught by Leonardo was a new sort of game. They ran at him one after another, or tried to climb up him, or asked him to hoist them up. Leonardo turned them away with dignity.

"Playing with kids isn't a hero's job. All right, get out of the way, clear the road."

Half-heartedly messing with the kids who were still swarming around him, Leonardo made for the outskirts of the village with leisurely footsteps. He was headed for that big boulder. It wasn't that he'd taken a particular liking to it or anything; he just couldn't handle getting swarmed by kids. The top of that thing would be a perfect place to take shelter.

As he walked, he ate the misshapen bread. It wasn't as hard as he'd thought it would be, and the flavor was faint and simple.

In that sense, it reminded him of the unseasoned, half-dried auto meals from just after the Catastrophe. However, as he chewed, a sweetness spread through his mouth, and he decided the flavor wasn't half bad. Tiny pieces of what was probably dried, minced mutton were mixed in, and the crunchy texture was terrific.

There was already somebody on top of the boulder.

It was KR.

His shape resembled a horse, but as he was now—with his knees folded, lying on his side on the rock—he didn't look like one. When he'd thought that far, Leonardo corrected himself. Real horses might actually look that messy when they slept, too.

KR glanced over with his third eye, spotted Leonardo, then blissfully closed that eye again.

"You're going back to sleep?"

"I'm not sleeping. This is a morning nap."

"That's sleeping."

"Not quite. It's not that I desperately want to sleep or anything. Good morning."

Even as he sensed the slight blur of the translation function, Leonardo gazed steadily at KR. He'd said he was getting up, but he apparently didn't plan to change position. He probably wanted to spend the morning idly.

Leonardo didn't really feel like getting in his way. He ate the bread-like thing in his right hand in silence.

Come to think of it, KR had said that mare was making eyes at him.

Leonardo thought he might have spent the whole night feeling the same thing Leonardo had felt when the kids were mobbing him. In that case, he did sympathize with him a bit. Well, not asking him about it was probably the mannerly thing for an adult male to do.

The brisk morning air caressed the two of them on its way by.

Time passed slowly.

Leonardo gazed at the thin road that ran far away to the southeast, but he didn't see any travelers or caravans making their way up it. Yagudo had said that a caravan would be here in the next few days, but apparently, things weren't going to go that smoothly.

"What's that?"

"They gave it to me. It's breakfast."

KR sniffed loudly; the motion looked exactly like that of a real horse. "Want some?" Leonardo held the poorly leavened bread up to his mouth.

"Thanks. I'd appreciate that."

KR didn't refuse. He obediently took a bite.

"Ah, damn. That's good. Grass is bitter and nasty-tasting. Did you know that? That's Soul Possession's worst point. You may be a mystical beast, but your sense of taste doesn't change. This body really isn't suited to having meals. It's awful."

KR's tone was thoroughly disgusted, and Leonardo was impressed. He hadn't known about that problem. When he'd heard Soul Possession explained, he'd thought it was an incredibly convenient ability with a wide range of applications, but even so, he didn't think he'd be able to handle two whole months in that shape.

"You're in Japan, right, KR?"

"Yes."

"...And there are level-91 Adventurers there."

"Some have levels that are even higher."

"I see..."

In the gaps in their conversation, the two of them ate the lightly salted bread.

In the midst of the dazzling morning light, Leonardo was remembering Big Apple. Inside his mind, the hometown where he'd holed up in a Midtown apartment and worked as an engineer and the comfortable room he'd made for himself in the sewers in *Elder Tales* blurred together into one New York.

"I bet things are pretty ugly in Japan, too, huh?"

"No, not really."

"Oh yeah?"

Leonardo hadn't expected to hear that, and he sent another question back at him.

He was thinking of the cold, paranoid times that had hit Big Apple after the Catastrophe. He'd overheard things about South Angel on a telechat, and although the details had been different, the situation had been similar, so he'd been convinced that Adventurers were hurting one another in all the major cities around the world.

"Well, it depends on where you are in Japan, but yeah. It's not as bad as the continent. I've seen all sorts of things since I came over here. There are some cities that are dominated by brutal violence. Dadu's so bad it makes Susukino look like a joke. There are things that make the situation in New York you told me about seem like child's play."

At KR's words, Leonardo tried to imagine the atrocities he'd mentioned, then shook his head, stopping himself. There was no point in thinking about them. He wasn't there. Right now, hearing this story came first.

"Japan's situation is a bit different. It's isolated, see. Most of the players are Japanese, and the ocean blocks exchange with the districts under the jurisdiction of other servers."

▸2

Come to think of it, that was completely natural.

When he visualized its shape on a map, it was clear that Japan was an island nation. It might be close to the eastern coast of the continent, but there was an ocean in between. That kept it insulated from other regions.

On top of that, Japan was the only area under the jurisdiction of the Japanese server.

In terms of the world map, the North American server managed Canada as well as the United States, and the European server covered more than ten countries. Unlike those, the range Japan's server managed was incredibly small. In addition, if Leonardo remembered correctly, Japan was a country with very few immigrants. Maybe the eruptions of racism he'd seen in North America had been comparatively less common there.

Or, no, was there a more fundamental reason?

Leonardo asked a question, looking for confirmation:

"Is that because of the new patch? Was there some sort of new element that maintains public order in there?"

"No, as far as I know, it's nothing to do with the new patch. It's probably because Japan is full of fanboys, hermits, and nervous types."

"Wait, really?"

KR lay down on the cool rock, shutting his eyes halfway. He looked completely relaxed.

Gazing at him, Leonardo fell into contemplation.

That must have been the peculiar Japanese "modesty" he'd heard about.

He'd always thought it was cool, and here he'd been given a demonstration of its greatness once again. Not only had they developed cup ramen and the rotary engine, they were managing to maintain order under circumstances like these. He would have expected no less from the country of Zen Buddhism and the samurai code.

"So Japan's peaceful, huh…? I'm jealous."

"No, it's not all that."

"Hmm?"

"Japan… Well, no, it's called Yamato here, but…"

Equine muzzle snuffling, KR drew a deep breath.

"Japan was in tatters when the transference happened, too. It was confused, and the depression was worse than the confusion. Talk about being desolated and down in the dumps. From the general mood, the future looked pitch-black. That day, I think there were about thirty thousand Japanese players logged in, and…"

Thirty thousand. That was a larger number than he'd expected.

Considering the area of that island country, it seemed like it would be overcrowded.

"Well, all thirty thousand of them got depressed all at once. Some players just crouched down and couldn't really move anymore. Some got desperate and tried to kill themselves. Then there were a certain number who started player killing, without a thought for anyone else. However, there were heroes who didn't think despairing forever was a good plan. In both eastern and western Japan, at that."

"Does an island that tiny even have an east and west?"

"It's not a matter of area. It's about population."

When he put it that way, it made sense.

The "size of the world" Leonardo and other modern humans felt was technically a network, the connections between people.

The only world a lone person could sense was the scenery in front of them. No matter how wide the world was, there was a limit to the range you could explore—and use—on your own.

In that case, the total size of the world was proportional to the number of observers. You could say that the world you were able to sense was dependent on your number of companions and the people with whom you shared information.

"Not that population alone is enough. Anyway, from what I've seen all over the place, the more people there are, the bigger the fights get."

"Conflicts, huh?"

"That's right. Although it hasn't heated up all that far yet. Eastern Yamato has banded together around a town called Akiba. It governs itself; all the guilds in Akiba participate. The top eleven guilds have formed something called the Round Table Council and are working together in a neighborly way. At this point, their representative is a player named Krusty. A good-looking guy, that one. They've probably got about fourteen thousand participating members."

KR broke off for a moment and glanced at Leonardo.

When Leonardo nodded, encouraging him to go on, he continued matter-of-factly, "Meanwhile, the West is centered around a city called Minami. That one's more radical. All the western Adventurers have been absorbed by a single guild called Plant Hwyaden. Plant Hwyaden claims to have done away with discrimination between Adventurers and established a fair and just society. Officially, they've got about twelve thousand participants."

"Those are some bold strokes."

"They had to be. They needed to state their ideals boldly to get the confusion under control. You understand that, right?"

"So it was like a presidential election."

"That's about the size of it."

"The leader in the West is powerful, and they managed to handle the circumstances skillfully. So the East is a republic? I get the impression there's a faction struggle going on. Is that right?"

"No, well, I guess you could call it that. It seems to me that 'republic' isn't a word they're real familiar with in Japan. Either way, those two are both working to get back to the real world, but they're rivals."

Something about KR's words felt strange to Leonardo.

"Are they? They're not fighting with each other—they're rivals?"

"They're both Japanese organizations. They don't have any particularly hard feelings toward each other. I'm not very confident, but I think that's true for everybody except Indicus. I couldn't tell you what it'll be like in the future, though."

"Then why are they rivals at all? If they're working toward the same goal, couldn't they just integrate? The Plant Hwyaden guild could participate in that eastern council. Or, no, all the eastern guilds could participate in Plant Hwyaden and act as administrative staff."

At Leonardo's words, KR smiled faintly.

"An excellent idea, but it ain't that easy. There are too many people. More than five hundred thousand..."

"Five hundred thousand?! But you just said there were thirty thousand Adventurers in Japan!"

"That five hundred thousand includes the People of the Earth. They've got their own circumstances and organizations. In the first place, due to past history, Yamato's People of the Earth are split between the East and the West. Akiba and Minami's rivalry is being influenced by the social structure of the People of the Earth."

"Why would you bother with them? They're just NPCs. C'mon, KR. You know *they're not human*, right?"

"......"

Leonardo realized that KR was gazing at him with eyes as cold as glass beads.

Under that gaze, Leonardo abruptly felt ashamed. He didn't understand why it had happened, but he felt as if KR was feeling contempt for him, as if he thought he were a slow little kid.

"Leonardo. You'd better hurry up and adjust."

"Huh? Uh..."

"Without information support, modern humans are just an undisciplined mob. My personal preferences aside, humans are all about numbers. Our true power first appears when we form groups. Groups are societies that have some sort of lifestyle and technological support. If you think back to life on Earth, you'll understand. Most people wouldn't even have been able to win a fight with a stray dog, right? Leonardo...I'm not bragging about it, but I'd even lose to a stray cat. We're fragile, but because we banded together, we managed to conquer the world. It wasn't our knowledge. After all, early humans weren't even really able to write... It was society. It's because we banded together and made a system out of it."

KR spoke fluently, as if giving a lecture from a podium.

"Knowledge, society, and information are a trinity. In order to create a society, you need to exchange information, and the surplus heat from that exchange generates knowledge. Put another way, if humans didn't build societies, there would be no need to exchange information, and the civilizations we got would probably have been low-level. That's clear from a look at history, isn't it? Information exchange is a weapon. Now that we modern human Adventurers have lost the Web, we're suddenly back in the Stone Age. We're being divided, fragmented, here in this other world. Are you aware of that, Leonardo? Can you borrow somebody else's wisdom at this point?"

A sharp pang ran through Leonardo's chest.

KR was right.

There were no computers or Internet here. Forget those; they didn't even have phones or a postal system. They had telechats, of course. Telechats had been part of the game system, and they had survived. However, this wasteland was on the Chinese server. None of Leonardo's old friends were here. In order to place telechats, you needed a live friend list, but his entire list was dark and silent. Telechats wouldn't connect unless you were on the same server.

Leonardo remembered the anxiety and hopelessness he'd felt when it seemed as if he'd meet his end in Tekeli—that loneliness.

If he'd had access to a solutions wiki, he probably would have searched for a way to get out of Tekeli. Or, no, even before that, he might have searched for dangerous information and then steered clear of the place to begin with. Even if he'd been unlucky enough to fall into that trap in Tekeli, if he'd had bulletin boards and e-mail, he could have called for help.

But what had actually happened?

He'd been on the verge of starving to death alone.

It was true that Adventurers had rare combat abilities. In terms of their old world, they were in the same position as wolves and panthers. There was no doubting their superiority as living creatures. However, his individual skills hadn't been enough to let him tear his way out of a single ruins trap. Not only that, in this world, there were all sorts of beings whose strength was higher than Adventurers'. Most of the party monsters encountered in dungeons were sturdier and had greater attack abilities than aboveground monsters. After all, they'd been designed on the assumption that parties of six Adventurers would be fighting them.

If Leonardo was ten levels above them, he might be able to win, but he didn't have a chance against a party monster on his level. Similarly, raid monsters were designed to be tackled by twenty-four Adventurers of the same level, or by even bigger groups.

Dragons, giants, behemoths, land worms—there were all sorts of enormous, terrifying monsters here, and unless Adventurers banded together, they couldn't display their abilities. Not in a world without online support.

"What I'm saying is that the People of the Earth aren't like that. Sure, they may be NPCs… At least to you, Leonardo. But so what? They're the residents of this world, and they've spread their roots much farther than we have. They have their own society. Compared with the electronic network back on Earth, it might be clumsy, but even so, in their own way, they've built a society."

"They…have?"

"Yep. From things that have been used since medieval times, like post horses, messengers and rumors, spies and bureaucrats. They even have a magical information network that uses crystal balls, transmission tubes, and lightning spirits. They aren't Adventurers, but they're not idiots and morons, either. And—bonus—they've got more than ten times our numbers."

"Still, that doesn't mean..."

Even if that was true, People of the Earth were People of the Earth.

Wasn't it nonsense to compare them to Adventurers? So what if they had ten times the players' numbers? Leonardo was confident that he could conquer this village all by himself if he felt like it. It didn't matter if there were two or three hundred villagers. Even Thekkek's strongest member was only around level 30. Leonardo couldn't imagine losing to somebody like that.

"Of course, I see what you're getting at." KR nodded sagely. "I could dominate this village myself. But what would you do then? Would you become village chief? What would you do if you got hungry? Would you defeat a monster and eat its meat? Would you seriously do something that tiresome? You want to eat wheat, right? You want seasonings, too. For those, in the end, you'd have to associate with the producers, wouldn't you? Do you think Adventurers could provide all that on their own? For example, even Chefs rely on People of the Earth markets for their ingredients. Even if you took meat from your prey, if you wanted grain, you'd have to buy stuff grown by the locals. If we're going to have a certain standard of living, we can't avoid getting involved with the People of the Earth. In the end, that's where the road forks."

"Where the road forks?"

"I mean we can't just think about ourselves, as individuals or as a group. It's the same with worsening public order, and with the enmity between guilds. If we want to solve our own problems, our only choice is to solve the problems around us. All of them, People of the Earth included. We can say they've got nothing to do with us and toss them aside, but in the end, that would royally screw up our own lives, too."

KR's words hurt Leonardo.

That was exactly what he'd seen in Big Apple, on the North American server.

In a mildly disgusted voice, KR concluded his lecture:

"In other words, do we and the People of the Earth acknowledge one another, or do we use each other? It doesn't matter how we do it, but there's nothing we can do but live with them. As long as we treat them like NPCs, no matter what kinds of guilds we have, even if we're Adventurers, we'll have an end-of-the-century conqueror's legend here, and then society will collapse. The end. That's all."

▶3

Two days had passed.

Over those two days, on the whole, the villagers had welcomed Leonardo's group.

In response to the villagers' request, Elias had cleared away several thickets, helping to reclaim land. Coppélia gave blessings and treated injured people when asked, and Kanami's natural charm made her hugely popular. KR himself absolutely refused to admit it, but half of the horses—and there were more horses than villagers—watched him with fervent eyes.

However, unexpectedly, the one the children took the greatest liking to was Leonardo.

Boy or girl, whenever the kids saw Leonardo, they seemed to get very excited and happy.

What really irritated him was the fact that the kids always tried to climb him. The slightly older ones hung back, but they did so out of what little juvenile pride they had, and he could tell that what they really wanted was to put their sticky mitts all over him.

To Leonardo, most of the younger boys and girls looked like babes in arms or little ones who'd just begun to walk, and they were far less shy about causing him trouble. In other words, they climbed on him, and if they were in a good mood, they'd smack his green mask. If they were in a bad mood, they'd throw tantrums and cry.

Leonardo fled this way and that, trying to stick to places where there were as few children as possible. Even so, in this small village, there was no way to completely avoid them at meals and when he washed his face in the mornings and evenings. He ended up having to spend a lot of time dealing with children whom he couldn't admonish.

Because the mothers who lived in the village understood that Leonardo was an Adventurer and that his combat abilities were far greater than theirs, they bowed to him apologetically over and over. *We're terribly sorry our children are causing trouble for you*, they said again and again.

However, according to what Leonardo's imagination told him, this was just for show, and the ladies enjoyed seeing the kids attack Leonardo as well. If that wasn't the case, he couldn't believe they'd let the little tyrants have this much freedom.

As a result, while they waited for the caravan, Leonardo had to spend his days hiding from children.

That huge boulder on the outskirts of town was a big help. It was two meters tall, and with an area about as big as a large room on top, it made for a perfect shelter.

After meals, Leonardo scuttled away from the little ones, ran through the streets to lose any pursuers, then crept up to the top of the boulder and hid.

Once he'd fled to the boulder, Leonardo spent most of the day up there, swinging his swords. It was the first serious training he'd done since the Catastrophe had brought him to this other world.

Leonardo executed monotonous techniques over and over, checking every single one and progressing with slow steps, like a frog. He was an engineer by trade, and once he'd made up his mind about something, he was extremely tenacious. Most of the time, he achieved his objectives through perseverance and patience, using his instincts like a hunting dog to bring the problem to bay. Right now, he was using those two weapons to deduce the answer to a riddle.

On the morning of their fourth day in the village, travelers arrived.

Leonardo, who was up on the big boulder, saw them first, and he went out to a spot fifty meters from the village to meet them.

They were a much smaller caravan than the caretaker Yagudo had said they would be.

A middle-aged Person of the Earth led a horse loaded with cargo, and a woman wore scarred-up leather armor. Even though she was on foot, the woman, who wore a fur-trimmed mantle, was carrying on her back more cargo than the horse. It looked like they might have been journeying for a long time; there was pronounced fatigue in her expression.

Leonardo confirmed that she was an Adventurer, and he knew she'd recognized him at very nearly the same time.

"Are you an Adventurer, sir?"

"That's right. I'm Leonardo."

The woman bit her lip, clearly wary. She looked young, but her voice was calm, and most telling of all, her expression was experienced.

In the world of *Elder Tales*, due to the influence of the game's 3-D models, everyone tended to be good-looking. As a result, people who were middle-aged or older often ended up looking as if their youth had been restored. In terms of simple appearance, this woman seemed to be about twenty, but from her self-possession, it wouldn't have been odd for her to be in her thirties.

"My name is Chun Lu. I am a traveling guard affiliated with the Lelang Wolf Cavalry. My strength was insufficient to protect the other members of the caravan."

The middle-aged man was a merchant with black whiskers and strong-willed eyes. Introducing himself as Ju Ha, he asked to be taken to village chief Yagudo.

Technically, Leonardo wasn't in a position to take requests like that, and he didn't have the authority to grant permission. However, Chun Lu seemed to think that he was an Adventurer who'd been hired to guard the village. Either way, he couldn't just leave these two on the outskirts of town. Leonardo returned to Yagudo's house, showing the pair the way.

At the chieftain's abode, the two travelers were given a warm welcome, and in the large hall, Chun Lu told them what had happened.

The Lelang Wolf Cavalry had accepted a request to guard Ju Ha's caravan. This sort of guard duty was routine for the Cavalry. There had been four members of the caravan and six guards from the guild. In the beginning, she said, the journey had gone smoothly.

"However, on the eighth night, while we were southeast of this place, we encountered some gnolls. Lately, gnoll sightings in this region have grown more frequent. We had been watching for them, but…there were too many."

Chun Lu and Ju Ha, who'd been offered plain hot water by the villagers, spoke in leaden voices, but they told things just as they'd happened, with no apparent reluctance.

"We couldn't tell their exact numbers, but I think there were more than eighty of them. Since we are a guard unit, there is no meaning in simply winning battles. We have to save our clients. We defended, but there was no way for us to block that many gnolls completely.

"Gnolls tend to attack Adventurers. Knowing this, we distanced ourselves from the caravan, but in the end, our efforts were in vain. My Adventurer companions were annihilated. After I'd managed to escape, I went around searching for the members of the caravan, but there was nothing to do but mourn their passing. Ju Ha was the only survivor I found."

Chun Lu's face was grave, and the merchant she'd called Ju Ha seemed to be trying to comfort her.

He was a virile man with chiseled features and black whiskers. Although his voice was tired, it was still firm.

"Life on the road is always dangerous. That lot knew something like this could happen. The Wolf Cavalry risked their lives to protect us. They won't hold a grudge against you."

"But—!"

With so much force that she seemed in danger of biting through her lip, Chun Lu swallowed her words. Leonardo and the others knew what the rest of the sentence would have been as clearly as if she'd said it.

But we'll come back to life. We're Adventurers.

That was only natural. If Adventurers died every time a monster got them, it wouldn't be much of a game. That was why they revived in the temple. However, this wasn't true for the People of the Earth.

People of the Earth died.

Because they were NPCs.

That was just as ordinary as it was for Adventurers to revive. However, even though Leonardo knew that death was natural, he was unable to accept it as such.

Ridiculous... You know there's no helping that. That's just how it goes...isn't it?

The things KR had said rose in his mind.

The symbiotic relationship between People of the Earth and Adventurers. He understood that.

There were more People of the Earth in this world than Adventurers, and there was work that only they could do. Therefore, Adventurers couldn't get by all on their own. In that case, why not just use the People of the Earth as servants and live that way? The way Plant Hwyaden—the guild from Minami that had come up in the conversation—did things was perfectly logical in this world.

Even so, something just didn't sit right with him, and Kanami, Elias, and even Coppélia were listening to Chun Lu as if that "something" was only natural.

He'd never been good with this sort of dreary emotion.

Leonardo was a genuine New Yorker, and as a city-dweller, he was a believer in dry, hard, urban survival. In New York, everyone had their hands full just trying to save themselves. Working to help yourself was the heart of liberalism.

The weak died. That was simply how the world worked.

However, by that same logic, Leonardo sensed nobility in this middle-aged merchant, Ju Ha.

In the midst of this harsh battle for survival, they risked their most valuable asset—their lives—by trading in this dangerous wasteland. Ju Ha had survived, but his companions had lost their lives. On the whole, it was probably safe to say that the caravan had lost this bet. Ju Ha had been defeated, and he'd lost a lot of property and irreplaceable friends. However, that didn't decrease his nobility in the slightest. After all, he'd *tried*.

"So what are you planning to do now, Ju Ha and Chun Lu?"

"Your companions are gone, and I doubt you'll be able to travel any farther west."

It looked as if Ju Ha had already been thinking of the things Leonardo and Elias had said. He had only one horse left, and he'd lost most of his guards. Journeying farther would be difficult.

Chun Lu had been about to say something, but she faltered and glanced at Ju Ha. Her employer's wishes probably took priority.

"You're right. I'll have to start all over again. I'm planning to sell off as much of my cargo as possible in this village, then return. If I make it to the City of Mare's Milk, Dadu may be far, but I think I'll be able to pull some people together and make a fresh start."

Chun Lu was a Cleric. That had probably helped them survive. The wounds both Chun Lu and Ju Ha had sustained when fleeing from the gnolls had healed already. If Ju Ha had been on his own, he would have had to stay in this village and recuperate, possibly for as long as six months, but fortunately, he could depart the very next day.

His voice was stern, but it held the energy to move forward again.

"My guild, the Lelang Wolf Cavalry, is planning a raid to wipe out the gnoll group. As a result, they don't have the leeway to send additional guards for the journey home..." Chun Lu sounded apologetic.

"That's fine," Kanami said. "We're on our way east, too. We'll be your traveling companions. The five of us... Or—no, I guess one of us is a horse. Anyway, with you, Chun Lu, that's six. Perfect, right?"

Just as she'd done when she picked up Leonardo and made him a traveling companion, Kanami settled the matter with a lightness that held no hint of sarcasm.

Elias nodded, and Coppélia's expression looked vaguely happy. This relieved Leonardo. He didn't know why he felt that way, but Kanami's decision seemed to have swept away the slight pain he'd felt.

▸4

Chun Lu belonged to a guild called the Lelang Wolf Cavalry. From what she said, the guild had left Dadu in China and fled west. Dadu was a city in the game that corresponded to real-world Shanghai. It was a player town on par with Yandu, aka Beijing, on the Chinese server.

She recounted her circumstances to Leonardo's group as they traveled together. Apparently, the Lelang Wolf Cavalry had gotten fed up with the way society was deteriorating in the central area of the Chinese server—the regions along the coast—and had been the first of the guilds to move their main base westward.

On hearing her story, Leonardo thought, *That makes sense.*

The Lelang Wolf Cavalry was probably a homey outfit. From what he'd heard, they had about five hundred members, which made them huge, but not *super-huge*. In other words, they'd had enough members to ride the situation out, but they hadn't been big enough to control the struggle for supremacy on the server. In that case, evacuating seemed like a sound move.

Most of all, Chun Lu knew a lot about this region.

Of course, the wasteland was a vast expanse of unexplored territory. After all, it was the center of the immense Eurasian continent. Even though its size had been halved by the Half-Gaia Project, the Chinese server covered an enormous region that included the Tian Shan Mountains, the Taklamakan Desert, and the Pamir Mountains, among other things. Even on Earth, you really couldn't say the region was completely developed.

In addition to the gigantic country of China, the area under its jurisdiction included Uzbekistan, Kazakhstan, and the other countries of Central Asia.

There was probably no one, Adventurer or Person of the Earth, who had complete knowledge of each and every zone in its entire map. Even the developers couldn't possibly have a comprehensive picture of the whole thing.

That said, there were people who did use the narrow paths that linked trade routes, villages, and oases, and Chun Lu and Ju Ha were two of the select few.

"I'm glad we went with you!"

On the night they had left the village, as she sipped hot water they'd boiled in a tin can, Kanami made that declaration to her traveling companions with a smile.

Leonardo had to agree with her.

True, in terms of fighting ability, the People of the Earth merchant Ju Ha would hold them back. The man had a virile, bearded face and a sturdy build, and for a civilian, he was comparatively tough. He might even be as strong as the average soldier. However, his physical abilities were far below Leonardo's and those of the other level 90s.

Moving forward in accordance with Ju Ha's orders, the group traveled for ten hours each day.

If he hadn't been there, they could have spent an additional two hours traveling, plus they would have doubled the distance they covered.

However, nobody was unhappy about this.

If the Adventurers hurried ahead on their own, they'd probably be able to shorten their travel time by a week or two, but the odds of losing their way or running into trouble would be far greater. Leonardo, Kanami, and Coppélia were all Adventurers who'd spent a long time living in cities, and it was highly unlikely that they'd be able to find an oasis.

As a matter of fact, when Elias spotted a watering hole from a sandstone ridge and tried to climb down to it, Ju Ha stopped him.

Although the water in the oasis they saw from up on the ridge was perfectly clear and sparkling, he said that if they climbed down to it they'd get trapped in an enormous hollow.

On hearing that climbing up a cliff of brittle, crumbling sandstone was next to impossible, and that they'd waste a full three days before reaching the next oasis, Leonardo and the others gave up on the idea. Additionally, by evening they reached an abandoned village, and while the place was small, it was comfortable and had an old well.

When traveling across deserts and wastelands, experience was vital.

"True."

Elias responded to Kanami's carefree comment with his deep, resonant voice. Of course this Ancient hero, who was as handsome as a picture, even had a beautiful voice.

"You said it."

Leonardo also responded, shrugging.

Ordinarily, it wouldn't have been at all strange for him to develop some sort of complex about Elias's high specs, but weirdly, he didn't feel anything of the sort. Maybe they'd just boggled him to the point where he had no idea what to do.

This is the *Elias Hackblade, after all. Even thinking about it is probably pretty dumb...*

The flames of their campfire snapped and crackled.

They'd built it out of solid fuel made from dried livestock dung and a little kindling. The deep red, flickering light shone on the party, who were sitting close together in the shadow of the rock.

"Yaaaay! I call the back today!"

Quickly, Kanami burrowed into the very back of the tent Leonardo had set up. The tent was something Ju Ha had had with him; apparently, it was a travel necessity. It was made of a sturdy felt cloth draped over a lattice framework of plaited bamboo, and even though it was collapsible, it was incredibly good at keeping out the cold.

If you ignored the fact that it made for crowded sleeping conditions, it was perfectly possible for six people to lie down inside.

Earlier, Leonardo had let his Adventurer body's capabilities handle everything and had traveled without making proper camping preparations, but now he was very impressed, both by this camping equipment and by the skilled campfire-building method Coppélia had used.

In every situation, there were logical actions to take.

"You're okay there again, KR?"

"I don't mind. I can handle the cold better than humans. Being a horse has its advantages."

KR had already moved his equine body to the tent's entrance.

Even if it was a high-performance felt tent, at night, the plateau wind sometimes crept in. The area near the entrance was cold, and Kanami had fled to the best seat in the house in order to avoid it. Picking up on this, KR had apparently taken the spot by the entrance.

Pulled in by Kanami, Coppélia also went to get ready for bed. From inside the tent, Leonardo heard inappropriate words like *hug-pillow* and *boff, boff,* but thinking that was okay because they were both girls, he let it slide.

Elias, Chun Lu, and Ju Ha, who were still near the fire, planned to stay awake a bit longer.

Traveling while fatigued was dangerous. Even so, it couldn't be much past seven in the evening yet. Since they'd started to make camp a little before sunset, it would be a while longer before they felt sleepy.

"Would you care for another cup?"

At Chun Lu's suggestion, Leonardo held out his mug. Dexterously using two sticks to take down the brass pot that hung over the fire, she picked it up with the tail of her mantle and poured boiling hot tea into the cup.

"It's hot, so please be careful."

“Thanks,” he told the woman, who filled another mug in the same way and handed it to Elias.

“It’s amazing, isn’t it?”

“This area’s always like this.”

Elias’s gaze was turned upward to the sky. Ju Ha was the one to reply.

“Full of stars” was the only way to describe that sky. It was high, infinitely clear, and adorned with a sparkle like scattered diamond dust.

“You said the Lelang Wolf Cavalry is planning to subjugate the gnolls with a raid?” Leonardo asked as he sipped his tea.

In response, Chun Lu nodded. “That’s correct.”

“What’re the odds are their of success?”

“The odds? The Lelang Wolf Cavalry is a guild with slightly under five hundred members. This operation will be conducted by a century unit led by Zhu Huan, our guild leader, in person. I can’t imagine we’ll be defeated.”

He’d never heard the term *century unit* before, but he understood that she was probably talking about a legion raid. That would mean ninety-six people. You could certainly call that “roughly one hundred.”

Generally speaking, Adventurers’ combat abilities jumped as their numbers grew. The total combat abilities of two Adventurers weren’t double what one Adventurer had—they were two and a half times that, at the very least. Three times, if they fought in close cooperation.

This was a manifestation of the ability generated by the fact that parties weren’t just groups of multiple Adventurers; they were single life-forms that coordinated their fighting. Some Adventurers specialized in defense, some in recovery, some in offense, and some in disturbing the enemy. If Adventurers who knew their own strong points exercised them and compensated for each other’s weak points, Adventurer parties could display terrifying combat abilities.

Of course there were several prerequisites for this sort of coordinated teamwork. The Adventurers in the party had to know one another’s abilities and work together appropriately. They also had to attempt to respond reliably to the other members’ hopes.

These principles applied to raids as well.

Full raids, which were made up of four six-member parties, had twenty-four members. Legion raids, which brought four full raids together, had ninety-six members. With units that large, a cohesive understanding among the groups, vital for cooperation, was difficult to achieve. That said, if they overcame that difficulty, these Adventurer "armies" were probably the strongest military force in the world of Theldesia.

Gnoll levels ranged from about 20 to 50. Although there was no telling what sort of tactics the beasts would use, if the Lelang Wolf Cavalry had gone through even modest team training, against a gnoll force forty times their size—yes, four thousand gnolls—they would be able to fight without giving an inch.

Considered normally, that was enough military strength to power through the game's content on the grandest scale.

Of course, after the Catastrophe, combat had changed.

The terror of violence, in which steel clashed with steel, emitted a burnt smell. The horror of death, where something gradually transformed into a bloody lump of meat before your eyes.

The influence these things had certainly wasn't small. Even people who had grown more resistant to pain, thanks to system assists, could break. Leonardo had seen many Adventurers crumple. However, if he believed what Chun Lu said, these fears were groundless. He got the impression that the Lelang Wolf Cavalry was a band of skilled veterans with an excellent leader, so they had nothing to worry about.

...Except for the phenomenon known as "plague demons."

Leonardo still didn't have any firm ideas about what the plague demons actually were. He'd told Chun Lu about them, but she hadn't heard of them. The merchant had said he'd heard rumors among the People of the Earth, but he didn't know details or the actual truth, and of course he'd never seen one in the flesh.

What had that crazed Person of the Earth boy been?

The boy's behavior patterns had unmistakably matched those of a gnoll.

It seemed almost self-evident that whatever had made the boy like that had something to do with gnolls. For that reason, he felt a trace of unease about the Lelang Wolf Cavalry's gnoll subjugation as well.

However, in that case, what was the specific relationship between the plague demons and the gnolls, and what sort of mystery did that hold? Leonardo had absolutely no clue.

He'd given Chun Lu a summary of the incident and had suggested she instruct her headquarters to be on the alert, but with no definite proof at that moment, inspiring caution was the best he could do.

"I hope it's nothing."

Elias's comment seemed somehow undependable. Apparently, even the words of a hero weren't much help at a time like this.

Leonardo and the others were keeping to the ridge as they traveled, over a hundred kilometers away from the Wolf Cavalry, which was advancing across the plain to the south. Besides, they hadn't been asked to help, not in so many words. They'd pray for their safety, but it wasn't as if they could do anything.

This was a natural conclusion, and it was a view Elias and Leonardo shared.

Far to the south, the Lelang Wolf Cavalry advanced under the night sky.

They were headed straight for the Ruined Colonnade of Tonnesgrave.

▶5

Two days later, the fighting began.

Led by Zhu Huan, the ninety-six legion raid members thickly encircled Tonnesgrave and attacked the gnolls.

From their scout reports, the legion raid knew the gnolls had vast numbers. There were ten thousand of them assembled there, at the very least. In terms of numeric fighting power, there was more than a hundredfold difference between them.

However, a hundredfold difference in fighting power didn't mean that a hundred monsters could attack a single Adventurer at once. In fact, the gnolls encircled the ruins as if trying to protect them, taking up positions on the opposite side of the structure from Zhu Huan's legion raid.

That meant the gnolls weren't making full use of their numbers. All Zhu Huan's unit had to do was fight the several hundred gnolls that surrounded them, and an encirclement on that level wouldn't be enough to stop them. The gnolls' individual fighting power was far below that of each assembled Adventurer.

A song welled up from within the unit.

It was Nocturne of Meditation.

In this land, the song was called "Ying Shi Ye Qu." Ordinarily, the melody the Bard was playing had the effect of recovering—albeit gradually—MP, which wouldn't normally recover during battle. It was slow, but in protracted combat, the accumulated recovery amount meant a lot. It was a strategic special skill.

Additionally, the green light of Pulse Recovery, the Druid spell, was visible here and there within the unit.

In terms of the relationship between HP recovery amounts and MP consumption, it was more efficient for each of the Recovery classes to use their unique recovery technique—in other words, Reactive Heal, Damage Interception, and Pulse Recovery—instead of instant recovery spells. In particular, while a Druid's Pulse Recovery couldn't recover instantly, it was a convenient spell that continued to recover HP for a set amount of time.

As these two points show, when putting together this legion raid, Zhu Huan had emphasized continuous combat ability over instant offensive ability. If the enemies were gnolls, they'd be able to consign them to oblivion without maintaining vast attack power.

On the contrary, it was more likely that they'd use their numbers to surround the legion raid and wear them out by force.

There was a rear guard unit stationed three kilometers behind the Ruined Colonnade, but Zhu Huan thought they'd be able to settle this with the ninety-six members of this large unit.

"Unit Three is exhausted. Pull them back to the inside! Right wing, switch! Unit One, advance!!"

He issued orders loudly, in a voice that was hoarse and roughened from living in the wilderness, but still full of dignity. The unit advanced in response, slashing through the gnolls.

In battles like this one, Swashbucklers and Taomancers were the leading players. Since their attacks pulled in the beings around them, they were able to suppress monsters on broad planes, instead of merely at points.

Lightning Nebula, a Taomancer wide-range spell, struck the gnolls. Electricity writhed, shining bluish-purple, gleaming like a nebula as it closed a dozen or so foul dog-headed monsters inside itself.

Coolly ignoring the gnoll screams that welled up all around them, four Swashbucklers leapt from the left and right of the unit, walking in a manner that looked like something out of a classical Chinese opera. Every time the twin swords they held flickered left or right, gnolls that'd been bound by the lightning fell comedically.

The swordsmen's dance of blood went on, and when space opened up in front of the unit, the heavily armored suppression unit made up of Guardians immediately filled the gap. The Swashbuckler class was specially designed for offense. Before they could sustain needless damage, the unit took them back in, in preparation for the next attack.

The unit advanced steadily toward the center of the ruins, using tactics that, while plain, were true to the basics.

"One hour since combat began, hmm?" Zhu Huan muttered.

In his mind, having his unit wipe out the gnolls had never been an option.

After all, there were more than ten thousand of the creatures, possibly even twenty thousand. If he decided to, he didn't think it would be impossible to destroy them, but it would take far too much work, and it wasn't realistic.

The gnolls looked like they'd encircled Tonnesgrave with a formation that was several rows deep. They were also camped on the other side of the ruins, opposite the north side, where Zhu Huan and his army had launched their attack. He really didn't feel like running an operation to annihilate them after they'd mustered all those backup forces as well.

Zhu Huan's instincts told him it was better to aim for the center of the ruins.

* * *

What was this gnoll army, anyway?

In terms of typical gnoll behavior, he knew they formed packs, but these numbers were abnormal.

Something—probably a raid quest or some similar event—had happened among them. That *something* had assembled them and was keeping them together.

And there was no doubt that the Black Dragon mentioned in the report was somehow connected to that *something.*

Zhu Huan thought that the key to unlocking those mysteries had to be in the center of the Ruined Colonnade that the gnoll forces had surrounded.

"Rear rank Taomancers! Crush the enemy on top of the hill ahead of you! Open fire!!"

Even if there were several tens of thousands of gnolls, if the Adventurers were simply punching at right angles through a balanced defensive net, they probably wouldn't encounter even a thousand of them. As a matter of fact, the Lelang Wolf Cavalry was currently tearing through that net.

But something was wrong.

The first ones to notice the initial signs were the Swashbucklers who'd carved their way into their foe's ranks. The special skill Green Mountain Wind had expanded the Swashbucklers' swords; their offensive abilities were no different than normal, but the attack range was wider, and when they swung, they pulled in the surrounding monsters as well. The way they slipped into the enemy's dense ranks maximized the damage being inflicted.

The four Swashbucklers, running to provide support attacks for their Taomancer allies, increased the damage by making their range attacks overlap, and they'd succeeded in turning the area in front of the unit into a killing field.

However—

Their swords' agile dance was blocked by gnolls they could have sworn had been lying on the ground. Hairy hands they knew they'd already defeated caught the Swashbucklers' wrists.

A young dwarf Swashbuckler with a boyish face choked back a scream.

Even if this was a subjugation battle in which they were sowing damage across a wide range, that didn't mean they weren't checking the creatures' HP. Gnolls the Swashbuckler was sure he'd finished off had gotten up again. In fact, the monsters' arms were shredded, and he could see pale viscera through the gaps in their broken scale armor.

Still, what really terrified the boy wasn't their grotesque figures. It was their status displays.

The displays were blinking, cycling back and forth between GNOLL: WARRIOR and GNOLL: DARKMANCER. Even the monsters' HP values wavered in time with the blinking. To the boy, they seemed to be supernatural creatures.

They really were ghoulish demons.

"Gsshara!"

With an indescribable cry that had blood-tinged saliva in it, the gnoll bit the boy's ankle. It was Blood-Starved Bite, an attack method specific to gnolls. Even as he felt the fangs sink into the tendon in his ankle, the boy desperately swung his sword, bringing the blade down on the thing's neck.

But its HP didn't fall.

The gnoll didn't die.

Of course it didn't. Its HP was at zero already; it couldn't fall any farther. In spite of that, an instant after the attack, the figure on its status bar rebounded, and the thing glared resentfully up at the boy with dull, yellow eyes.

The pain was akin to being squeezed in a red-hot vice, and the boy panicked.

He swung his sword again and again.

"Hghk! Hghhhk!!"

Stifling screams in his throat, he kept on hitting it as if he were running it over with a car, and as a result, the gnoll finally fell silent. A Druid he knew came running over, looked at him, then cast Pulse Recovery.

The spell healed the wound on his ankle as they watched, but the boy's expression was still taut, as if he was about to burst into tears.

The actual damage hadn't been enough to put his life in danger.

Instead of damage to his HP, the boy had been harmed by a colder terror—as if wind had blown into him and chilled his heart.

Similar confusion was occurring all across the battlefield.

Gnolls stood up, even though fighters could have sworn they were dead. Gnolls the army had assumed to be magic users began brandishing axes. Gnolls that had been swinging swords cast magic spells.

But no matter what petty tricks they used, in the end, gnolls were just gnolls.

If dealt with calmly, they were no match for the Lelang Wolf Cavalry, and as a matter of fact, even in the midst of this confusion, damage to the guild hadn't increased explosively.

However, the irrational phenomenon whipped up a primitive terror in the hearts of the Adventurers.

The Catastrophe had been an unfair disaster. No reason or explanation had been given for it. One day, out of the blue, they'd been plucked from their familiar homes on Earth and flung into this other world. At present, when they had no prospects of finding a way to return, it was safe to say that they'd been exiled.

Under those terrifying circumstances, the Adventurers had managed not to fall into the worst possible panic because, although this might be another world, it bore a very strong resemblance to the world of the *Elder Tales* game they knew.

What did it mean to "strongly resemble a game"?

It meant that there were certain set rules, ones that were comprehensible.

It was possible to decipher this other world using the game rules and common sense— the principles—that they'd picked up during their days of playing *Elder Tales*.

Just the existence of those principles meant their knowledge was valid here. It led them to hope that "Someday, this will make sense." That was precisely what had allowed the Adventurers to get by in this strange, stress-filled other world.

However, the demons in front of them flew in the face of the system they believed in, the *Elder Tales* game system.

HP was stamina, the power to exist. If that value hit zero, you went down.

That was the rule, or it should have been.

Special abilities, skills, or the circumstances of an event might recover a creature's HP and revive it. However, statuses must not be chaotic, and multiple classes must never be displayed by turns. Those phenomena violated the rules, and they seemed to predict the breakdown of the *Elder Tales* system.

The panic that awareness triggered among the Adventurers was quiet, but its roots ran deep.

If they acknowledged what they just observed, they would lose the rules they'd believed in up until now. Specifically, this world would truly become irrational nonsense. Humans couldn't handle a world that was consistently impossible to understand.

"Withdraw the Swashbucklers! Summoners! Hit the front line with close combat types, and hurry!!"

Zhu Huan, astutely picking up on the mood, rapped out new orders.

The enemy's attacks weren't ferocious. For a short amount of time, it would be possible even for summoned creatures with combat abilities inferior to the Adventurers' to hold the front line.

The panic was bound to subside eventually. However, in order for that to happen, they'd need a little time.

If they were hit with an additional shock now, the front line might collapse. However, conversely, if they got through this situation, they'd be able to compensate for practically any loss.

The Wolf Cavalry still had sufficient combat resources and spare fighting strength; they didn't have to win right now. The best course was to stick to defense and let the unit recover from its mental disturbance.

Zhu Huan had gotten questionable reports from his scouting units, but he hadn't expected an occult phenomenon like this one. Wiping a spot of bloody sludge off his Three Kingdoms–style armor, Zhu Huan continued issuing stern orders.

Right now, the most important thing was to raise his voice and inspire his troops.

Zhu Huan's instincts told him that commanding was more important than personal bravery at this point, and in order to reassure his subordinates, he kept calling out in a voice so full of confidence that it seemed he understood everything.

However, even Zhu Huan's voice was drowned out by the sound of the Black Dragon's wings.

▸6

The local People of the Earth called the pillars "demon's fingers thrust into the heavens," and just as the name indicated, their sharply pointed tips were silhouetted against the sky.

They were roughly thirty meters in height.

In terms of real-world buildings, the structure would have been about ten stories tall, but in this area, where it was surrounded by wasteland, the Colonnade looked like enormous fangs sunken into the earth. Three pillars stabbed the sky. Two stood sharply, while the third had broken partway down.

The pillars seemed to be made of metal. That said, they had been melted down, and now there was a strange softness about them, almost like a living creature. On top of that, untold years had left them rusty and mossy. As a result, instead of the cold sharpness of metal, they struck anyone who saw them as a forgotten ruin.

If you ignored their size, what they resembled most were ancient iron spears that had been stuck into a battlefield and abandoned.

Two black shadows stood at their base, on top of the fallen rubble piled against the iron pillars, about ten meters off the ground.

The tall shadow carried pitch-black darkness with it, beneath its feet.

That black swamp changed shape constantly, and sometimes viscous bubbles burst. The tall figure, whose face was hidden by a hood, was standing on top of a swamp that looked like coal tar.

The shorter figure was a girl, no taller than a child.

Like her companion, the blond, small-boned girl had turned her even-featured face toward the battle below her.

The gnolls that had gathered around the ruin were in the process of being driven away by a group of Adventurers.

The girl gazed at the sight. She didn't seem terribly interested.

She was playing with the ends of her bangs with her fingers—she might not even have been aware she was twirling her hair. She wore frilly, impractical clothes that made her look like the daughter of some aristocratic family. However, her expression was utterly alien, and although her appearance was unmistakably female, the aura she wore made it impossible to state with certainty that "girl" was her actual gender.

The group of Adventurers was closing in on them, slowly but surely, and the tall figure pointed at them. The robe hid its shape from head to toe, and even the protruding bony finger was covered in a black, sticky membrane. A darkness that resembled filthy sludge dripped from it into the swamp under its feet.

"______"

There was a sense that some sort of order was being issued. Bubbles rose from the shadow at the tall figure's feet, adding an accompaniment to that feeling.

They welled up one by one, the sound of bursting methane bubbles forming a sequence. It was a muttered sound, like a faltering imitation of human speech: "**GO.**"

A gust of wind welled up behind the two.

The corpse of a Black Dragon, which had been dozing as if guarding the ruined base of the iron pillars, rose easily into the air with a single flap of its wings, becoming a black curtain that blocked the bright Aorsoi sunlight.

Turning even its torn, hanging wing membranes into symbols of terror, the Black Dragon made for the group of Adventurers.

"A splendid banquet, don't you think?"

"**That is a reasonable judgment.**"

A tall shadow responded to the girl's mechanical-sounding question. However, its voice was the static that rose from the unclean bubbles of muck at its feet. The sticky bubbles had to have been bursting incidentally, but by the time the popping noises reached the ear, they sounded like words.

Apparently, the speech this tall man used was the result of this bizarre phenomenon.

The girl fell silent for a while. She was completely motionless, and she used that short span of time to think.

"True…or possibly that way would be more certain."

"**How many?**"

"For that Black Dragon—"

At this point, for the first time, a thin smile appeared on her face.

"I drew one thousand two hundred souls to it in exchange for your theft of one thousand two hundred souls."

"Rasfia."

"Hmm?"

In a doll-like gesture, the girl—Rasfia—looked back, moving only her head. She was looking into the hood, which was packed full of thick sludge. The sludge wavered as bubbles slowly welled up through it.

"How many?"

"Let's see."

There was no telling what intent she'd read into the question, which was exactly the same as the one that had come before it, but the girl's lips warped. In ordinary terms, the expression would probably have been categorized as "a smile," but her face was masklike, and there was nothing approachable about it.

"If we pull in another two thousand..."

"Two thousand, hmm?"

The tall man abruptly grew thinner.

In the midst of the wind, at first glance, his shape didn't seem to have changed, but the viscous darkness that streamed from under the man's feet ran up the rubble like a shadow. It flowed over the slope, then over the ruins, slaughtering gnolls that were outside the pair's view.

"We mustn't lose the Black Dragon. Without it, we won't be able to break these iron towers."

"Into powerless models— The inconvenience of this bound body."

The Black Dragon crossed the far edge of their vision, descending over the heads of the Adventurers. From where the pair stood, the motion looked smooth and slow, but when size and distance were taken into account, it was clear just how overwhelming its speed and weight were.

The dragon's flailing tail and the jet-black electricity it spat out dragged down many Adventurers.

"My, my."

The girl smiled ironically.

Her oval face had a clear-featured beauty that was as tidy as a bisque doll's. Of those classic features, only her dull amethyst eyes gleamed, dark and intense, seeming to relish the phenomenon before them.

"Again… Heh-heh. It's dispatched thirty-two of them already."

"Rasfia."

The volume of the robed black shadow had decreased, but even so, just as before, he reproved the girl who seemed to be his partner with noises like bursting bubbles. Listening to the popping sounds, which should have been no more than static, slowly revealed expressions in the voice, and that was even creepier.

"Never fear. They took ten or so of those Adventurers or whatever they're called along with them. Drunk on the power they've been given. This should serve to pay for their ignorance."

"That is true for us as well."

Something in the bursting bubble-voice seemed to have irritated her: The girl commented by stamping a shoe that looked as if it was made of enamel, then narrowed her eyes into a smile and beckoned as if embracing the air.

Across a vast distance, as if manipulated by her slim, white fingertips, the Black Dragon rampaged.

If someone with remote viewing abilities had been present, they would have seen the dragon infused with gnoll souls raging as its instincts dictated, greedily devouring Adventurers, its cruelty starkly visible.

Originally, in the vast land of Aorsoi, this dragon wasn't a particularly enormous or difficult enemy. It was a level-85 full-raid monster—twenty-four Adventurers around level 80 could have defeated it. It was a monster that the Lelang Wolf Cavalry should have been more than able to deal with.

However, some mysterious art had given the Black Dragon a false immortality.

Of course, that didn't signal a decisive loss for the Adventurers.

In extreme terms, even if the Lelang Wolf Cavalry members were annihilated, they'd only be forcibly returned to their headquarters.

At present, the Adventurers were struggling against the Black

Dragon's immortality, but gradually, they seemed to be finding ways to deal with its attacks.

That said, as you'd expect, the fact that the Adventurers had lost a dozen or so members in that initial surprise attack was significant. The pressure from the countless gnolls that flooded the earth and the repeated lightning attacks from the dragon in the sky seemed to be clashing with their line of defense.

The Black Dragon used its disposable lives to render all attacks meaningless, paying out attacks so powerful they should have been mutually destructive, and it was steadily paring down the Adventurers' numbers.

The situation had turned into a battle of attrition.

However, the pair didn't issue any new orders regarding the combat situation. They simply continued to observe coldly.

"Idleness..."

"**Understanding of the layers seems to be limited.**"

"Give them the fate of inferior beings."

"**If they slept, rest would come to them, and yet...**"

Their conversation blended into the sound of the wind and was hard to follow, but eventually, the girl broke into an unbecoming smile.

"Fu-fu-fu! Could this be joy, perhaps?"

Delight surfaced in her dull amethyst eyes.

This was the girl's first true smile; she'd only warped her expression before. However, the smile was far too twisted and ugly. The fact that her features were passably neat and cute lent it a shudder-inducing malice.

It was an incredibly human smile, yet it was quite clearly inhuman.

"**The personality in the avatar's communication dictionary seems to be eroding.**"

"...You're right. My self-diagnosis suggests something similar."

"**It is not necessary in the collection of Empathiom.**"

"Still."

The girl had been reproached for her smile, but even so, she kept laughing, a light, muffled chuckle deep in her throat. The sound seemed to be connected on a fundamental level. Its source was different, but it had a quality identical to the sound of the tall, lean shadow's bursting bubbles—meaning, it was a grotesque expression of emotion.

"Our duty is nearly complete. We mustn't leave the corridor to the heavens here. Toying with unaware actors is quite entertaining."

"We are no different."

"And that is precisely why it's entertaining. Eleven hours remain. Our time will end, and Hora Octava will come. Keh-keh-keh. Fu-fu-fu-fu! Aah, what delight! Hurry, hurry. Quickly, quickly. I can't wait. I can't bear it. These lives, in which we're merely Rank 2… I want to end them. I want to end. I want to die. I want to kill!"

The girl flapped her gothic dress in the plateau wind. A pale vermilion line marked her neck.

The line was no thicker than a thread, but as she danced, the movements of her body widened it. The "line" made anyone who saw it uneasy, and on top of her neck, the girl's head wobbled like a decorative paper ball that had lost its rhythm.

"I can't take it. I can't wait. Hurry, hurry. I beg, I plead. Hora Octava! Trihorium! My siblings, my half sisters from another father. Come, awake, bring the end, the beginning!"

On the altar of the pointed fang at which empty-eyed gnolls worshipped, the girl spun and spun. Her laugh was clear yet ugly, like a piano that had fallen out of tune, and it echoed through the ruins of Tonnesgrave, seeming to lick them, to cling to them.

This land, which on Earth was called Baikonur, seemed to have exchanged its master for a nightmare.

▶7

"Wiped out?!"

It was evening when Leonardo's group received the news.

Chun Lu, a Cleric affiliated with the Lelang Wolf Cavalry, had been contacted by one of her companions, and she reported the content of the telechat to her current group.

"Unfortunately, our legion raid was annihilated. The surviving unit seems to have been some distance away from the site."

"By 'surviving unit,' you mean…?"

"A unit that had been kept in reserve as rear support personnel. That said, there are only a few dozen members. They were effectively annihilated… I never dreamed this could happen."

Chun Lu answered Elias's question, her voice gloomy but not despairing.

After all, it was a confirmed fact that Adventurers did not die.

From what Chun Lu said, the Cavalry had chosen their headquarters' current location because it had a temple. This meant, while they might have been wiped out, the members who'd fallen and hadn't been able to revive at the scene would be back at the temple.

Annihilation didn't mean that the guild itself was beyond all hope of recovery.

Elder Tales had begun as a game. It had consisted of sword-and-sorcery adventures in the world of Theldesia. Of course, production and interaction were also a big part of the fun, but the majority of the game had been combat.

However, even combat had existed on several different scales.

First, there was solo play, where lone Adventurers fought monsters on their own.

The next step up was party play, in which as many as six companions fought in cooperation.

Most of the combat in the *Elder Tales* game had consisted of these two types. There were no actual statistics, but to Leonardo, it felt as if about 80 percent of the content had been playable with those two methods.

Raids were what players tackled when they'd been through enough of that sort of game content.

Full raid content was played with twenty-four members, and legion raid content was played with ninety-six members. Combat for large groups like these had been considered high-end game play in *Elder Tales*.

Naturally, the difficulty levels were high, and it wasn't unusual for a single dungeon capture to take close to half a year.

Since the opponents this time had been gnolls, considering the level difference between the two sides, everyone had assumed the battle would go quickly. However, if they thought of it as a raid, getting wiped out wasn't all that rare. Even for top-class guilds made up of elites, it was hard to break through a high-difficulty raid on the first try.

That was probably why, although Chun Lu's expression was surprised and disappointed, it held no trace of despair.

The concerning thing was…

"It does sound as if they saw that double status display phenomenon."

"I see."

When Leonardo checked with her, Chun Lu nodded.

"I knew it…"

"So the phenomenon is spreading."

No one in Leonardo's party—not Kanami, who shrugged, or Coppélia, whose expression didn't change, or Elias, who was frowning—had any acquaintances at the Wolf Cavalry headquarters. Since they hadn't been registered as friends, they couldn't contact them by telechat, and so all of their information had to come through Chun Lu.

"Their numbers were great, and in the latter half of the battle, they say it was observed in almost all enemies…"

Leonardo wanted to know exactly what sort of phenomenon this was, and he did want to solve the mystery, but he had no likely sounding hypotheses or methods, so he curbed his curiosity.

It sounded as if the enemy's total numbers were close to ten thousand.

According to Chun Lu, they'd defeated quite a large number of gnolls, but during the battle, an unidentified black dragon had appeared as well. That dragon had spelled the beginning of the end, and the Lelang Wolf Cavalry had been routed.

There were only six Adventurers in Leonardo's group, and there was nothing they could do. For now, it was probably best if they kept heading east and, if possible, picked up more information at Cavalry HQ.

At the time, Kanami and Elias had been satisfied with that as well.

That night, Leonardo slipped out of his sleeping bag.

For the duration of this journey, Leonardo's group was keeping someone on watch at night. They weren't just a party of Adventurers.

Ju Ha, the Person of the Earth merchant, was traveling with them, and they'd decided they should be appropriately cautious as they went.

They took turns keeping watch, but one of the companions kept stealthily sabotaging the turns system. "Sabotage" didn't mean that they ducked their guard shift. On the contrary: They intentionally forgot to switch with the next guard.

It was Coppélia.

Yawning, Leonardo sat down next to her.

Coppélia had set a cushion she'd bought in the village down on the desiccated, brittle sandstone and was sitting on it. A magnificently embroidered, quilted garment peeked out from under the hem of her maid outfit.

"Good morning. Do you wish to be healed?"

"It's still the middle of the night. You didn't wake me up again."

"Coppélia does not yet require sleep. She is capable of staying on guard."

That was probably true.

Adventurers' physical abilities made it possible to shorten the time they spent sleeping. Their tough bodies had excellent powers of recovery, and they seemed to be able to get by on three hours of sleep a night without any ill effects.

That said, keeping watch at night all alone was a different story. They were companions, and they wanted to keep this journey fair.

Leonardo, turning silent and sullen, muttered only, "I'll keep watch, too."

Their surroundings were swallowed by darkness.

This was partially because the group hadn't lit a fire tonight. Fires were handy for keeping animals away, but there was a good possibility that they would attract intelligent monsters. In addition, when you considered the loss of vision that would follow if the light suddenly went out, you couldn't say there was no downside.

However, it wasn't that there was no light. The moon that floated in the crystal clear Aorsoi sky cast its pale light over the earth. The glow was more than enough to let him examine Coppélia's profile as she sat next to him.

"It sure is quiet."

"Coppélia detects no hostile monsters in the area."

At Coppélia's response, Leonardo nodded. According to the contact from Chun Lu, after that incident, the gnolls had stepped up their activity. They were probably far enough away, but there was no such thing as being too careful.

The moonlight shone over Leonardo and Coppélia.

He averted his eyes from the softness of her illuminated cheek's smooth contours, looking at the ground instead.

The two of them sat quietly, not really talking.

Leonardo was watching the moonlight shift gradually into darkness, as if it were crawling over the earth.

It was an odd feeling. Shadows moving—that was all it was, but Leonardo realized it stirred up a curious emotion inside him.

Considered in terms of real-world Earth, the fluctuating shadows would be caused by the movement of the moon, or more specifically, the rotation of the earth. In terms of the game world, it would happen because the light source set in the sky's texture was moving.

Either way, the shifting moonlight that fell over the wasteland was the passage of time made visible. Leonardo felt something curious in the perfectly normal fact that time did not stop.

He was deeply, quietly affected, in a way he couldn't put into words, by the fact that he existed as an individual in the midst of the flow of time.

This feeling soon shifted to the girl beside him. It was curious that he was here with Coppélia under the night sky of Aorsoi. If it hadn't been for the Catastrophe, this sort of thing would probably never have happened. After all, Leonardo was a geek from New York. The Catastrophe had changed everything. All sorts of things had happened. Apparently, this was true where fate was concerned as well.

"Coppélia will loan you this cape."

The next thing he knew, Coppélia was offering him a cloth that looked like a quilt. It was covered in embroidered grapes, violets, and flowers whose names he didn't know; it seemed like a mantle, and it looked warm.

The predawn wasteland was cold. She was probably concerned about him.

"You got this in Thekkek, too?"

"Yes. It was given to Coppélia."

Coppélia took a similar cloth out of her magic bag and wrapped it around her narrow shoulders.

"Those people gave you a thing like this, huh?"

Still sitting, Leonardo picked up a nearby pebble and tossed it. Coppélia had treated sick and injured people at the village; it was only natural that they'd thank her. That wasn't a problem.

It wasn't a problem, but it was a little irritating.

I fielded those annoying little ankle biters, but I... Well, I guess it's not like I didn't get anything.

Leonardo hugged his knees and dropped his forehead onto them.

A round, pretty rock. A weird scrap of cloth. A branch carved into the shape of a wooden sword. Half-eaten bread. A dried-out dead bug. An amulet made out of hairs from a horse's tail. None of the things Leonardo had gotten had been any good.

"You're lucky, Coppélia."

"?"

"I meant the cape. It's nice and warm."

"Yes. It is a folk craft with excellent heat retentive properties."

Only half listening to the off-key response, Leonardo sighed. However, he wasn't actually in a bad mood.

"In that village..."

"Hmm?"

It was unusual for Coppélia to start speaking of her own accord, and for that very reason, Leonardo was able to wait without hurrying her along.

"The boy we encountered in that village recovered."

"Yeah."

That double status display. The boy who'd been driven feral by some enigmatic disease. He was still in Thekkek. Now that he was no longer savage, he was just a Person of the Earth boy. He didn't have the strength to cross the wasteland alone. If he was going to return to his home village, he'd have to make proper preparations. Besides, even if he made those preparations, the odds that his home village was safe were only about fifty-fifty.

If that strange phenomenon had affected everyone in the boy's village, the villagers had probably already scattered. In addition, if that disease had been brought in from elsewhere, like some sort of plague or curse, it was naïve to think that whoever had brought the disaster in hadn't done any damage to the village.

If both those possibilities were groundless fears, and if all the members of the boy's village were still ordinary People of the Earth, then there was a significant possibility the boy had hurt the people of that village—his companions, including his parents and his old friends—through his transformation.

Leonardo thought that continuing to live as a resident of Thekkek might be the happiest possible future for him.

"That boy was…orange and green."

"Huh?"

Leonardo had been thinking about the kid's future, and he couldn't fathom what Coppélia's odd words meant.

"Monsters have green light, and People of the Earth have orange light. That is how it appears to Coppélia. Adventurers have blue light, and Elias has purple."

"That's…"

"Coppélia believes it is the color of their souls."

At that abrupt remark, Leonardo's eyes went round.

"Coppélia is not equipped with sight in the ordinary sense of the word."

Without waiting for Leonardo to ask his question, Coppélia went on, and what she said was something he hadn't even dreamed of.

"Sight? Huh?"

"Coppélia is unable to see. —To be accurate, Coppélia's sight is incompatible with yours and the others'. Coppélia is aware of her surroundings through data streams, tags, and the colors of souls."

The conversation was nuts.

However, at the same time, he couldn't completely deny it.

If this world was based on a game, then there had to be tags of some sort in the masses of data that were part of objects.

The Adventurers' status displays were one easy-to-understand example. If he concentrated on Coppélia, even Leonardo was able to make her name, main class, and level display, layered over his visual field.

The name, level, and class were "tags."

Monsters had monster tags. People of the Earth had People of the Earth tags. He didn't know the logic behind it, but could Coppélia be seeing those tags as different colors? He didn't understand the bit about souls, but if that was what she meant, it would technically make sense.

Is her sight maybe…?

A special device for people who'd lost their eyesight had been developed some time before. Research that had managed to make people sense images by connecting sensors to their brains had been reported about a decade earlier. Leonardo didn't know the details, but he'd heard that, at this point, they'd developed a device that let people recognize several different colors and images.

Had Coppélia been using that sort of device to play *Elder Tales*? Leonardo wondered about that, but he wasn't able to say it out loud.

He didn't think he and Coppélia were close enough for him to bring up personal stuff like that yet. Immediately afterward, he laughed at himself, thinking that that sounded like a coward's excuse.

"Coppélia has no color. That does not mean that Coppélia is transparent. It means she lacks the vibrating body—in other words, a soul—that generates color. Back then, Parallel One disappeared because Coppélia, who is structurally void, approached, and the more unstable soul was attracted—"

▸8

"Sorry to be an oaf and disturb your date, but—"

"KR?!"

The white horse had thrust its muzzle in between them. The voice of the Summoner who'd possessed the mystical beast hakutaku broke into Leonardo and Coppélia's conversation.

"What is the matter?" Coppélia asked calmly.

As Leonardo watched her, he mulled over her earlier words. *"In other words, I lack a soul.*" What did *that* mean? It made him feel as though there was something hard lodged deep in his throat.

Even when she'd said that, there had been no pain or sadness in her voice. Leonardo's heart felt heavy just thinking about it.

"They're close. It's the gnolls."

"Huh?"

However, Leonardo's thoughts were instantly interrupted.

"They're marching through the ravine in the northeast," KR said.

His back was wet. Wiping it down with a cloth, Coppélia said, "Requesting an explanation of the situation."

"Well, I've been out doing recon, and I saw 'em with my own two eyes."

Did that mean KR had spent all night running across the Aorsoi wilderness? Come to think of it, Leonardo didn't think he'd seen KR's big white body at the entrance to the tent when he'd woken up.

"They're advancing down a riverbed below sheer cliffs. I don't know what their numbers are. This body doesn't have good night vision. Moonlight alone wasn't enough to let me check. We're not talking a dozen or so, though. There are five hundred of them at least."

"Five hundred?!"

"At least. They've got those broken statuses."

"Meaning they're gnolls, but they're People of the Earth?"

"No, not that."

KR's voice was calm, and in the shadow of it, Leonardo felt ashamed. His own words had sounded rather frightened.

"It was more like there were two types of gnolls mixed together, but… Uh… How do I put this? It's hard to explain. Anyway, the displays seemed to have two monsters layered over each other. It was like that Person of the Earth boy, except a fusion of two monsters."

He was able to visualize the phenomenon.

However, as before, the cause was beyond him.

"A slew of gnolls, huh?"

"Five hundred, you said?"

When had they woken up? It was probably the faint sounds of their voices talking to KR that had pulled them out of sleep. Kanami, who'd only poked her head out of the tent, and Elias, who was looking down at her as if to reproach her for it, joined the conversation.

Not long afterward, Chun Lu and Ju Ha also emerged from the tent.

"Anything besides gnolls?"

"All I saw were gnolls and gnoll subspecies of different classes. I wish I could do a more detailed recon, but in this body, I can't summon a servant."

"Why...?"

Chun Lu's question was understandable.

Why were they moving as a group at this time of year? It was the first thing Leonardo had thought as well.

One possible explanation was that they were looking for food.

Or rather, it was safe to say that gnolls' *only* reasons for moving were to find food or claim territory. Their objective was to provide the main group of gnolls—the ones assembled at the ruins, the group Chun Lu's guild had attacked—with food: That seemed to be the rational explanation.

The Aorsoi wasteland was barren. The land was dry, and chill winds blew even in summer. Huge, deep green forests spread over the vast wilderness in places, and a wide variety of creatures lived there, but even they probably wouldn't be enough to sustain ten thousand gnolls over a long period.

In this wasteland, he couldn't think of a reason for forming an army of that size other than to provide the main group with food. Small groups of a dozen or so members were a lot more efficient at surviving and hunting creatures for food. When you thought about the size of hyena or wolf packs back in the real world, this was self-evident.

On top of that, gnolls were supposed to be monsters that gathered in dungeons and lived in groups of several hundred. They were predators that lurked in caves and ruins, killing and eating creatures that passed by—

That's game knowledge, though, huh? Leonardo admonished himself. This world was a game. Well, it should have been a game, but for some reason, he'd been summoned into it, body and all, and he did seem to be existing according to its laws.

* * *

"The direction they're heading puts them on a course for Thekkek."

When Ju Ha pointed this out, he heard Elias catch his breath.

Food…

In that sense, the village's sheep would probably be pretty appealing.

No, there was a possibility that they would see even the People of the Earth as food. Their habit of avoiding them certainly wasn't rooted in goodwill. It was because they knew that, if the People of the Earth banded together and defended their village, it would be more difficult to steal sheep and other prey.

If their forces were great enough to surround and wipe out an NPC village or town, they wouldn't have a single reason to hesitate.

"Are they aiming for the villages?!"

"I don't know if they're actively going for them, but if they pass one, they'll probably attack it. Look at their numbers. I seriously doubt they'd turn back."

Elias was bristling with anger, but KR responded coolly.

It had already been four days since their departure from Thekkek. Since Ju Ha, a Person of the Earth, was with them, they'd traveled slowly, so they were probably about 140 kilometers away.

If the gnolls kept marching along the ravine, it wouldn't take them a week to reach Thekkek.

Of course, if they felt like it, the Adventurers could get back to the village before the gnolls reached it. However, even if they got there, what could they do?

Chun Lu and Ju Ha were probably thinking the same thing.

A heavy, wordless silence filled the area.

"Okay. Hup. Hup!"

Kanami completely failed to read the atmosphere. She'd had her face stuck out of the tent, and now she wriggled and crawled the rest of the way out. *Why is she crawling?* Leonardo wondered, but as it turned out, she was still in her sleeping bag. She inched forward, looking like a caterpillar, then agilely hopped to her feet. Possibly because she was embarrassed (and rightly so), Kanami shucked off the sleeping bag with Elias's help.

Though really, if she was embarrassed, she should've just walked out to begin with.

* * *

"Mm. Good. Good? Five hundred dogs. That's good luck."

He had no idea what was lucky about it. Maybe it was some sort of Japanese folk tradition. As Leonardo wondered what the hell Kanami was saying, she punched a fist up into the sky.

"Sounds like a worthy opponent to me!!"

"Hey, moron! Don't you dare!"

"M-moron?! Did you just call me a moron, Croakanardo?!"

"Uh, sorry. Perhaps I went too far."

Kanami was planning to pick a fight with five hundred monsters—monsters with unknown abilities, at that—and in spite of himself, Leonardo verbally smacked her upside the head. He apologized, but he really did think she was a moron.

"Still, there's five hundred, you know? It'll be fun to charge in and kick 'em to pieces," she added.

"If you manage to kick 'em to pieces, yeah."

"I can do it if I really try."

"Like you could ever actually do it, you idiot!"

There was a level difference here. A difference that was probably more than ten.

Warrior classes existed to attract the enemy. They used their abilities to protect the Recovery and Magic Attack classes, and to give Weapon Attack classes like Leonardo the perfect chance to strike.

However, when they attracted the enemy, naturally, they became the target of their attacks. In exchange for not wearing proper armor, Kanami's class, Monk, had overwhelming evasive abilities. Most attacks from low-level gnolls probably wouldn't even scratch her.

That was "most," though.

It wasn't a guarantee.

On top of that, when the enemy's numbers were vast, there was the possibility that her MP would be drained during battle. If she ran out of MP, she wouldn't be able to use special skills. For a Warrior class, Monks had good attack power and well-balanced abilities, but these were only possible because they paid out lots of special skills rapidly, one after another. If her MP ran out, her fighting potential would drop drastically.

With Monk evasive abilities and Kanami's unique combat abilities, she might actually manage to drive off five hundred gnolls. Leonardo was training with the goal of surpassing her. There was hope. However, the risk was too great.

No, risk wasn't even the problem here. The problem was her motive.

"And anyway..." As if laughing at Leonardo's thoughts, Kanami grew enthusiastic, striking up a beat with her fingernails. "Five hundred is apple pie when your stomach's all grumbly, Croakanardo."

"Just for the record, I'm not Croakanardo."

Besides, he hated girls who scarfed down apple pie like that.

"Real Adventurers just blast their way through five hundred! Double up and do twice that."

"Don't make up crap about Adventurers."

And Kanami wasn't allowed to gamble. What was this "double up" business?

"We punch clear through the enemy and then, um, what was it again? Tone-deaf grads?"

"It is Ruined Colonnade Tonnesgrave."

"Yeah, that! We charge into the grave-thingy and behead the enemy!!"

"Are you nuts?! There are more than ten thousand of 'em!!"

Leonardo's shoulders slumped.

He hadn't held out much hope of their beating even five hundred of them. What was this woman thinking? He'd thought there was just something weird about her, something odd, but no, she was flat-out crazy.

"Weren't you listening? They wiped out the Lelang Wolf Cavalry's legion raid. Understand? That's one hundred level-90 Adventurers. *Wiped. Out.* All right?!"

"That's because they fought them head-on, with no intel."

"Wha...?"

"So we won't fight. We'll just attack and behead them. Then we run. A perfect game! We are the champions!"

"Mo—"

This girl had to be a moron.

What was that stuff about "champions"? Your brain is the world champion of stupidity.

That was probably why there were ten thousand gnolls protecting the ruins: so that sort of thing didn't happen. They'd tried to capture them with a raid because they hadn't been able to do it the other way. That was what Leonardo thought, but Kanami's attitude was so cavalier that all he could do was flap his mouth uselessly.

"So, Kanami."

"Hmm? What, KR?"

"You mentioned intel."

"We heard quite a bit from Chun Lu, remember?"

"Hmm. So, what sort of intel? And how are you going to use that to defeat the gnoll boss, assuming there is one?"

"You figure that out, KR!"

Kanami spoke decisively, with a smile so bright it almost made you think dawn had broken in the Aorsoi night.

"———"

"There's literally no way he can do that, you idiot!"

KR had gone speechless for a moment, and Leonardo hit her with a few strong words in his place. As things stood, he felt much too bad for KR, who dexterously bent his horse's neck, snickering as if he couldn't quite hold back. He was muttering things like, "B-bus guide. There it is, the bus gas explosion..." It was creepy.

"Hmm. I don't think it's a question of being able to do it or not."

"Then what—?"

"We need to go."

"And I'm asking you why we need to do that!"

As Leonardo pressed her, Kanami took a few light steps on tiptoe and gave a little smile. She didn't seem to be teasing Leonardo; it was a soft smile.

"It's a reason I can't say out loud."

That kept Leonardo from putting the rest of what he'd been planning to say into words.

Chun Lu and Ju Ha probably thought this was their party's problem; they were watching, but they didn't say anything. Leonardo and the others wouldn't get anywhere like this. He wanted Elias and Coppélia to scold Kanami, too, but they betrayed his expectations.

"I agree with Kanami."

"———!"

"I'm not saying we should depart for the jaws of death because I have an obligation to her. You may have forgotten, but I'm an Ancient. I have a duty to protect the People of the Earth. That has been the mission of the thirteen global chivalric orders ever since they were established. It may be trite, but even so, I sense the weight of truth in it. On the pride of the fallen fairy tribe, I will not abandon the People of the Earth."

Come to think of it, that's true, Leonardo remembered.

Ever since Leonardo became their companion on this journey, he'd forgotten that Elias was an Ancient, an NPC. He wasn't a player. He seemed to be rich in emotions, but he was basically a high-performance robot.

The same went for the People of the Earth.

They were only NPCs.

That was why everything they did was so dumb.

"What the hell are you thinking?! If it's dangerous, you get away from it. Isn't that obvious? You people don't know New York; that's why you're spinning castles in the air like this. What happens if you do something like that? This world is weird. It's a crazy dystopia. Adventurers aren't invincible. There are things you can save and things you can't, you know? The People of the Earth aren't human. We can't save them. Just leave them!" Leonardo shouted, spitting the words out.

They tasted like blood. Like regret.

"Coppélia will go, too."

"Why—?"

After Coppélia responded to him, she moved her thin arms, packing her belongings into her weight-reducing bag.

Leonardo couldn't condone the gesture, and he caught her wrist. There was no help for Kanami and Elias. However, Coppélia served Kanami as a maid, and she had to be different. It gave Leonardo a terribly unpleasant, pathetic feeling.

"Why? You know there's no way to win that."

"Are you certain?"

"Just think about it! Why would you do a thing like that for NPCs?!"

"Coppélia feels that there is a chance for victory. Coppélia termed that phenomenon 'Parallel One.' That condition is likely to be unstable in the extreme. If Coppélia, who has no soul, approaches, the broken, copied things will rush Coppélia. Coppélia's defensive gear has anti-spirit capabilities, and she suspects that may prove to be an effective countermeasure for Parallel One."

"Even if your logic's sound, it won't cut down the enemy's numbers! You don't have to sacrifice yourself, Coppélia!"

Her deep indigo hair swayed, denying Leonardo's words. Her large eyes reflected him like polished mirrors.

Fixing that innocent gaze on Leonardo, Coppélia spoke.

"Coppélia is not a player, either. A money-laundering group headquartered in China established several bots to collect capital inside the MMO. Coppélia is one of them."

Those quiet words pierced right through Leonardo's cowardice and escapism.

CHAPTER. 4

DOGFIGHT

▶ NAME: COPPÉLIA

▶ LEVEL: 90

▶ RACE: HUMAN

▶ CLASS: CLERIC

▶ HP: 9626

▶ MP: 8587

190
180
170
160
150

▶ ITEM 1:

[WHITE MAGIC STEEL SHIELDS]

HIGH-LEVEL, PRODUCTION-CLASS GREAT SHIELDS MADE WITH THE ADDITION OF SUNLIGHT BRIGHT-STONES, WHICH STORE LIGHT FROM THE SUN AND SPECIAL METALS SUCH AS MITHRIL. IN ADDITION TO BOOSTING THE THE AMOUNT OF RECOVERY GAINED FROM HEAL-TYPE SPELLS, THEY HAVE THE MUNDANE EFFECT OF AMPLIFYING ILLUMINATION SPELL BRIGHTNESS.

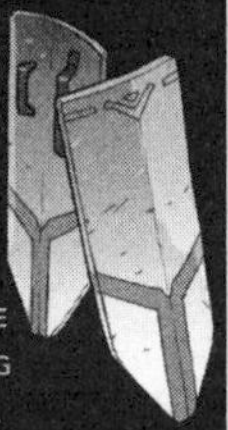

▶ ITEM 2:

[VIRTUOUS APRON DRESS]

PRODUCTION-CLASS HEAVY ARMOR WITH A DISTINCTIVE SHAPE THAT MIMICS A MAID OUTFIT. THE INTERCONNECTED, FLEXIBLE COMPONENTS ARE FINE METAL PLATES, AND THEY HAVE BOTH HIGH DEFENSIVE POWER AND A HIGH MOBILITY THAT PRESERVES THE PRETTY SILHOUETTE NO MATTER HOW THEY MOVE.

▶ ITEM 3:

[SAIERIKA'S TRUNK]

A STORAGE BAG THAT HAS SEVERAL TIMES THE CAPACITY OF DAZANEK'S MAGIC BAG BUT WHICH POTENTIALLY RESTRICTS MOVEMENT. IT ISN'T IDEAL FOR WALKING AROUND WITH, BUT COPPÉLIA STORES HER TRAVELING KIT IN IT AND CARRIES IT AROUND AS IF IT DOESN'T BOTHER HER AT ALL.

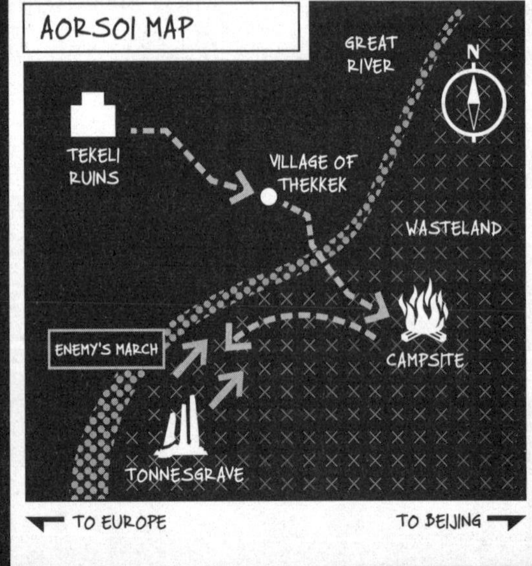
AORSOI MAP
GREAT RIVER
N
TEKELI RUINS
VILLAGE OF THEKKEK
WASTELAND
CAMPSITE
ENEMY'S MARCH
TONNESGRAVE
TO EUROPE
TO BEIJING

▶1

The light of daybreak shone down upon Leonardo.

In that flat glow, the wasteland looked terribly bleached out.

Kanami and the other two had headed for the ravine.

Saying they were going to warn the village of Thekkek about the emergency, Chun Lu and Ju Ha had also left without waiting for dawn.

Leonardo sat alone in the wasteland of Aorsoi, feeling as if he'd swallowed rocks. Before long, the indigo dawn passed, and the sun poked its face up over the horizon, but the day didn't feel all that bright or warm.

The light illuminated all of creation impartially, but it only served to make the world look counterfeit.

In a world flooded with that luminosity, Leonardo kept thinking.

Even now, he couldn't support Kanami's course of action at all. The fact that he couldn't understand it made it even worse. He had no idea what there was to be gained from confronting an army of more than ten thousand.

He just didn't know what her eyes were focused on.

People of the Earth were People of the Earth. They weren't human.

Couldn't she understand that logic? They weren't human. Every time that question rose in his heart, echo-like, Leonardo desperately shook it off, trying to convince himself that he was right.

"There we go."

"Huh?"

When he turned around, he saw KR. He still looked like a beautiful white horse, but he'd folded all four of his elegant limbs and was lying on his belly on the ground, relaxing almost like an enormous canine.

"KR… You didn't go?"

"Why do you ask that?"

"I mean, you're… You and Kanami go way back, right?"

"Sure, but… Well, I've got something on my mind, too."

Eyes half-closed, KR spoke lazily, as if he was savoring the temperature of the air.

Leonardo couldn't agree with Kanami's group.

What they were doing was folly, throwing their lives away for no reason, and he couldn't go along with that. However, if asked whether he could continue the journey east alone, he had serious doubts he was capable. As if he'd seen straight through Leonardo's hesitation, KR glanced at him with those intelligent eyes.

"What're you going to do from here on out?"

"What am I…?"

He tossed a question at Leonardo, and sure enough, the man wasn't able to answer it.

If he'd known the answer to that, Leonardo thought he probably would have been able to say a little more to Coppélia.

A capital collection bot.

That was what Coppélia had said.

What were bots, anyway? The history of the MMO-type online games that were *Elder Tales*' predecessors went back to the 1970s. At first, due to poor communication channels and computer performance and to the cost of those facilities, the user demographic was small, and this had made the genre a minor hobby. However, as the Internet flourished, it had undergone major development.

In the early 1990s, ambitious titles that had formed the foundation of current MMOs were released, and from then up until the 2000s, they'd acquired many fans.

MMOs were characterized by the experience of multitudes of users interacting with one another within the game world. In such games, it was routine for the owners of items to either give or sell them to other players who wanted them.

When it came to selling items, at first people had used the in-game currency or had bartered other items for them, as the developers had assumed they would. However, as the popularity of MMOs heated up, players who wanted to buy high-rarity items and in-game currency with real-world money appeared.

Whether a thing is real or imaginary, if there is demand for it, prices will be set, and it will evolve into a market. The information that movable property in MMOs could have real-world monetary value rapidly became the new understanding in the neighborhood of the Internet.

Resources in the game had more value in the real world than most of the still-young players thought.

In the early 2000s, when the scale of economic activities in currently popular MMOs was stated in real currency and revealed to be larger than the GDPs of some small real-world countries, the trend became known around the world. The interior of the game world was semi-independent from the real world, but since it was linked to that world through the desires of its players, perfect freedom wasn't an option.

In this way, the sight of in-game currency and items being bought and sold with real money became routine.

Of course, this practice was criticized for warping the normal game experience, and a significant percentage of game administration companies exposed it constantly. However, as long as there were people who wanted it and people who sought to profit by it, exposure was a Sisyphean task, and it wasn't possible to prevent it completely.

Bots were a kind of program that had been thought up against the background of this era. They were a type of autonomous AI, and they were used to run an MMO character without a player.

Naturally, they weren't capable of the sort of complex actions players performed, but they could continue simple, programmed actions for long periods of time. Bots were characterized by the ability to play in ways that humans were physically and mentally unable to handle, such as continuing to collect money and items in the same hunting ground for twenty-four hours straight.

There were a few players who used these bots on an individual basis, but the vast majority were used by traders.

In order to create points of connection with the daylight world, the underground society based in China and Southeast Asia used bots to win myriad items and money in MMO games. After all, neither taxes nor criminal investigations could reach them inside an MMO. It was the perfect place to collect untraceable capital and to convert underground money into respectable funds.

Since these bots ravaged hunting grounds and the game environment, serious MMO fans had come to loathe them.

A capital collection bot, set up in the MMO by a money-laundering group headquartered in China—that was what Coppélia's words had meant.

If she was a bot, her vaguely mechanical way of dealing with things, her blindly repetitive hunting, and probably even her unconditional obedience to Kanami made sense.

It wasn't a big deal.

She was a mechanical doll, just like the People of the Earth.

"Forget me, KR, what about you? You're sure you don't need to go?"

"It doesn't matter."

"It...doesn't?"

"Kanami's— She's going to do what she wants, you know? If it gets her killed, she won't have any regrets about it. She's got a Pollyanna brain. The girl's a serious pain in the butt."

"Why is she so reckless? That idiot."

"That's not recklessness."

"———?"

KR's laid-back attitude always came off kindly.

"It's...all the power she's got. She's accepting everything with all her might. That's what it is. That's important. It's kind of sad, isn't it? Kanami has no concept of gears or brakes. That's the sort of person she is."

"So, she's dumb."

"Well, I'm not saying she isn't."

KR said the words with a snort, but he looked satisfied.

"Do you think she can win?"

"I think she's got a good shot at it. I think that other young lady's the one who's worried. Kanami may not look it, but she's got plenty of raid experience."

"……"

"Did somebody say something to you?"

Back then…

When Leonardo had caught Coppélia's wrist, she'd confessed to him that she was a bot. Leonardo's words had frozen up on him, and she'd whispered to him in a transparent voice:

"In that village, Coppélia treated eighteen People of the Earth. She blessed forty-nine people. Coppélia did not know if either action had any effect. With regard to these actions, Coppélia was thanked three hundred nineteen times."

Coppélia hadn't said, *And that's why.*

She'd only turned on her heel and followed Kanami.

He knew that. There was a thorny lump in Leonardo's chest. A prickly, oppressive sensation. It irritated him and harassed him and made his chest heavy. It seemed to be urging him on.

The sensation was taking the beautiful wasteland of Aorsoi, illuminated by the flat morning light, and rotting it into a mess of hackneyed textures, and Leonardo knew what it was.

Those nasty, totally uncute, selfish, snotty little brats in Thekkek who hadn't shown him the tiniest bit of consideration—it was the same sensation he'd gotten from them.

That prickly warmth had turned inside out and was raging inside Leonardo.

He knew.

He'd really known the whole time.

What would not the part-timer geek, but the unbeatable ninja-hero that Leonardo loved the most, do at a time like this? He'd known from the very beginning. After all, he idolized heroes more than anybody. He hadn't even had to think about it: It was self-evident.

Leonardo was the one who'd been warped.

He'd been a coward.

He'd abandoned his hometown because he was afraid.

He'd hesitated to take the hand he'd been offered.

He'd had lots of warnings. This world was beautiful and abundant. They, the Adventurers, were the ones who hadn't admitted that, who'd behaved insolently, and who'd turned it into a lawless wasteland. Leonardo and others like him had taken something that was correct and had ruined it with their selfish assumptions. They were the worst.

What would *he*, the coolest guy in the world, do?

He wouldn't just stand around in a situation like this, looking on and doing nothing.

So what if the other people were machines or bots? He wouldn't hesitate.

He wouldn't blame his own cowardice on the other person's value.

Master is a person like first light, Coppélia had said.

What had she meant, exactly?

Coppélia hadn't said, *Master is a person like the sun*. First light was what came before the dawn. It was a sign that the sun was on its way. The messenger that slashed permanent darkness apart. It was a voice that said, *It's all right. Keep watching for just a little longer.*

In that case, what was the "sun" that Kanami foretold? He didn't know. He didn't know, but that sun had shone into Coppélia's soul. That was why she'd left on a journey with Kanami.

Leonardo turned it around, asking himself what he was. Not the sun; not first light, either. A gloomy, defeatist geek. However, *He* was different. *He* would probably leap over any darkness, bantering and cracking jokes as he went, and run off through the light. Leonardo knew.

The ambition inside Leonardo showed him his path.

If he thought he wanted to save something, then that meant the something was worth saving. Human, dog, cat, or bot, it didn't matter.

On the contrary: Who cared about that stuff?

It wouldn't hurt to have one more idiot who risked his life for AIs in the world, would it? Leonardo was a geek. However, he was a geek who worshipped heroes.

"I'm going."

As Leonardo stood up, KR chuckled, deep in his throat.

"What? Got a problem with that? Huhn! If you want to laugh, go right ahead. Maybe my going won't change anything, but I don't plan to just shut up and let 'em hit me. I've got a new power, too."

"No, I wouldn't laugh. I'm not Indicus."

KR got his white horse's body to its feet, then stretched his neck out a long way and neighed. His voice echoed for a long time; the neigh shifted into a sound like birdsong, then into a high-density chant—and white light filled their surroundings.

"Things are heating up. Is this the endgame? It's the endgame, right?"

When Leonardo opened his eyes again, squinting in the light, a man he didn't know was standing there.

He was an elf, a skinny young man with his hair pulled back in a ponytail. His face was as pale as an invalid's, and there was an entertained smile plastered over it. His equipment was unique: He was wearing a resplendent mantle with a tattered hem over a tracksuit. On top of that, he held two staffs, one in each hand. As magic-user equipment, staffs weren't unusual, but using two of them at once was.

"Are you…KR?"

"Uh, yes?"

"—So you're actually human?"

"What did you think I was?"

Snorting, the young man dexterously stuck his staffs into the ground, swung his now-free arms in circles, then stretched hugely. Considering the resulting, almost gratifying sounds, he seemed to have spent quite a long time hunkered down.

"How did you do that, and what was it?"

"Castling… You know: the emergency evasion spell that lets a caster switch places with a summoned servant creature."

"What, *that*?!"

"I just teleported to this server from Japan."

Leonardo was taken aback.

He'd been surprised by the fact that spells worked across server boundaries, too, but he was more startled by how versatile summoning magic was.

"All right, okay. Things are heating up. I'll go with you."

"Why?!"

"Well, this is interesting, isn't it?"

"Don't phrase that as a question."

"I'll make it a statement, then: This is interesting. Kanami's pulling out all the stops. It's a moronic explosion. Raging stupidity. On top of that, you're going to give it everything you've got, right, Leonardo? In that case, I'll shoot the works, too."

Oh, Leonardo thought. *This guy's another idiot.*

"I can't use magic well while I'm possessing something else, see. If I'm going to experience something live and in the flesh, my human body is where it's at. Mm-hmm!"

Even so, to have left Yamato, where he'd probably been safe, and come to a foreign land so easily, with no insurance… KR, who was wearing sandals, was grinning.

"—Even I…"

An enormous magic circle made of light radiated out from the staves he'd stuck into the ground and began to revolve three-dimensionally.

"I recognize that mask, y'know. I liked 'em."

Even as he smiled bashfully, sounds like whistling wind and the resonance of the magic array continued.

"I want to brag, too. If a hero's going to show off his new power, I have to show my stuff as well, don't I?"

The shining lines that were drawn in the air twisted together in complicated patterns. As they watched, the outlines formed a complex wirework figure, sketching a vivid shape.

"A summoning…?"

"Awake, crimson dragon. Graceful, supreme ruler of the contract, wake from your garnet sleep and soar through the heavens!"

The deep crimson dragon he'd summoned picked the panicking Leonardo up in its jaws, then set him on its elegant neck. KR, who'd settled in behind him at some point, whistled sharply through his fingers, and a moment later they were racing up into the sky.

With the two of them on its back, the dragon flew higher and higher, almost as if it were melting into the Aorsoi atmosphere.

▸2

However, at this point in time, there was something that Leonardo, naturally, but also Chun Lu, who should have been familiar with the area, and even KR, had overlooked.

This was the fact that Thekkek wasn't the only village in the region. There were People of the Earth villages over toward the ruins as well.

If, as Leonardo thought, villages in this other world were distributed randomly by an automated program, then there was a certain consistency to that distribution. The blasted wasteland of Aorsoi was dotted with many small, independent villages like Thekkek.

By this point in time, the incident had already caused a lot of damage.

Multiple gnoll units had crawled away from Tonnesgrave like tentacles, spreading out farther and farther, like wine spilled on a tabletop, until they'd engulfed several villages.

No disciplined will was evident in their movements. They were aimless, haphazard, irresponsible, and wild.

That was precisely what made their actions terrifying. After all, even if the gnolls had a mastermind or commander, that being obviously didn't care about the current situation.

It didn't care whether the several thousand gnolls won or lost their invasions.

It had no interest in how many People of the Earth died or were plunged into despair in the process.

The will that was visible behind the invasion seemed to state this eloquently.

"Rraaaaaaargh!!"

For that very reason, Elias howled.

He was an Ancient, and to him, this was an unforgivable evil.

Elias was an Ancient who had been raised by the fairy tribe. Ancients were spontaneous mutations born among the People of the Earth, and their origins varied. In most cases, they were born into People of the Earth family lines by coincidence, but there were quite a few who had special backgrounds.

However, whether they were born into ordinary families or, like Elias, came into the world as orphans, at a certain point in their lives, Ancients parted ways with the People of the Earth.

Their powerful combat abilities made it difficult for them to live in regular society. Many Ancients' talents appeared when they were in their teens, and they were welcomed into the community of Ancients before they turned twenty. Some became aware of their identity as Ancients while they were still happy, but many gained that awareness in the midst of sorrow and pain.

One type of resignation all Ancients shared was a sense of isolation:

the feeling that, while they had common roots with the People of the Earth, they were different beings. They probably got this idea from their combat abilities and their treatment by People of the Earth society, which, although it did respect them, treated them as aliens.

What's more, Elias was a "forbidden child" raised by the fairy tribe, and that loneliness had dogged him with particular intensity.

As a result, he didn't interfere in battles concerning People of the Earth. This was true of all Ancients. They had excellent combat abilities, and they had pledged to have nothing whatever to do with wars and political conflicts among the People of the Earth. To them, all such beings, from commoners to royals, were fragile creatures. There was no point in participating in their struggles.

As far as they were concerned, People of the Earth who killed other People of the Earth were not evil.

They were simply foolish.

People of the Earth were frail, short-lived, and weak, and they fought with one another and died because of this foolishness. That was the general view among all Ancients, Elias included.

To the Ancients, the People of the Earth were a bit like unwise children who had to be sheltered. When you watched them from a distance, they seemed precious and you wanted to protect them, but when you got closer to them, you were met with wariness and cold reservations. That was what they were like.

Of course, there were those who were high-minded and worthy of support. There were others who were innocent and lived ethical lives. When it came to saving them, Elias felt no reluctance; however, lending his strength to their power struggles was something quite different and—to him—inconceivable.

Ancients were guardians of the People of the Earth race, not of individual People.

"*Hiyaaaah!* Spirits of clear water, transform yourselves into a ten-thousand-foot blade and shine! Aqua Thousand Rain!!"

Elias's roar became a long, crystal spear, blowing away the gnolls who stood in his path.

In this incident, his nose had sniffed out "evil" for the very first time.

This wasn't the struggle for survival or predation that was seen among monsters, and it wasn't based in greed, like the territorial struggles powerful People of the Earth sometimes conducted. Elias had detected the first indiscriminate evil he'd ever encountered.

Killing from a desire to destroy and steal.

He was familiar with that sort of murderous intent, but this was different.

Killing because nothing really mattered.

That disgusting sensation made the Ancient shudder.

For that very reason, he'd been fighting with everything he had.

Since he was under the fairies' curse, he wasn't able to finish off anything, even monsters. His attacks couldn't drop his opponents' HP to zero.

However, as if to compensate for Elias's weakness, Kanami raced over the ground.

With smooth, feline motions, she leapt into the midst of the enemy, thrusting both her fists into separate opponents. From Dual Fist, she shifted into Wildcat Stance, executing a serial attack.

Choosing opponents whose health had been pared down by Elias's wide-range offensive sword techniques, Kanami steadily paid out attack after attack. By nature, Monks were Warrior classes. They were supposed to draw the enemy's attacks to themselves, but Kanami had abandoned that role.

Monks had very versatile abilities to begin with, and they were able to use "stances" to drastically change their own performance. By making skillful use of Iron Reno Stance, which was excellent for defense, or Tiger Stance, with its outstanding attack power, Monks could change their tactics to match the situation. This was one of their strong points.

Wildcat Stance, the stance Kanami had chosen, improved her movement and the ability to execute serial attacks. From a low stance that nearly hugged the ground, she paid out sweeping kicks and punching attacks that used both hands, finishing off enemies whose HP was already low.

Elias and Kanami advanced, moving ever forward, as if they were competing with each other. Fortunately, there was a ravine. A high river flowed along its bottom, and the banks on either side were about ten meters wide. Along these banks, a dense crowd of gnolls pressed toward the pair.

Both Elias and Kanami charged ahead without thinking about what would come afterward.

Not far from them, Coppélia was sporadically forcing her way forward.

Coppélia was a Cleric. Since she was a Recovery class, her attack capabilities were low. However, Clerics were able to use heavy armor, and in terms of equipment, among the twelve main classes, their defense was second only to that of Guardians.

Coppélia was currently wearing plate armor that was also reminiscent of a maid outfit. It was heavier than what she usually wore, and its "skirt" was reinforced with a series of iron plates. Even the puffed sleeves were made of magic-tempered metal, and they were distinguished by being lined with lace.

Today, unusually, Coppélia had equipped a large kite-shaped shield to each hand. This combat build, which was known as Double Shield Style, boasted the mightiest defense among Clerics.

Her move speed wasn't anything impressive, but she used the weight of the gear she'd equipped to mow down the gnolls.

Using the shields almost like walls, she protected herself, simultaneously pushing the dog-headed monsters together as if they were bread dough. The fate that waited for the compressed creatures was Elias's range attacks and Kanami's serial attacks.

Their three-person combination was efficient, and the gnolls' numbers fell before their very eyes. Coppélia's presence on the front line likely contributed to the trio's success.

Elias couldn't see it clearly, but when Coppélia closed in on a gnoll and touched it, an obviously savage energy dissipated. Of course, on its own, that wasn't enough to defeat the enemy. Thanks to Coppélia's participation, though, they were managing to keep this within the bounds of a *normal battle*.

However, on the other hand, this also meant requiring Coppélia to continuously participate in close combat even though she was only a Recovery class. She was using plate armor and two shields, but that didn't mean her basic abilities and special skills were suited to hand-to-hand combat. Even if they managed to recover damage, when their MP ran out, there was a risk that the battle line would collapse.

Little by little, Elias was growing more anxious about the circumstances.

True, the combat situation wasn't bad at all. On the contrary, things were going their way, and they hadn't taken much damage.

However, it was built on a balance in which all three of them were giving everything they had. As proof, when his spirit, which was like a taut thread, disturbed that balance just a little, a gnoll raced past Elias and leapt at Coppélia, who'd had her back turned.

Responding quickly, Kanami punched right through that gnoll with Wyvern Kick, but they ended up expending quite a lot of MP to repair the ragged battle line.

"Vanish! Vanish! Disappear!! Aqua Stream Hurricane!!"

The day his Ancient companions had vanished...

A day his comrades, the thirteen global chivalric orders, had fallen. Howling Moon had lasted only a moment, but it had brought a long sleep with it.

Half of his companions had departed, and the other half would probably never wake from their slumber. The Words of Death had destroyed the Ancients.

Kanami had been the one who'd saved him from the deep sleep of loss. Her brightness had warmed him, her light had illuminated his footsteps, and her fingers had pointed out his path.

However, he was still Elias, as he'd always been.

Elias Hackblade. Guardian of the world. The strongest Ancient.

In order to save this world...

In order to protect the souls of all People of the Earth and Ancients...

Elias used everything he had to carve his way into the throng of gnolls.

In the midst of a wind that seemed liable to tear his ears off, Leonardo shouted. There was a hardness in the passing air, and he couldn't talk to KR without yelling.

"Hey!"

"What, Leonardo?"

"Where are we going?! The ravine's right over there!"

"I thought we might as well go scout out those ruins or whatever they are."

The back of the red dragon wasn't all that big.

It was probably over fifteen meters in length, but its long, elegant neck and slender tail took up two-thirds of that. Besides, although KR was securely straddling it in what seemed to be his usual place, Leonardo was clinging to its neck.

However, this was Leonardo's first time flying, and he was completely fascinated by the wide land of Aorsoi as it streamed below them at high speed. The wasteland, the wind, the light: Everything raced past him, and the speed captivated him.

The membrane of air held a violent pressure, and there was a primal joy in blasting through it.

In just ten minutes, black spires came into view on the horizon.

Leonardo and KR knew in an instant that they were the ruins in question: the Ruined Colonnade Tonnesgrave.

For one thing, they were bizarre structures sticking up out of empty wasteland with nothing else around them. The other reason was that a jet-black dragon launched itself from the base, snapping off the structures with one sweep of its powerful tail.

"Hold the phone!! Hey!"

"Wow, that's really something. Is that a raid enemy?"

"Why are you being so laid-back about this?!"

"You think it's a full-raid monster for twenty-four players, or a double-raid rank for forty-eight?"

It looked as though the visual scale had been skewed.

When KR had summoned the dragon, Leonardo had thought, *Now we'll be able to win this!* but the mere sight of the destruction on the distant horizon made it clear to him that he'd only been dazzled by how cool the crimson dragon looked.

Even though both were dragons, there was an overwhelming difference between the Black Dragon on the horizon and the red dragon the two of them rode. To begin with, their sizes didn't match. Because of the distance, they couldn't compare the two properly, but that dragon was easily twice as big as the crimson dragon.

"What're we gonna do about that thing?!"

"We'll use, you know…that thing you wanted to show off. The hero's new power."

"Don't be an idiot! That's a Raid-rank monster!! How are we supposed to take it down with just the two of us?! Or, what, is this dragon small but high-performance, like a Honda?!"

"Gar-gar's a Minion rank."

"So?"

"That means she's cute."

This was hopeless. Leonardo squeezed his eyes shut.

In *Elder Tales*, there were two axes that showed monster strength. One was level. Each monster had its own individual level value, as Adventurers did.

The other was rank, and it showed a monster's strength by stating how many people it was best to fight it with.

The rank for ordinary monsters was Normal.

At that rank, Adventurers on the same level as the monster could fight it one-on-one. For example, it was optimal for Leonardo, who was level 90, to fight a Normal rank monster on the same level.

Of course, even among Adventurers at level 90, strength varied depending on equipment and how well they'd mastered their special skills. Normal rank monsters of a certain level were designed so that an average Adventurer on that level could beat them without trouble. For an experienced Adventurer like Leonardo, hunting Normal monsters that were a few levels above him wasn't all that difficult.

The next most common rank was Party. These were divided into subcategories such as "x 2" and "x 4," and the maximum was "x 6." "Party x 3" meant that three Adventurers on the same level could fight it on equal terms. These enemies were mainly fought in dungeons and similar places by Adventurers who'd formed a party. They were characterized by having HP and attack power that differed from Normal rank monsters, even if their levels were the same.

Above these was Raid rank. In order to subjugate Raid rank

monsters, you needed a large-scale unit on the same level as the monster, so "x 1" meant a full raid, or twenty-four people, and "x 4," the highest rank, required a legion raid of ninety-six members.

Since monsters of these ranks tended to show up on high-difficulty quests or be found lurking in the depths of megadungeons, even encountering them was hard to do.

On the other hand, there was a rank that was weaker than Normal.

This was the rank known as Minion, and it was seen mainly among the monsters Summoners could call with servant summonings. If a Summoner had been able to summon a Normal rank monster on their own level, it would have given them twice the combat strength of other Adventurers on that level. As far as the game balance was concerned, that wouldn't be a good idea.

That was why the Minion rank had been created. Minion rank monsters were one-third as strong as Normal rank monsters. Since Summoners had only two-thirds of the abilities of other classes on the same level, they weren't balanced until they'd summoned a servant—or that had been intentional design of the *Elder Tales* game, at least.

The red dragon the two of them were riding was apparently a Minion rank.

"You mean it's weak!"

"Did you hear what he just said about you, Gar-gar?"

"Why are you talking like this is somebody else's problem?! You're such a— Aaaaaaaah!"

While the two of them squabbled pointlessly, the dragon they rode had sketched an arc across the Aorsoi sky, drawing closer and closer to the Ruined Colonnade. Naturally, the Black Dragon and the two figures on its back had spotted them. With a great flap of its wings, the jet-black dragon spat several gnolls it had had in its mouth onto the ground. The wind from its wings sent the gnolls nearby scurrying this way and that, but it didn't even glance at them. In the space of a single breath, it closed in on Leonardo's group.

"Whoa!"

"You're going to bite your tongue."

Heaven and earth flipped for Leonardo.

The crimson dragon they rode folded its shining, garnet-colored wings tightly so that its body was dagger-shaped and dove rapidly, spinning as it went. It was traveling faster than a fall, heading for the ground like a bullet shot from a gun.

As it turned out, that speed saved them.

A thunderclap boomed.

Pitch-black smoke charged with lightning blew through the space where Leonardo and the others had been just a moment before. It was Dragon Breath, a legendary attack belonging to the tremendously powerful monsters classified as dragons.

As an experienced player, Leonardo had seen that attack many times, but it had been nothing more than well-rendered computer graphics on a wide, liquid-crystal monitor.

Children often draw pictures of cars and airplanes with crayons, but it's not like they comprehend the terror of a crashing airplane or of having a car plow into them just from looking at those pictures. Now, Leonardo felt the impact from the depths of his soul.

Electricity and black smoke streaked through the air not three meters away, and he felt a trembling as though the air had spasmed. His nose caught the burned stench of ions. *Those past game experiences were a total lie*, Leonardo thought. *Hey now, hey, hey, hey. The air just got broken down.* He'd known that was where the rumble of thunder came from, but he hadn't thought it possible to sense these things with his nose.

Okay. He'd admit it—

This might be a game world, but he'd temporarily retract that knowledge.

If they got hit by that lightning, it seemed as though that philosophical doubt would evaporate, too.

There are tons of things city geeks don't know! Oh my God!

Still carrying them on its back, the crimson dragon fell in a tailspin, but when they got close to the ground, it opened its wings wide and beat at the wind. It glided to maximize aerodynamic lift, then used the layers of air generated by the slope of the hill to shoot up into the sky again as if launched from a catapult.

"What is that?!"

"Judging by its appearance, probably a Black Dragon, right?"

"Not that! Those two on its back!!"

Even in the midst of their tailspin plunge, Leonardo's excellent eyesight had burned the two figures' shapes into his eyes. A thin, mage-like figure in a hood and a golden-haired girl as delicate as a bisque doll.

"Considering where they are, they're probably not allies of justice."

"Just looking at them, I can tell they're bad guys."

"The masterminds behind this incident, I presume?"

Even as Leonardo and KR conversed in shouts, several bolts of lightning skimmed by them. The electrical bolts' trajectories were straight lines, but they reached a long way, and although the black, smoky gas that clung to them only went partway, it spread out and was hard to avoid.

The red dragon was smaller than the black one, but it was agile, and at this point, it was managing to evade through dramatic trajectory changes that didn't give a thought to its riders. That said, the red dragon was a Minion rank at level 90.

Even though the Black Dragon was level 85, and therefore lower in the hierarchy, it was a Raid-rank monster. One solid attack from it would probably be fatal.

The red dragon probably knew this as well. Either that, or KR had given it instructions in a way Leonardo hadn't been able to see. As it evaded several bolts of deadly light, the red dragon circled around behind and above the Black Dragon, capturing its back.

Dragon Breath was a range attack and a powerful threat, but it had a weakness as well:

Since it was emitted from the dragon's mouth, the directions in which attacks could be made were naturally limited. On top of that, the Black Dragon was currently airborne. If it bent that long neck carelessly, it would end up turning. If it had been braced on the ground like a gun battery, things might have been different, but its build made it incapable of attacking behind itself.

"Great, good position!"

"It looks like we're better at accelerating."

"We've got its back. Attack with Breath!"

"We don't have Breath."

"Huh?!"

"Gar-gar doesn't have Dragon Breath. I told you, she's a Minion."

"What, seriously?! Talk about useless!"

As if protesting Leonardo's abuse, the red dragon gave a deafening roar. The only way Leonardo could handle the sudden howl was by clinging to its neck and riding it out.

"If you're going to go that far, why don't you attack?"

"Don't be an idiot. We're in midair!"

"Where there's a will, there's a way. 'Yes, we can.'"

"That's old. Whoa!"

Leonardo ducked, avoiding a tentacle that stank like sewage.

It wasn't the Black Dragon.

The Black Dragon was flapping and twisting left and right, up and down, trying to chase the red dragon out of its blind spot. However, like a well-made trace macro, the small, elegant red dragon was sticking close to it, right behind and above it.

The attack had come from the hooded figure on the Black Dragon's back.

Still standing on the dragon's back, the hooded shape had pointed a hand up at Leonardo. Even if the Black Dragon's back was broad, that attitude was absurd, and—unusually for him—KR swore. The threads that poured from the man's finger were clearly tracking Leonardo and the others, and a thoroughly scorched, acidic stench hung about them.

"Cut them down!"

KR hadn't needed to tell him that.

Having registered that threads wouldn't work, the tentacles had morphed into something like exposed animal viscera and were stretching out toward the red dragon. The black and red dragons were about ten meters apart. Their objective was clear.

If the villains damaged the red-dragon team with the attack, fine. Even if they didn't, if Leonardo and company retreated to avoid an attack from the tentacles, their pursuers were probably intending to switch to a Breath attack.

"Don't screw with me!"

Leonardo drew his Ninja Twin Flames and lopped off the tip of a tentacle. The additional effect activated, drawing tracks of flame, and the tentacle burned down, streaming backward.

To the right, to the left. Straddling the dragon's neck, Leonardo slashed down the tentacles that stretched up one after another. Fortunately, the tentacles seemed pretty fragile. One slash was enough to shred them and send them flying.

However, they were also pipes that carried acid.

When the red dragon failed to avoid one of the slashed remains and the acid landed upon its scales, there was a sound like meat sizzling on an iron griddle, and white smoke erupted.

The red dragon forced down a low moan, but it managed to stick to its current position, and Leonardo felt a huge respect for it. The structure of dragon wings was similar to bat wings; they were made up of a thin membrane. If acid struck its body or neck, it could probably tough it out to some extent, but if the membranes burned away, its evasive abilities would diminish. In the worst-case scenario, it would go crashing to the ground.

The red dragon knew this, and in order to protect its wings, it had intentionally taken the acid on its neck.

Responding to that spirit, Leonardo stepped up the ferocity of his slashes, trying to deal damage to the owner of the tentacles as well.

Whizzing into a rolling scissors maneuver, the two dragons raced across the Aorsoi sky, sketching complicated trajectories. As he swung his swords from the dragon's back, Leonardo forgot about the shredded, speeding clouds and the distant earth and became one with the battle in front of him.

Leonardo saw the two figures on the dragon's back clearly.

The beautiful girl with the derisive smile was Rasfia. She was a level 89 of Normal rank. The hooded being who was tenaciously attacking with the tentacles, over and over, was Papus. He was also a level 89 of Normal rank. Neither of them had a main class or were affiliated with a guild. They had human shapes, but monster displays.

If they'd been on the ground, fighting one-on-one, he wouldn't have lost to stats like theirs. However, under these circumstances, when they were teamed up with a Raid-rank monster, they couldn't have been more of a problem.

Inversion.

In the midst of an intersection that switched the positions of heaven and earth, Leonardo cut the pursuing tentacles away again. Even the scattered acid was evaporated by the flame attack he thrust out.

The battlefield had shifted, and before they knew it, the wide earth had been exchanged for a valley like a thin green path. The single great river that crossed this wasteland had carved the ground away, forming a ravine. Dense, vivid green forests grew on either side of the water at the bottom of the canyon.

Attempting to shake off the red dragon, the Black Dragon skimmed just above the treetops.

The trees were flooded with light and gleamed as if they were wet, and small, startled rainbow-colored birds burst from them all at once. The flock of birds filled the sky, and the two dragons shot through it like arrows.

The banks of the river were littered with countless gnoll corpses. When he saw them, Leonardo lowered his gaze. As if being guided by some miracle, his eyes met Coppélia's, who happened to be looking up at him from the midst of the gnoll horde.

Coppélia's clear, calm eyes reflected the red dragon, soaring against a background of blue sky.

A sound echoed in Leonardo's heart, and he cemented his resolve.

"If those two are gone, can you draw that Black Dragon away?"

"What are you talking about?"

"I'm asking, if that overblown pair gets off the Black Dragon's back, can you tow the dragon over the horizon?!"

For a moment, Leonardo's yell seemed to render KR speechless.

"Leonardo."

"What?!"

"I just got to Aorsoi a little bit ago."

KR spoke carefully, spacing his words out so that their meaning was sure to get across.

"That means, if I die, my body will resurrect in a temple in Yamato, aka Japan. Whether we win or lose—this is probably good-bye."

"Bring it on!!"

Leonardo turned back, thumping KR's chest with a fist that still held a sword. KR coughed, then struck Leonardo's chest with his slender magic-user's hand.

It was an exchange of war cries, and encouragement, and friendship. It wasn't the sort of thing that belonged to a New York geek. It was a promise between heroes.

They went through a series of steep climbs and sharp dives. Irritated by the red dragon, who stayed stuck to its back no matter how it twisted, the black one tumbled through the sky, sometimes scraping its wings against the trees of the forest, sometimes trying to fling itself into the sun.

Before long, spotting a moment's opening in those movements, Leonardo bent down onto the red dragon's neck, storing up strength.

"KR!"

"I know!"

There was no time to say more.

Taking advantage of the moment when the Black Dragon's unfurled wings hid him from the grotesque pair of adversaries, Leonardo leapt into space.

"Cowabungaaaa!!"

Mimicking the legendary hero's yell...

Leonardo slammed into the two on the Black Dragon's back, clinging to them, and then, according to plan, as the acid burned him, he plummeted toward the ground.

▸4

"He did it! He actually went and did it! He's awesome! That's the spirit! Right, Gar-gar? This front-row seat is a bargain, isn't it? Thank you, O great and glorious Lady Kanami!"

Tearing off his scorched robe, KR cackled loudly.

The enemy was a tough customer, too: Even as he got tangled up in Leonardo's body blow, he'd left a parting gift. He'd intentionally severed ten-odd tentacles, and the fragments acted as midair mines loaded with acid that engulfed KR and his red dragon.

COWA-BUNGA!!

Even as he took significant damage, KR was in high spirits.

To him, being on the scene for the moment when the world began to move was the greatest joy there was. And that was why he'd been Kanami's defender and devotee: because he'd seen that power in her.

Something changed, and somewhere gears began to turn, moving the story, the world.

Sometimes, things happened that couldn't be described any other way. The goal of KR's life was to be there for such moments, witness them, and help those people along. That was just as true in this other world as it had been back on Earth. Or rather, since it was flashier here, he could even say it was better, easier to understand.

There was a scream like several thousand bowstrings snapping.

It belonged to the aggravated, and now masterless, Black Dragon.

Leonardo didn't seem to have noticed, but its status display was blinking kaleidoscopically. MIASMIC LIGHTNING BLACK DRAGON, GNOLL, MIASMIC LIGHTNING BLACK DRAGON, GNOLL—the speed was so great that the display itself seemed to blur. Those two riders must have been influencing the Black Dragon in some way: The dragon had clearly lost its composure and was acting insanely aggressive.

It was so bad that it had even forgotten to aim, and lightning leaked from its mouth, scorching the tops of the trees.

The wind was blowing out KR's mantle and making it flap, and as he clung to the red dragon's neck, he yanked it in, wrapping it tightly around himself. In a mobile fight like this, no matter how excellent Adventurers' physical capabilities were, he couldn't afford getting yanked around by it.

Lightning gathered in a black, warped space, then shot from the Black Dragon's mouth. It was the creature's Negative Thunder Breath, and the Garnet Dragon avoided it by a hairbreadth. She evaded, veering as if there were a track in the air.

However, that didn't negate the entire threat. It had been a violent choice, made possible by the fact that, with a dragon's tough defensive abilities, she could ignore damage to a certain extent. That said, even if he was an Adventurer, KR was only human, and the damage was too great for him to shrug off with an *Ah, I see, is that right.*

Adventurers and monsters had different approaches to combat

abilities. Most monsters were born strong. They had combat abilities that were above a certain level right from the start. Meanwhile, for Adventurers, growing and changing was an adaptive strategy. Leveling up and learning new techniques were part of it, but improving their chances of survival by acquiring equipment made up a percentage that couldn't be ignored.

Gwaaaaaah. Cold air endurance equipment, air pressure endurance equipment, pressure endurance equipment—I don't have enough of anything!!

In the midst of the wind that roared and blustered at him, violent wind that was practically a rigid body, KR clung desperately to his dragon's neck.

The Black Dragon didn't pursue them.

In a short span of time, the other had climbed savagely to a distant height from which it could look down on KR and his mount.

Aerial battles were sophisticated mental battles in which you had several choices and worked to rob your opponent of theirs. The red dragon's mobility far outstripped that of the Black Dragon, in fact overwhelming it. She could probably win on speed in a straight line as well. However, that difference wasn't absolute. It was affected by wind direction and air pressure, and most importantly, a difference in altitude could easily turn the tables.

The speed that could be gained from falling was far greater than what one could gain from flapping wings or magical propulsion. That is, being at a higher altitude than your opponent gave you greater positional energy than they had. In aerial battles, having gravity on your side was an overwhelming advantage.

The red dragon had KR on her back. Dragons could withstand the reduced air pressure and lower temperatures at high altitudes without trouble, but this wasn't true for KR. In a dogfight, KR's presence handicapped the red dragon. This was most obvious when it came to taking up positions at high altitude. Relying on its toughness, the Black Dragon had climbed to an altitude with low air pressure, then made up for the difference in speed by diving.

"Gar-gar, up, up!"

Going pale at the sight of the Black Dragon's power as it sliced through the wind on approach, KR put his ride on the alert. Even though both creatures were the same species, their attributes and personalities were completely different. Compared to the Garnet Dragon, which specialized in aerial battles, the Black Dragon was a heavyweight raid monster. Although not very mobile, it had outstanding range attack capabilities and endurance, and it was excellent at defending strong points and at trampling down and charging.

And now its huge body, which could have been described without exaggeration as an airborne fortress, was plunging toward them with gravity as its ally. Not only that, but as if determined not to let them get away, its jaws gaped and its front legs stretched out, their halberd-like claws fully extended.

With a sharp whistling noise, the two dragons intersected.

"———!"

There was a dull thud, and the stink of ions scorched their surroundings.

KR gave a goofy smile. He'd managed to last through the Black Dragon's dive attack.

When they'd crossed paths, those short front legs had swung at him. As the price for having beaten back that attack, KR's right arm was burned black and hung limply, dangling. It was a miracle that he was managing to hold on to his Staff of Scorpius.

"Sheesh, Gar-gar. That's cold," KR grumbled at his partner, who was making quiet, dissatisfied noises. Seemed she thought she'd been made fun of.

That's not true. KR laughed.

The Aorsoi sky was high and blue. Against that ultramarine, with the light shining through them, the red dragon's wings were pretty enough to provoke a sigh. Like the "pomegranate" from the Latin root of her name, they shone transparently. That didn't mean he'd been protecting her or anything. He just couldn't let those wings fall prey to dirty talons.

As far as compensation went, this was fair. In the first place, they were up against a raid monster. If you wanted to take its attacks, you'd need a dedicated tank with multiple healers and the support of buffers in order to match it. If KR, a Magic Attack class, had gotten by with losing only an arm, that cost was actually pretty cheap.

* * *

"—Let's go with a Japan-US showdown special."

Marvel versus Ishimori Production.

With that big statement in mind, KR lured a little animal out of his jacket.

The animal, which looked like a white mouse, was a Crew Rat. It was a level-3 monster and an event creature.

Summoner was an unusual class.

Adventurers earned experience points by fighting and completing quests. When they'd acquired a certain number of experience points, their level went up, and they learned new techniques. In addition to experience points, there were things called mastery points, and it was possible to select special skills and make them even stronger.

However, a certain type of special skill was acquired on quests outside of leveling up, and it was Summoners who had the most of this type of quest.

Summoners' main special skill was Servant Summoning.

To be accurate, this wasn't a single skill. It existed as a separate special skill for each summoned subject, like Servant Summoning: Hakutaku and Servant Summoning: Siren. Most of these skills were acquired through quests. This was why even Summoners on the same level used different servants, depending on the quests and the progression of the adventures they'd completed to date.

Quests in *Elder Tales* were independently designed by each server administration company. As a result, countless distinctive summoned creature acquisition quests were said to exist across the world's thirteen servers, and it was hard to grasp just how many there really were.

However, as far as the balance with the other main classes was concerned, it wouldn't be good if individual Summoners were able to acquire dozens of special skills. For that reason, there was a maximum number of special skills that could be acquired on quests, and that maximum was twelve. If a Summoner wanted to conclude a new contract that put them over that number, they had to choose one of their existing contracts and cancel it.

KR muttered a short, simple spell, and along with a shining green magic circle, the Crew Rat in his hand disappeared. The cute little mouse had just concluded a contract with KR, becoming his servant.

A magic system which KR himself knew nothing about had stored it away until he chose to summon it with Servant Summoning: Crew Rat. At the same time, since he'd gone past the limit, one of KR's contracts was dissolved.

"You fool!"

There was a brief flash of light. In the blink of an eye, the unleashed light particles formed a magic circle centered on KR, who was flying through space. The enormous red magic circle looked a lot like the one used to form contracts, but its properties were reversed, and it signified release.

"So you finally summoned me, did you?! You half-witted elf magus! Bravo! Bravo! To think you'd be my sacrifice again!"

"Gar-gar, are you kinda hyper?"

"I was subjected to an acid shower in a body that couldn't talk!! That tends to excite the nerves!"

"Now that you mention it, you're right."

"What wretchedness! Why must I accept your protection?!"

"Huh? That's the problem?"

"Don't give me a trite comeback, dullard!"

"No, you were completely right, Gar-gar, so I just—"

"That blasted red-headed frog. I have no Dragon Breath? How dare he join you in mocking me!"

"Y'know, you might be more popular if you just called him an ignorant human, laughed, and forgave that stuff."

"You imbecile! I have not forgotten that you made me into a trivial, ignorant, pseudolizard pet!"

KR was on the verge of retorting, *Well, it was that kind of contract, wasn't it?* but sensing the forceful change in mobility and the vast amount of heat she was gathering, he shut his mouth.

The red dragon KR was riding had just more than doubled in size. She was twenty-five meters long. Her body, the elegance of which belied its huge size, held energy that seemed equivalent to an active volcano, and she climbed all in a rush.

The speed of her ascent was filled with an overwhelming sense of power. There was an extraordinary amount of mana in her wings. The dragon was a single streak that led to the sky, a line the color of shining blood.

"'Draw the Black Dragon away'... What a small-minded thing to say."

"That frog-man is the very essence of ignorance and unenlightenment."

"That sounds like a new type of demihuman."

"Do not blame me if you bite your tongue!"

The red dragon, who fired something like a shining, crimson crescent moon from her mouth, had finally shown her true worth.

A level-90 Raid-rank monster.

KR's partner, the Garnet Dragon, raced across the sky.

Becoming Raid rank hadn't simply doubled the size of the Garnet Dragon's body. Her HP was several thousand times greater, and her attack power, defensive power, reaction speed, and spellcasting abilities had all risen prodigiously.

Her speed and mobility were no exception, and as she flew through the sky, she looked like red lightning. The difference between her and the Black Dragon, which had been slight up to a few moments ago, had clearly widened.

"Unless I show 'em something impressive, I don't get to appear in the final episode, see."

"What are you talking about?" the Garnet Dragon hissed.

"It's how supporting characters fight."

Speaking defiantly, KR raised the staff in his undamaged left hand like a gun turret.

A complicated magic design surfaced in the lantern portion at the tip of the long staff, beginning to draw in tiny light particles from the space around it. It was Hive of Evil Spirits of the Abyss, a phantasmal equip item that had the tears of Elreida of the Fifth Prison closed inside it. Against a beautiful, somber noise of moving mechanisms that was in sharp contrast to its name, KR wove a spell.

The basic performance of Hive of Evil Spirits of the Abyss was high as well, but what set it apart was its ability to temporarily seal a servant. Sealing a servant with recovery abilities in the "Hive" at its tip raised the baseline for the special abilities of other servant summons.

"Gar-gar!! Goooo!"

"Right!"

With that war cry, the man and the dragon unleashed a crimson ray of heat filled to the brim with magic.

▶5

"It seemed like something out of an incredibly gallant epic poem, but after that, you passed out from the pain and returned to Yamato, did you not?"

"Heeeeey, Gar-gar. We promised we wouldn't talk about that, remember?!"

"I made no such promise."

"Ah-ga-ga-gah! Ooooooh. Seriously, ooooh. Ow! That really hurts, I mean it!!"

"Hmph. Gutless."

When the ribs the girl had lightly jabbed played "do-re-mi" and reached "fa," KR flung himself away and ran. The girl had already occupied the deck chair.

Unfortunately, what she'd said was accurate: Although KR had won the battle with the Black Dragon, he'd pushed himself too hard and had passed out. He'd fallen, hit the ground, and died, and as a result, death had returned him to his shelter on the Yamato server.

If you said one couldn't look cool that way, you'd be right, but he had taken on a raid boss as a lone Adventurer. There was probably no helping the outcome. Even if he'd had a raid-boss level ally on his side, he'd been pulled into that fight. Coming out unscathed would have been too much to hope for.

KR and his partner were in a place called Ikoma. Specifically, one of the House of Saimiya's second residences, located about eight kilometers to the east of the city of Minami. However, its current master was Plant Hwyaden, the enormous guild that controlled Minami. They were using this mansion as their guild headquarters.

Having returned to Arc-Shaped Archipelago Yamato, KR had taken three days to get himself back into shape and had then gone to participate in Plant Hwyaden, the giant guild that governed Western Yamato. This secondary palace in Ikoma was the hub of that guild, and it held the greenhouse where KR and his partner were living.

"Merely asking you a question is an utterly foolish endeavor, but..." The girl, who was swinging her feet, addressed KR: "Why do you belong to such a backwater guild, anyway?"

"Aagh. Ooooh..."

KR was curled up in an odd position, rubbing his side, but when she asked him "Why?" again, he answered slowly. The slowness certainly wasn't because he didn't want to answer, or because it was a difficult answer to give. It was simply that his kicked side hurt.

"Well, getting meals ready and cleaning rooms is a pain in the butt, you know?"

"An answer from a direction I never even suspected!"

The girl was so startled by this that her words overlapped the end of KR's statement.

Still, it wouldn't do to have people startled over a thing like that. While he might not look it, KR was the type of person the world called "a pampered rich kid." It wasn't something he was proud of, but he'd never even touched a vacuum cleaner. On top of that, this was another world, one in which electrical appliances like vacuum cleaners didn't even exist. Cleaning was a professional's skill.

"I can't cook or clean to begin with, see?"

"What incompetence. Have you absolutely no talent?"

Hearing that said directly to my face is kind of a problem.

Communication abilities that let him chat about the latest chocolate offering at the doughnut shop with unfamiliar high school girls probably didn't count as "talent," and although he'd technically had a command of four languages in the old world, this world was equipped with an automatic translation system, so that didn't seem like much of an advantage to KR.

"Taking care of small girls, maybe?"

"I am a *girl*. Not a *small* girl!"

She'd evened out the number of (undamaged) ribs on his right and left sides, and KR rolled around again. The ground was close. More specifically, his cheek was pressed against it. *So this is what being "down for the count" is, huh? Down for the count because a girl broke your ribs. What sort of game is that?* KR desperately hit himself with verbal jabs, trying to distract himself from the pain. Even if you were an Adventurer with recovery abilities, unless you had a specific sort of fetish, painful things hurt.

"So you're saying you can do that stuff, Gar-gar?"

"I am a dragon. As if I'd ever do anything so petty."

Holding his sides, KR nodded. *I see.*

Come to think of it, that made perfect sense. As a Garnet Dragon, in the natural way of things, if she got hungry, she caught prey and devoured their meat, and if she got dirty, she dove into a lake. She was a monster in the shape of a girl, so trying to make her do things the human way was probably egocentric.

Her violent behavior might also be some form of dragon communication.

"I would like stew with shrimp for dinner tonight."

"You're letting human society rub off on you, Gar-gar." Completely disgusted, KR changed the subject. "So, Leonardo—what do you think of him?"

"Why would I think of him?"

KR sat down cross-legged on the floor, which was designed to look like a beach.

He had the elation he'd felt. It was fact. Leonardo was definitely one of the chosen ones. Someone with a protagonist's destiny, one that was different from KR's. Someone who'd been born under stars that let them do uncommon things, like Kanami and Soujirou. One of the people KR idolized and wanted to help.

Leonardo was an interesting guy, too. If he gave the sympathy he'd felt during that one moment a name, he'd probably be able to call it "friendship." That word had gotten harder to say as he'd grown older. Coming to share that feeling with someone else through hero stories was embarrassing, too. However, KR had no intention of ignoring what he'd felt.

"His prospects, that sort of thing."

"That's a foolish question."

The girl stretched hugely, then said, as if it didn't matter, "He uses the skills of the great ones. I can't imagine he'll die easily." She probably really didn't care.

The skills of the great ones: That was how the girl had rated Leonardo's training. The skills of the great ones were training, plus resolution strong enough to warp that training. At the time, KR hadn't managed to grasp the meaning of that word completely, but now he thought it might mean techniques like Overskill and the Mysteries. It seemed likely that the same phenomena and techniques were called by different names, depending on the region and the community you belonged to.

"Well, that lot are pretty much strangers to 'safe travels.'"

"That's just as true of this city."

She's not wrong, KR thought.

Plant Hwyaden, the guild he was affiliated with, and Minami were currently enjoying prosperous times.

The People of the Earth ruling class had long traditions, and as a result of those long traditions, it had governed Western Yamato with an ossified bureaucratic system. Their rule had been useful in asserting their legitimacy, but on the other hand, it was true that things had remained unchanged.

Then the Catastrophe had occurred, and many Adventurers had appeared in this world. When you took a broad view of things, the arrival of the Adventurers had brought positive changes to Minami's governing organizations.

Simply by existing, Plant Hwyaden had improved public order, cut down on damage from monsters, and dramatically developed the economy. In a way, the Catastrophe had triggered a breakthrough for the country.

However, abrupt changes couldn't help but produce distortions.

Not only that, but Plant Hwyaden was a single enormous guild. It had an internal class system, and the guild's top-level members, who were known as the steering committee, ran it autocratically.

KR didn't think autocracy was a bad thing. Even in Japanese society back on Earth, there had been countless examples of dictatorships in the form of "one-man" corporations and similar things. In fact, there were a multitude of cases where, during the development process, it was more efficient for the person in charge to take decisive, authoritative action.

He'd seen cases on the overseas servers where everyone had become equally unhappy because no one had tried to take responsibility, and the misery had spread to the People of the Earth. To him, Plant Hwyaden seemed to be doing incredibly well.

The majority of the Adventurers who'd holed up inside the Japanese server might not understand, but KR had journeyed around the other servers, and he did know: The lack of chaos and orderly recovery on this server were miraculous.

However, even so, there were those who were left without a place in that dictatorship and system of command, and the city's ordinary People of the Earth were often trampled on. In the first place, Plant Hwyaden's control had been established when a few capable Adventurers formed an alliance with the People of the Earth nobles. No one had included the perspective of protecting citizens' rights for People of the Earth. In that guild's system of self-government, newbies and low-level Adventurers were weak, too.

KR knew that Kazuhiko was tearing around all over the place, unable to just stand by and watch the unfairness that had begun to run rampant in Minami. However, viewed from a high perspective, even that was no more than a drop in the bucket, and it was actually making the situation worse. The harder Kazuhiko worked to save people, the easier it was for Plant Hwyaden to govern unjustly. Precisely because Kazuhiko's Miburo rescued the people that Plant Hwyaden's tyranny oppressed, no decisive complaints ever exploded.

There had been no need for the girl to point it out: The situation here was far from "safe."

Now that they'd solidified their bonds with the Adventurers, most of the Holy Empire of Westlande's nobles seemed to be openly enjoying their glory days, viewing the situation as unparalleled prosperity and the opportunity for a great leap forward. However, to KR, all this prosperity and advancement seemed to rest on thin ice. He honestly couldn't fathom how they could be so giddy about it.

Of course, their carelessness was due to Indicus's manipulation of information and Nureha's skills, but even so, KR thought it was far too irresponsible and thoughtless. Either that, or it could be due to the deterioration of the Yamato nobility, which had lasted for too many generations.

"That sounds likely," the girl agreed with KR. "That strange pair we met on the continent… They radiated a curious air of intimidation unlike any enemy I had met before. I don't believe that I would lose against beings like them, but I can't declare that I could win, either."

Those weird monsters, the ones Leonardo had taken along with him on his screaming leap to the ground…

Afterward, with a sure premonition in his heart, KR had continued to search for information about them. This was one of the main reasons he'd decided to participate in an enormous guild like Plant Hwyaden. He'd risen to a position of authority as a Ten-Seat and had used it to gather information. As a result, he'd managed to confirm several things.

"Geniuses." New monsters by that name had been striding about this world, unnoticed, since the Catastrophe. KR had confirmed that information through one incident in Nakasu and two in Akiba.

Since it was something KR could detect, it was likely that people with a rank similar to his, or those who had a means of gathering information, would notice the incidents soon. In other words, it was about time for the People of the Earth nobles to pick up on them. If they couldn't do that, they were pretty much asking people to criticize them for being lazy, and in fact, KR thought they were probably in denial about the fact that things weren't as peaceful as they seemed. Of course, as a modern Japanese citizen, he was in no position to criticize someone else for that, but even so.

KR didn't know how the battle in Aorsoi had ended.

From the back of the Garnet Dragon, after Leonardo had jumped off, KR seemed to remember catching a brief glimpse of him landing on the ground and fighting. However, it had only been for a moment, and KR and the dragon had had their own job to do. Leonardo's fight was part of Leonardo's destiny, and this time, it hadn't been KR's role to see it through to the end. This was true for Kanami's fight as well.

However, KR was confident that they hadn't lost.

He couldn't imagine Kanami losing in an all-or-nothing bout like that one. The more decisive and highly anticipated the game, the better she did. Even if she'd lost that moment's contest, she was sure to resolve the incident itself, and she'd save as many as she possibly could.

Those were the stars that belonged to Kanami and Leonardo. It was what set them apart from supporting players like KR and Kazuhiko. For that very reason, along with a faint pang in his chest, he felt a greater sense of expectation. Someday, Kanami's group was bound to appear here on the Yamato server. She'd promised to visit this place, so it was practically an established fact already.

It was also likely that war would break out. He didn't know what that fight would be like.

Would Plant Hwyaden, which had grown grotesquely obese, begin creaking and trigger it? Would the nobles lose their heads and launch a war against the Adventurers, or would their opponent be the East's Round Table Council in Akiba, which was supported by Shiroe? Would the Geniuses threaten KR and his people again?

He didn't know, but some sort of fight would probably flare up. This was more than just a vague premonition. There were sparks all over the world. Right now they were hidden, but to KR, it felt as if those sparks were growing bigger by the moment.

In preparation for that time, he had to get stronger on his own.

Even if he was a Summoner who could never be more than second-rate, giving up on that final performance wasn't an option for him. If Kanami was coming back and if Indicus was going to meet her, then he intended to be there for it, no matter what sort of sacrifice he had to make. To that end as well, KR had to acquire the ability to intervene—even if that meant drinking all the Black Dragon's blood.

In order to see the storm that was to come and the achingly clear blue sky that would follow it, like the one over Aorsoi… Here, in this secondary residence at Ikoma, KR continued his solitary battle.

CHAPTER. 5

GO EAST

▶ NAME: KR

▶ LEVEL: 90

▶ RACE: ELF

▶ CLASS: SUMMONER

▶ HP: 8476

▶ MP: 12714

▶ ITEM 1:

[STAFF OF SCORPIUS

THE PROTECTION OF SCORPIUS, WHICH IS SAID TO GOVERN REBIRTH, BEGINNINGS, AND INSIGHT, SHRINKS THE RECAST TIME FOR SPELLS. IT ALLOWS THE USE OF A SPECIAL BUFF THAT LOWERS THE ENEMY'S CRIT RATE WHEN TARGETING YOUR ALLIES, AND ITS EFFECT IS GREATEST ON HIGH-DIFFICULTY RAIDS.

▶ ITEM 2:

[HIVE OF EVIL SPIRITS OF THE ABYSS]

A LONG STAFF WITH A LANTERN-LIKE TIP THAT HAS THE TEARS OF ELREIDA OF THE FIFTH PRISON SEALED INSIDE IT. IN ADDITION TO BOOSTING CHANT SPEED, IT STRENGTHENS MAGICAL BEASTS THAT DO NOT HAVE RECOVERY ABILITIES. THE PROBLEM IS THAT ITS USES ARE EXTREMELY LIMITED.

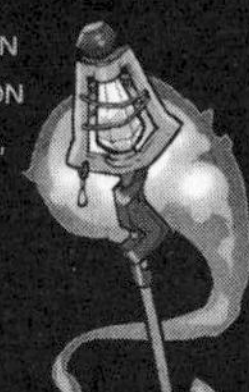

▶ ITEM 3:

[COTTON HAMMOCK]

A PORTABLE BED WOVEN FROM HIGH-QUALITY COTTON ROPES. IT'S STURDIER THAN IT LOOKS. THE PERFECT PLACE TO SUN YOURSELF AND TAKE A NAP. IT'S MADE TO BE USED BY ONE PERSON, BUT IT'S TECHNICALLY POSSIBLE TO LET SOMEONE ABOUT GAR-GAR'S SIZE LIE ON YOUR STOMACH (SHE'LL BREAK ME...)

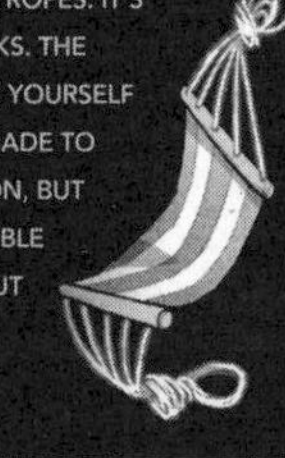

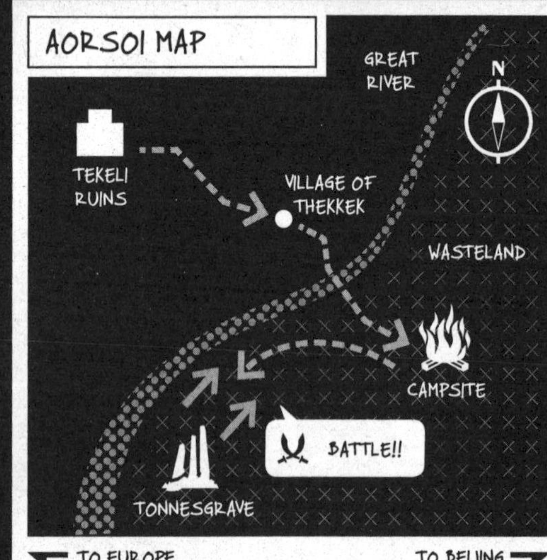
AORSOI MAP
GREAT RIVER
N
TEKELI RUINS
VILLAGE OF THEKKEK
WASTELAND
CAMPSITE
BATTLE!!
TONNESGRAVE
TO EUROPE
TO BEIJING

▶1

However, unlike all the different memories KR was reviewing back in Yamato, Leonardo really was just a force of one, and that fight of his was thoroughly unpolished and clumsy.

"Cowabungaaa!!"

Having leapt from the red dragon with a war cry, Leonardo fell like a stone toward the Black Dragon, then pulled the man in the robe—who was waving his tentacles around, trying to tangle him in them—and the delicate girl along with him. They must have just been sitting astride the dragon, without using any special riding gear: Swept along by Leonardo's momentum, they were flung out into empty air with startling ease.

Naturally, Leonardo wasn't able to fly.

He'd only used his excellent Adventurer physical capabilities to leap from the red dragon's back, and all he did was fall, reflecting on the physical reality of gravitational acceleration as he did so.

"S-s-scaryyyyy..."

"What a strange thing you've done."

"Keh-heh-heh-heh. Embraced by passionate arms, scattering petals like a dahlia..."

The horror of his two nemeses—who were wriggling in a rather self-satisfied way—caused an abrupt premonition of danger that made him thrust out his short sword. There was a biologically repulsive sensation, as if he'd stuck the blade into damp mud, and the robed man melted, running thickly.

Leonardo clamped down a scream in his throat. This seemed to strike the girl he held in his left arm as funny. She gave a light chuckle.

"You amaze me, human. Are you an imbecile? Are you brave? From that height, like a red fruit, flung away. What delight. What joy."

"Shut up!" Leonardo yelled, feeling a horror that froze his spine for reasons he didn't understand. He hadn't been startled by the fact that the girl had spoken. It wasn't unusual for NPCs to have set lines to say at the end of quests and things. This was true even of monsters.

In addition, Leonardo knew that some monsters, such as lamias and nymphs, looked like beautiful women.

However, this girl was something entirely different from those. He felt a similar horror toward the swarm of worms inside that robe, but the fact that this girl appeared to be delicate and lovely made her abnormality stand out even more.

Compared with her, the People of the Earth seem way more human!

"My, my, whatever's the matter? Do you finally regret your foolishness, perhaps? How droll. How delightful."

"Hey, if I hadn't watched Episode 104, 'Fly, Froggers!' I never would've done anything this crazy, either!"

The gallant figures of the heroes as they leapt into action to put down an enormous pumpkin monster rose in his mind's eye. Come to think of it, that pumpkin monster had moved its vines like writhing tentacles. It was just like that robed monster. No, since this monster had a mucky stench and made sickening viscous sounds, it was much worse.

"A hot pulse. The scent of blood. Is this the resonance of factors in sympathy?"

"Save the sleep-talking for when you're asleep!"

"Ahhh… Heartless sweet nothings. Cold talk. How wretched."

While Leonardo was distracted by the girl, whose smile was both pretty and cruel, the robed figure slipped out of his grasp. It extended those gray tentacles that had caused him so much grief in all directions, casting several of them into the rapidly approaching treetops.

The green boughs were right in front of them. Leonardo had been planning to dash the robed shape to the ground and use it as a cushion, and as the figure slipped away from him, he groaned.

"Oh my God!"

"Two at once is extravagant. Immoral."

Drawing her lips into a smile, the golden-haired girl touched Leonardo's cheek with pale, bloodless fingertips, as if he were someone precious to her.

"My, my."

"Don't give me that 'my, my' crap!"

In that moment, spurred on by what felt like a ten-degree drop in his body temperature, Leonardo slashed upward with his Ninja Twin Flames.

Although their paleness made one anticipate the feel of porcelain, the girl's fingertips were desiccated, and the sensation he'd gotten had been one of dead wood or a mummy. Those fingers squirmed like arthropods with an intent to gouge out Leonardo's eyes, and he shoved the sword into them. In order to do it he let go of the girl, but the ground was already right there, and Leonardo didn't have the leeway to care.

His drawn swords cut a branch as thick as a child's torso in two. His speed slowed just slightly. Counting on this, Leonardo began cutting away all the branches within reach.

The great trees were like Japanese cedars, and it took four seconds to reach the ground from their tops.

"The end of our tryst is the ground's embrace."

"Go hug yourself, pervert!"

"U-fu-fu-fu-fu. Until death fills the world."

"Waaaaaaaugh!"

The girl seemed to have finally decided to take action: Emitting horribly cold air from her lips and numbing Leonardo, she latched onto the trunk of one of the big trees in a bizarre, spidery movement.

With a cruel sound that made you want to cover your ears, the girl's fingernails were ripped off, her fingers bent and broken, and blood rose to the surface of her white skin as if she'd taken a grater to it.

However, Leonardo didn't have the heart—or the time—to sympathize. Betting on the speed he'd dampened by cutting those branches, he also dashed his curled-up body against a tree trunk, drastically changing his direction.

I'm gonna die! I'm gonna die! Is this dying?!

But Adventurer bodies were sturdier than Leonardo had thought. Either that, or Feather Fall, an Assassin special skill, had had some influence. Leonardo survived. Not only that, but the damage was far less than what he'd steeled himself for.

This seemed to have been true for Leonardo's enemy as well.

The girl Rasfia, who was facing him on a branch five meters off the ground, dispelled the semitransparent phantasm that surrounded her with a wave of her arm. The illusion thinned and vanished, seeming to melt into thin air. From within its veil, Rasfia's pretty—and undamaged—body appeared.

"My God..."

Leonardo glared at her sharply, and the girl spread both arms mischievously and smiled. In the tops of the dense conifer forest, where the winds of Aorsoi moaned, Leonardo and Rasfia, the Genius of Necromancy, squared off.

▶2

"Wha—?!"

Elias looked up, mouth hanging open. He was watching two dragons intersect with each other like leaves dancing in the wind.

The echoing roars were enough to shake the ravine.

A dark mass fell from the two tangling spirals, racing toward him through the sky like a meteor. It approached Elias's group, crossing the sky over the ravine, then fell, shaking the treetops.

"There is a high probability that those are the enemy leaders."

Elias had sensed that as well, without being prompted by Coppélia's words. His eyes had clearly seen Leonardo slam into the robed man and the girl who were riding the Black Dragon, then fall along with them.

"Kanami!"

"I knooow. Wow. Croakanardo, that's fantastic! So he wanted the best part all to himself, huh? Well, well! If that's what that was, I wish—he'd said something!"

Even as Kanami spoke, she slammed a fist into the side of a gnoll who'd swung a rusty sword at her. Just before the gnoll whose attack she'd deflected could start to rampage, she jammed a pretty leg into it, exhaling sharply.

The monster flew as if it had been hit by a big dump truck, and Elias ran after it.

There was no way he was going to ignore the gap that had opened in the battlefield. Elias swung his crystal broadsword, which was nearly the size of a surfboard.

Elias's curse prevented him from defeating them. He couldn't finish them off. However, his attack power was immense, and the gnolls had lost the majority of their HP to it.

He seemed to be swinging his great sword haphazardly as he ran, but countless currents of water wrapped around its blade, rearing their heads like snakes with their sights set on prey. This was Tributary Blade, one of Elias's unique special skills. Even the gnolls who'd avoided the broadsword were unable to block the blades of water that attacked them from their blind spots.

Even if they didn't lose their lives, the beast-men were run through or had their arms and legs slashed apart, and their movements grew sluggish, as if they'd been pinned in place by a ferocious look.

"I'm going!"

"Yep, leave it to me!"

Kanami had also broken into a run, following Elias.

Moving on feet as nimble as a cat's, she destroyed the enemies to her right and left. As the gnolls' heads suggested, their behavior was close to that of hyenas or jackals. In other words, they moved in groups and used teamwork to hunt their prey. Now that Elias had slashed his way through their pack, it was in chaos. Under the circumstances, Kanami's individual kills produced maximum results.

However, Kanami was a Monk, and her class characteristics were different from Elias the Blademancer's. Having been designed as a true hero, Elias could use both sword techniques and magic, but Monks were lacking in range attacks.

To make up for that shortcoming, Kanami raced around the

battlefield at high speed. If Elias was a silver-blue sword that slashed the gnoll pack apart, Kanami was a streak of spring-green lightning.

"I have cast Reactive Heal and Slash Block on you, Master."

"Roger that, Coppé-cat! That means I wiiiin!"

In order to provide backup to the hyperactive Kanami, Coppélia was advancing as well. Spells had a range; if she let herself get separated from Elias and Kanami, it was possible that her recovery spells wouldn't reach them.

Even more than that, Coppélia was a Cleric. Since she was a Recovery class, her destructive abilities weren't high. If she ended up alone on the battlefield, she'd probably wind up in deep trouble. Moving together, the three of them advanced far into the enemy's ranks.

A disturbing cracking sound was coming from the deep green trees into which Leonardo seemed to have fallen. They didn't know what was about to come bursting out of there, but they wanted to finish off as many gnolls as possible before that crucial moment arrived.

Elias's misgivings proved to be correct.

"What is *that*?!"

Kanami's astonishment was entirely understandable. The thing that had appeared was bizarre. One might have called it a human set in a wooden frame; it was probably what had broken the trees in the grove. It was a skeletal die, constructed from trees that were about as thick as a human torso. It was about two meters to a side, and inside it was a man in a robe.

"Master. Lord Elias. The object in front of us is—"

"We know!"

—It wasn't human.

It couldn't possibly be human.

The robed figure was stooped and limp, as if it was exhausted.

Countless nauseating tentacles of a color somewhere between indigo and brown squirmed from that hollow figure, latching on to the wooden frame that surrounded the shape. Or rather, the wooden frame itself was being held together by those tentacles.

"Level 89, Normal rank. Name: Papus."

Coppélia murmured the words as if to confirm them.

It seemed out of place, but the sound of the mountain stream reached them very clearly.

The grotesque shape that had emerged from the woods seemed to have overawed the gnolls, as well as Elias's group.

"So you read my name. That must be the current special ability."

"———!"

With that one comment, Elias knew.

The mass of tentacles in front of him was one of *their* kind.

"He's a..."

"—Genius!!"

"You know that name, do you, survivor?"

The calm voice was a feint. Or, no, it might not have been consciously intended as a feint. That was the sort of beings they were. Contact, conversation, and hostility were connected almost seamlessly; they made no distinction between them. A lunacy with a type of life that corroded you if you so much as touched it.

Along with the mild question, tentacles as sharp as spears were thrust out at Elias. It would have been easy to knock them aside, but the Ancient didn't really want to.

"Aqua Soliton!!"

A thin stream ran over the ground from the great sword that had been stuck into it. Row upon row of wave-shaped spears of water shot up out of that clear stream. The ranks of spears that stuck up from the ground intercepted the tentacles that flew through the air.

They writhed, spewing out filthy liquid that scattered white smoke around the area. The severed tentacles were leaking strong acid. Acrid smoke rose up, stinging their eyes.

As Elias squinted against that haze, he saw Kanami charge into the white smoke, whipping up a wind.

"I call dibs! He's mine!"

Although there was no telling when she'd gotten over there, Kanami used the tops of the evergreens to perform a triangle jump, then sent a twisting kick into the tentacled apparition.

"Yeeek?!"

"What's wrong?!"

"Th-this thing! He's all squishy! That's disgusting!"

It wasn't clear whether Kanami's attack had had any effect, but the monster rotated the wooden frame that surrounded it. She jumped back in a move like a leaping fish in order to avoid getting caught up in the sharp rotation.

"What a curious combination, Ancient. I must not let any of you live. Rank 2. I will prevail."

No sooner had the monster Papus made that declaration than a flood of tentacles poured down over Elias and Kanami.

Enemy of my friends. Elias's soul was quaking with emotion, but he bit it back.

This being was an invader who had come to steal the world. Unleashing his anger would have to wait.

Wagering the Ancients' entire reason for existence, Elias intercepted Papus.

▶3

Elias.

Kanami.

And Coppélia.

Even though they were fighting Papus, they weren't able to let themselves be completely absorbed in that battle.

Papus might be a complete mystery, but he was only a Normal rank monster.

Elias and the other two were Adventurers and an Ancient on roughly the same level, and under ordinary circumstances, they should have been able to beat him handily.

After all, unlike Leonardo, Elias had Kanami and Coppélia with him. In terms of numbers alone, they had three times the enemy's forces, but they also had two close-combat fighters—one of whom was Elias—who could attack and defend on the front line, and Coppélia, who could take charge of recovery in the rear. It was common knowledge that a party with balanced offense and defense had greater combat potential than the sum of its individual members' abilities. The three of them shouldn't have had trouble holding their ground against a Normal monster on their level.

"Argh! Again!!"

"Master. Leave the right side to me."

Coppélia raised the shields she'd been holding at the ready. Her White Magic Steel Shields were heavyweight kite shields, and using them as counterweights to change her direction, she slammed into the gnolls at full force. Kanami tackled the ones that had charged in from the left.

...Exactly. The battle line had become deadlocked because the creatures were attacking in waves.

Single "tails" grew from the backs of the attacking beast-men's heads like strange pigtails. They wriggled like fish hauled up on land, bit into the gnolls' brains, and relayed orders from Papus.

The gnolls, which had become hosts for Papus's tentacles, attacked Elias and the others. Every one of them had eyes that were stained a dull, dirty yellow, and they were drooling profusely. Gnolls that were more savage than usual—that was what was making the battle difficult for Elias's group.

Coppélia and Kanami, who'd split to the right and left, were blocking the gnolls well, covering for each other. The combat situation certainly wasn't easy, but the two of them kept on fighting, not caring a bit.

Coppélia fought impassively.

Kanami fought boisterously.

By nature, Monks didn't have many range attacks, but Kanami seemed to have conquered that flaw: She was distributing the serial attack skills that were her specialty across the monsters around her.

The first attack, a right punch, went to a gnoll who'd leveled its sword. The second, a left palm heel, slammed into a gnoll mage who'd raised its staff and was just about to activate a spell.

In a battle of fists and blades, the angle and timing at which attacks were executed were important elements. For example, in the sport of boxing, all you could do was thrust out either your right fist or your left one. Even so, adjusting angles, timing, and trajectories has created an incredibly artistic system of techniques. This was probably evidence that, in combat, slight variations in attack techniques led to tricking your opponent and increasing hit accuracy and power.

In Kanami's case, Monks already had an abundant range of serial attacks. By using motions to activate them voluntarily, she explosively expanded their structures, delivery methods, and timing. As Kanami paid out combinations that were dizzying to even imagine, and in a baffling variety tailored to the number and condition of the enemies around her, she looked as if she were dancing her heart out.

Kanami activated chains of serial attacks with complicated structures, parceling them out to the surrounding gnolls. However, she looked far from meditative. Elias thought she was probably executing this complex fight through sheer instinct and muscle memory acquired during training.

As for Elias, he was facing off against Papus, the owner of the tentacles, who was still spinning in front of him.

"Glub-buh-bub! Glup-blub-bloop-blorp!"

With an unpleasant laugh like seething bubbles, Papus attacked Elias.

Papus's countless tentacles reached out for Elias, but Elias was the owner of the byname "the Strongest," and the number and speed of those tentacles were nothing he couldn't gauge. However, this was Papus he was dealing with, and if he avoided the tentacles, he'd sacrifice nearby gnolls. The tentacles took in foreign matter, and they were apparently capable of absorbing monster energy. If he did it, he'd only be giving Papus more underlings. It was a troublesome attack.

In order to prevent that, Elias used his two-handed sword to keep severing the tentacles that bore down on him. He intercepted tentacles he'd missed with the instantly activated Aqua Ripper, then slammed his sword into Papus, who'd closed in on his back.

"Useless."

"Tch!! Spawn of disaster!! By my fairy blade, I will end you!"

"Fairy blade? Blup-glup. Glorp-wah-ba-ba-ba-bah!"

The rapidly spinning log structure struck Elias and sent him flying.

Even as his abdomen took heavy damage, Elias closed the distance immediately and shifted into a counterattack. Papus's defense blocked his midrange attack spells, and they wouldn't reach him.

Having decided that he had a better chance of winning in close combat with sword attacks, Elias charged forward, believing in the protection of the water spirits that dwelled in him.

Papus must have known this, but he let him close in.

A wild dance of tentacles and water currents broke out at close range.

Elias's two-handed sword, Crystal Stream, bit into Papus's wooden fortress. The exchange became a contest of strength, and they locked up.

"———!"

"I know."

"You know—what?!"

"How your race met its end."

Elias's vision went red.

"Have your companions awakened? Impossible. Why do you not sink? Why do you not freeze? A mere hint of Empathiom. How can you move?"

He'd known.

He'd sensed it with his first glimpse of this tentacled monster.

As he'd suspected, he was a Genius. A rank-and-file member of the army that had destroyed half of the world's thirteen chivalric orders. Images flew into Elias's mind: his companions, who had been transported against their will to a battlefield under a foreign sky, and the grotesque army that had assailed them.

His blood burned.

Rage gathered at his throbbing temples.

The monster in front of Elias was one of the faction that had destroyed his comrades. Even though he tried to hold it back, his rage made the water magic boil.

"Enough!!"

"Why do you not stop?"

"Shut your mouth!!"

Elias howled. His arms, wrapped in his blue and silver surcoat, swelled up, and cursed blood raced through the magic circuits that were under fairy protection. Using only his aura, Elias repelled the layers of tentacles that tried to wrap around him. However, Papus spoke to him in a dripping sort of voice that was hard to make out, filling it with malice:

"I know. You Ancients— No, all People of the Earth as well. You are all dolls. Puppets with no will, mere character software."

A memory burst.

These were the Words of Death that had put half of the Ancients, Elias included, to sleep. A dreamless "sleep," from which there was no waking. To the Ancients, who had no concept of death, it was another name for "parting" that came very close to it.

You are dolls.

That compulsory awareness had devoured the thirteen chivalric orders like a plague.

The words had driven some insane, made others despair, and caused still others to lose all interest in everything. Some had been unharmed, but they were the ones who had disappeared from this world.

When confronted with those words, even Elias, who was known as the strongest, had fallen into a dreamless sleep. He'd been unable to bear the ridiculousness of his mission, its hollowness, that overwhelming truth, and he'd closed himself off.

"Fall, as a counterfeit. Shutting down is what's best for your kind. Those who were born from nothing should halt their timelines."

The Words of Death echoed.

There was no Ancient hero who had learned swordsmanship from the fairies.

After all, there were no fairies.

There were no Ancients.

There were no People of the Earth who must be protected.

There was no world.

The hum of the fairy village, which he could remember if he listened closely, was fake. The sword in his hands, his surcoat, the wind, the wide world—it was all false. Everything Elias knew was counterfeit, and the world was just a hollow vessel.

Even Elias himself was only...

"Like! That's! Even! True!!"

Suddenly, light was born.

Mowing down trees and breaking through both Papus's defense and the swarm of tentacles, Kanami howled. She'd shot through with a flying kick like a shooting star, and she didn't break that stance.

"Don't be an idiot! Eli-Eli's here, all right! He's right here! From now on, we're going to do tons of fun stuff! Don't take him away without permission, you—bike-tube guy!"

In the midst of the golden Aorsoi light that streamed through the pierced grove, she roared like a proud queen.

Just as she had on the day she'd resurrected Elias from the abyss of sleep.

"Kanami—"

"We're taking this guy down, Eli-Eli!"

"Understood!"

Elias nodded.

Strength returned to the hands that gripped his sword.

Mana overflowed. Kanami's trust was converted into physical warmth, and his exhilaration and sense of mission came back to him.

"Hup!"

"Aaah!"

Sending the mana and fighting spirit within him into Crystal Stream, Elias ran like a white tiger. The aggressive streams of water he unleashed attacked Papus like countless spears. As the tentacles reached up from the earth to intercept them, they looked like opposing ranks of spears, held at the ready. However, as Elias's water spears fell from the sky, the light passed through them, and they shone, forming a binary of light and darkness with Papus's mud spears, which intercepted them from the ground.

A single blow opened a vast hole in the conflict.

Giant-Killer Gauntlets groaned. A shift from Mantis Action to Aerial Rave had sent Papus into the air, and Shadowless Kick knocked him even higher, like a circle throw. He was a perfect midair target.

Elias, who had believed and held his two-handed sword at the ready, channeled a flood of emotions into it and brought it down.

"Begone! Back to your den!"

His main body must have been fragile. With nothing more than a sticky noise, a gaping hole that stretched from Papus's chest all the way through his upper body opened up. Robbed of both his mobility and the defense of his tentacles, Papus really was nothing but a Normal rank monster.

Exhaling roughly, the Ancient glared down at the monster's corpse and swung his sword to clean it. Elias Hackblade had been reborn, and this had been the attack that would touch off the war with the Geniuses.

▶4

Meanwhile, about a hundred meters from Elias and Kanami's fight, Leonardo and the blond girl, Rasfia, were confronting each other.

The forest, which had looked like a green ribbon from up in the sky, seemed to have sought out the water of the mountain stream and grown thickly. In the desolate wasteland of Aorsoi, it was likely that only the moist soil of the river basins could maintain stands of trees large enough to call forests.

The two who had been facing off in the branches of the woods were now racing through the trees, launching attack after attack at each other.

Leonardo was an Assassin.

Assassin, Swashbuckler, and Bard were known as Weapon Attack classes, and they were specially designed to inflict physical damage. They tended to fight in the vanguard, and not only did they have the physical strength necessary to deal massive damage, they acquired high-level agility in order to evade enemy attacks and claim locations that would give their attacks an advantage.

On top of that, Leonardo was a level-90 Adventurer. His physical performance was high, and he'd never let a Normal monster defeat him. This was true even if the opponent was level 89, very nearly his equal.

However, Leonardo hadn't managed to land a solid blow.

He was having this much trouble, even though he should have been the faster of the two, because of Rasfia's bizarre martial arts.

The girl's movements weren't human.

She'd stick an overarm stroke straight into a tree trunk or hang upside down, using freakish actions to toy with Leonardo.

They might not have been martial arts.

Her approach to movement paid no attention to the principle of getting around on two legs. Her abrupt, creepy motions were just like those of some sort of insect. Using her sharp nails and toes, Rasfia scuttled up tree trunks, facing backward.

"What pleasure. What joy." She laughed with a bell-like voice.

As she bent her joints in impossible directions and moved like an insect, the fact that she was a lovely girl with a doll-like beauty made her seem like something out of a nightmare to Leonardo.

There was one other thing that cemented that grotesque impression for him.

"Shut up!!"

"Gee-hee!"

Leonardo's slash had severed Rasfia's arm.

"Aah! The steel. It bites me, it rends me. So this is pain, or perhaps an ache. More vermilion than sunset, redder than the equinox flower, more scarlet than the false strawberry—aah, aah!!"

Immediately after that coquettish, singsong cry, Rasfia's severed arm struck back at Leonardo. Its fingernails grew like steel daggers, and cloaked in cold air, they slashed through his leather armor.

Tch!! Again?

Twisting to avoid the subsequent serial attack, Leonardo put some distance between them.

This happened again and again, and it was making Rasfia seem even more horrible.

That severed arm… When he looked, it had reattached.

The same was true for her legs and torso. The girl seemed to have a freakish sort of immortality. Possibly because she knew this, Rasfia brandished her four chilly, cloaked limbs, laughing elegantly as she did so.

Normal-rank monsters were defined as monsters with combat abilities that made them appropriate one-on-one opponents for an Adventurer at their level. However, in adjusting that balance, *Adventurer* indicated somebody who was at that level, who was equipped with store-bought weapons and equipment appropriate to their level, and who had not yet reinforced their special skills with mastery points.

Put that way, it meant "an Adventurer with minimum skills for their level."

Leonardo wasn't a top-level ranker-class Adventurer, but he'd still racked up more than enough experience to count as a veteran. The bulk of his equipment had come from raids, and at the very least, he had production-class items that filled in any gaps. His special skills had been reinforced to their maximums with mastery points.

The idea of Leonardo having trouble with a mere Normal-rank monster was ludicrous. Of course, he hadn't expected to settle things instantly, but the fight really shouldn't have dragged on for more than a few minutes.

Leonardo's and Rasfia's levels were roughly equal. In addition, Rasfia's rank was Normal. However, for that very reason, Leonardo—who was an Adventurer with a full set of equipment—should have slightly but decisively surpassed her in combat strength.

Is that the trick—?

That blinking, flickering status display. The name RASFIA was alternating with GNOLL. The blinking was irregular, and there was a mesmerizing rhythm to it.

He didn't know how it worked, but this Rasfia NPC seemed to be controlling that blinking at will.

Leonardo had picked up on something through their repeated clashes:

This woman was choosing which name took damage.

Would those be "souls," to borrow Coppélia's word? Coppélia had called the phenomenon "Parallel One," but from Rasfia's behavior, it was clear that "one" was a gross understatement. Leonardo's instincts told him that this woman had several dozen "souls," at the very least.

Rasfia was switching her "name" right before Leonardo's katana hit her, letting a disposable name take the damage for her, then discarding it.

...This is seriously not normal!

Twice, three times.

Rasfia thrust out her delicate hand with the sharpness of a raptor. True, there was something astonishing about that speed, and the execution was clean. However, her physical body was no different from that of a girl in her early teens. Leonardo evaded, using the difference in reach to his advantage.

A split opened up in his cheek.

Rasfia smiled, tilting her pretty face.

The tips of her outstretched fingertips had blurred like an illusion, morphing into a hairy hand. That hand held a roughly made scimitar.

The gnoll hand and the weapon it held flickered, just as they had when they appeared, then abruptly vanished.

Taking advantage of Leonardo's astonishment, Rasfia closed in.

Her gothic dress flared like a rose blooming in empty space. A lace petticoat peeked out from the generously full skirt. From within it, a pair of jackal's hind legs, spotted with gray, stretched out toward Leonardo.

If Leonardo hadn't avoided them at the last second, those toes would have gouged out his eyes. As he watched, they morphed into small pumps decorated with silk ribbons.

"Whatever's the matter? Have you given up? Have you shriveled up? Like a flower that never sees the sun, like a migrating bird that's lost its home?"

Rasfia's mocking smile settled Leonardo's resolve.

He still didn't completely understand, but he decided that this was no time to hesitate.

If I stay on the defensive, things are just gonna keep getting worse.

Close the distance. They were already so close that if either leaned in, they'd be able to touch the other. As if abhorring that distance, Leonardo thrust out his left hand. He wasn't attacking. It was an activation trigger.

With a flash, he unleashed Deadly Dance from that stance. It was a special Assassin attack skill. As a technique, it was a bit different: When used back-to-back, its power gradually rose, but if you messed up in the middle, its attack power would fall.

Leonardo had activated it not from the technique's icon in his mind but through gesture input.

In the world as it currently was, there were two ways to activate combat skills during battle. As in the days of *Elder Tales*, you could activate skills by selecting an icon. The other method was voluntary activation, in which you mimicked a motion to activate it, using your own body as an input device.

In an overwhelming majority of cases, icon activation was used.

"Fight" and "attack successfully" were easy to say, but there was a huge variety in both monster builds and battlefield terrain. The Adventurers were ordinary earthlings with no martial arts or combat experience, and no matter how much stronger their physical abilities were, their skills were limited.

As long as they selected an icon, their special attack skills would track the enemy they were facing and make their attack hit home using the most appropriate action. For the classes that fought in close combat, this was a core attack method.

However, instead of doing this, he'd activated the skill voluntarily, using his own body.

This was the secret of Kanami's "strength," which he'd noticed that day.

Monks were called "the combo class," and they had an incredible number of special skills that used one technique to execute multiple attacks.

Aerial Rave was one of the showiest serial special attack skills Monks had. It was a five-stage technique: In addition to using back-to-back left and right punches to knock the enemy into the air, you used a knee kick to toss the airborne enemy higher, then performed a heel drop, segueing into a rear spin kick in one flowing motion. The damage from each individual attack was slightly lower than it would be ordinarily, but when you totaled it up, the five-attack combo inflicted massive damage on monsters.

Then you had Triple Blow, which was a technique that unleashed three powerful punches—a right punch, a left straight, and a right hook—in a row.

Since Leonardo wasn't a Monk, it had taken him time to fully understand it, but those two special techniques had triggered his line of thinking.

In short, Kanami had used the two final attacks in Triple Blow as the first two punches in Aerial Rave, fulfilling its activation conditions.

While a special skill was activated, Adventurers couldn't activate another one. In *Elder Tales*, that had been common sense. As a matter of fact, even now, the mental icon went dark while a special skill was activated, and you weren't allowed to input anything.

However, when activating a special skill with a physical body, there was no time when input was invalid. Even if it did exist, a person could perform back-to-back input using something that resembled wait-listing.

Aerial Rave was a powerful combo attack, but its damage relied on the kicks in its latter half, the heel drop and the rear spin kick. The earlier punches were there just to get the enemy into the air, and as far as damage was concerned, they were practically nothing. However, when using icon input activation, the sequence flow was set, so starting or stopping it in the middle was impossible.

Even if an attack was unnecessary, it couldn't be left out.

Kanami had destroyed this common sense. By substituting the powerful Triple Blow for the early, low-damage attacks meant to break down the enemy's stance, she'd drastically increased the total performance of both special techniques.

Of course, this was easier to say than to do.

Special skills that were activated from the visible icon assisted the Adventurer's actions by instantly sizing up their own stance and the terrain, the enemy's body build, and the distance between them.

Voluntarily activated special skills didn't have that sort of assist function. To begin with, there was a considerable range of voluntary activations. For example, for a basic Deadly Dance, the Adventurer thrust their left hand out, charged up, then executed a rapid strike with the blade in their right hand. That was all there was to the technique, but there were seven different motions that could be used to activate it, and those were only the ones Leonardo had confirmed for himself. There were all sorts of angles and timings at which one could thrust out their left hand, as well as permissible charge time ranges.

Unless Leonardo himself selected one of these diverse variations to match the conditions in front of him, the attack probably wouldn't be effective in actual combat. Voluntarily activated attacks didn't have auto-tracking, so without a lot of training, their hit rate was lower than icon-activated attacks. The difficulty was too high, and the system was so complex that nobody felt like practicing them if there was no advantage in doing so.

However, there was an advantage.

Leonardo swung the blade in his right hand. The slash became a drawn line that was absorbed into Rasfia. The icon in his mind went dark and began slowly recovering, like an hourglass. It took one second. If he used Deadly Dance again one second later, the power behind that second attack would increase by 7 percent.

However, Leonardo didn't waste that second.

He added another attack, scooping upward with his left hand. The special skill was Quick Assault. Then, immediately after, Deadly Dance. Then Stealth Blade, leading into another Deadly Dance. Turning the simple pose of thrusting out his left hand into a method of attacking with the Ninja Twin Flames he held in both hands, Leonardo became a storm of blades.

Assassins didn't have the variety of combo attacks that Monks had. As a result, Leonardo couldn't copy Kanami's fighting style exactly.

Realizing this, he'd racked his brains and put together this fighting method, Parallel Plot. It used "charge" and the gaps between motions to turn a series of special skills that would normally only be processed in sequence into a double-layered attack method.

At this point, he could only use a combination built around Deadly Dance, but all of Leonardo's nearly thirty skills had to have the flexibility of voluntary activation. By combining them or honing them to perfection, Leonardo would probably be able to deal damage that surpassed the Assassin maximum.

Leonardo confronted his opponent with a fighting style that, while still far from perfect, was all his.

▶5

"What is this speed—?! That light—"

"Shut up!!"

Two. Three, four!

Rasfia was no longer silent. Countless mesmerizing blades leapt from the arm she drove forward. She was prepared to go down and take him with her.

Leonardo took these attacks, and sprays of blood went up from his chest and forehead.

He evaded with Gust Step, and no sooner had he appeared behind Rasfia's back than he hit her with his sixth slash. The destructive power in Deadly Dance was already up to 175 percent of the damage in its first attack. As she took nearly double the damage of a normal attack, Rasfia's limbs crumbled away easily, then immediately regrew.

Leonardo had no leeway, either. He was an Assassin, just a Weapon Attack class; he wasn't a Warrior class, whose mission was to take damage from enemies on the front line, nor a Recovery class, who could heal their own damage. He had better defense than a magic user, but there was a limit to his HP.

Take them down before they take you out. For the weapon attack classes, that was the principle behind solo combat. However, even as the monstrous girl before him smiled with charm, she slipped through Leonardo's attacks again and again, jabbing him with thrusts cloaked in cold air.

Ignoring his draining HP, Leonardo paid out more attacks. Either way, as an attack class, there was nothing else he could do.

—Nothing but attack and silence his target.

"What is that power?! You poor little lamb! You foolish, lost child of this transient world!"

"Shut up! I don't wanna hear that from a lousy raid boss!"

"Raid boss? Heh-heh! Heh-heh-heh-heh-heh! —Aah! How droll, what comedy! Just when I fancied you were an all-knowing god privy to the secrets of the cycle of transmigration, you prattle like a naïve child playing on the beach. How atrociously soft. That sin is worth ten thousand deaths!"

"What..."

...was she saying?

What did it mean?

Leonardo couldn't finish the question.

Rasfia had abruptly closed in on him, and in the instant his eyes were caught by her glossy lips, sharp pain ran through him. A gnoll head had appeared from a tear in her gothic dress.

The gnoll, which had sunk its fangs into the top of Leonardo's shoulder, disappeared, leaving only the inside of its red-stained mouth behind, like an illusion.

His shredded shoulder could still move, but his HP was nearly gone.

This is no time for talking!

Mustering his willpower, Leonardo continued his chain of attacks.

The permissible input time for Deadly Dance was a bit under two seconds. Unless he executed the next Deadly Dance within that time limit, the increase in attack power he'd accumulated up to this point would evaporate.

Tearing his mind away from his hot, throbbing shoulder—*Quick Assault. Deadly Dance*, as if slamming it into Rasfia's impudent words.

The attack power had increased to 212 percent.

Mental serenity led to skill. Leonardo did his best to keep his eyes focused on what was in front of him. The pain, which was like a ringing in his ears, receded. His own body temperature had been in the way, but it receded as well. The world held nothing but the twenty-odd types of special attack skills Leonardo could use. Combining their cast times, motion binds, and recast times, he raced down the shortest route.

There was no single right answer. The enemy's defense and evasions, the distance between himself and them, their weight and the positions of their dominant hand and foot. On the contrary, these were an RGB kaleidoscope that shifted with the passage of time with a lowercase *t*. Seeking the best move within it, avoiding dead ends that would shut down his attacks, Leonardo continued his internal sprint.

In the midst of a sense of time so stretched out that he could feel the delay in his own physical reaction speed, the method—the "code"—he'd assembled in order to attack caught fire.

* * *

"What ferocity! But even that is mere child's play."

"That's just fine!"

Leonardo thought this from the bottom of his soul.

"Child's play" was just fine.

Programs were dense trees and forests.

He could assemble tiny, simple codes, building functions. The accumulation created bigger, more convenient components, and before long, he had an app. He combined them even more dynamically, had them transmit to each other, and created a service.

Leonardo knew that, if you wanted results, you had to do very simple work and keep on doing it. In order to create a work of art that was the equivalent of an enormous structure, you had to put together the fragments that were in front of you right now.

Geeks were the people who understood that distance…

…and the ones who embodied its nobility were hackers.

Leonardo happily continued his detailed operations.

The attack power was currently at 245 percent.

If Rasfia wanted to call it child's play, she could do that all day. That child's play was cornering her. Leonardo believed that. He believed in geeks.

"As often as you like."

Beyond a salvia-like spray of blood that had bloomed in the air, he saw Rasfia's slender hand.

As Leonardo layered on another Deadly Dance, she aimed an attack at his neck, but he avoided it by simply twisting the trunk of his body, then pursued her. That counterattack had cost him three of the special skills he could have chosen for his next attack. He had four possible options left. From these, he chose the next attack, the move that would lead to the next exchange, and executed another strike.

"Paralyze Blow!"

"Keh-hee-hee!"

No, even those thoughts were in the way.

All that existed were nearly reflexive decisions, backed up by vast amounts of experience. Leonardo believed in the branching skills he'd unearthed. His training up on that big boulder was alive here, in the midst of this fight that would spell the difference between life and death.

"I've wearied of this. Die, ignorant lout. Dance, Reckless!"

Possibly she'd grown irritated: Without even avoiding Leonardo's swords, Rasfia unleashed a large attack.

Her sleeves swelled up like balloons, then released a torrent of gnolls. Claws, fangs, swords, and axes hit him like raging waves. It was Rasfia's certain-kill attack, one made possible by her ability to negate damage using her "names," and it was meant to take out both of them at once. The torrent was filled with the grotesque resolution to inflict a lethal wound, no matter which attacks he avoided.

But Leonardo had been waiting for that attack as well.

"'Reckless'?! Awesome, bring it!"

Activating Trick Step, Leonardo leapt into the attack. In the treetops, twenty meters above the ground, he danced fearlessly between life and death. With a calm heart, looking just like the heroes he admired, he unleashed his attacks.

If this was an attack that was determined not to let Leonardo get away when he fled, then all he had to do was not flee. In a group attack that surrounded you, the eye of the storm held a shot at survival.

"Deadly Dance!!"

Just as the name implied, it was a dance of life and death: Rasfia's switching advances; Leonardo's attacks. Victory drifted in the space between them.

"What delight, what joy! However, you're still—"

Leonardo had slashed Rasfia with the tip of his sword and sent her flying, and he raced after her. Her name blurred. He'd predicted that already, a moment earlier. He'd taken a lot of hits. Leonardo didn't have any time left.

Still, his heart was quiet.

He could even remember *her* voice.

Leonardo had hurt her. He'd treated her like a doll.

But there was only one way that heroes apologized.

Just one.

Rasfia's expression had warped into a smile. He wouldn't give her time.

Her torso disappeared, like a dim shadow. However, that was merely an omen of regeneration, and her eyes, half-closed in apparent delight, reflected Leonardo's figure.

One beat. The space of one-fourth of a breath. That was the amount of time Rasfia needed in order to regenerate. He'd gotten a feel for it during their long battle.

Leonardo sought out, then implemented, an attack with enough speed to force its way into that slight space.

"Sorry. I've got a previous engagement."

The fastest, strongest, ultimate secret move, using the residual tension after Deadly Dance as a portion of its activation gesture.

—Assassinate.

It was the Assassin's pride, a single special attack with astronomical output. It boasted the greatest power of all twelve classes.

"!! ——! ——"

The sensation of neatly bisecting a crimson world was as dry as if he'd cut a fragile clay vessel in half. Leonardo, who'd mustered all his strength for the pursuit, lost his balance and was left unable to do anything but look at the figure of the lovely girl whom he'd already cut in two.

"Get lost!!"

"Ah… Aah! —The hands of the clock—eleven more—"

The girl's expression looked taken aback, as if she'd just heard a magnificent joke, but she showed no pain. Leaving behind a delirious murmur, she turned into particles.

Leonardo watched it happen. A moment later, though, he remembered he'd also leapt off the branch into thin air, and he ended up enjoying a cordless bungee jump to the ground.

▶6

"Dammit. What kind of idiot bungees without a rope?"

Leonardo was lying spread-eagled on the leaf mold.

The trees around him had been mowed down and carried scars from his fight with Rasfia, but the area where he lay was quiet now.

At some point, birdsong had twined its way into the cool sound of the mountain stream.

The sounds that had echoed from far away and nearby up until just a little while ago, noises that had probably come from Elias and the others' battle, had also disappeared.

Apparently, they'd settled things somehow.

That said, Leonardo couldn't get up.

His HP was extremely low, in the red zone. Rasfia's freezing hand strikes seemed to have inflicted cold attribute damage. He hadn't had the leeway to check during the fight, but he'd racked up more than ten negative statuses. The continuous damage each one inflicted was minuscule, but the total was nothing to sneeze at.

That damage and the automatic recovery that occurred at times of peace were competing with each other on Leonardo's HP bar.

He didn't feel like he was going to die right this second, but he couldn't hope to recover naturally anytime soon. Besides that, his limbs tingled; they might have gotten frostbite.

Still. Hot damn, I did it.

Even so, Leonardo felt good.

He'd done everything he could do.

He wasn't sure, but at the very least, they'd probably managed to halt the gnoll invasion along this tributary. Leonardo was sure that the pair he'd seen had been the masterminds behind this raid.

Since he'd left the Raid-rank Black Dragon to KR, he didn't know what had happened to it, but Leonardo had no doubt:

This lowly geek had gotten through the fight. There was no way the easygoing KR would have wiped out. In any case, having lost the beings who'd been controlling it, the Black Dragon showed no sign of returning. That young guy probably didn't need Leonardo worrying about him.

Still, that didn't matter anymore.

This world wasn't the world of *Elder Tales.*

At this point, Leonardo was able to say that and mean it.

In *Elder Tales*, raids were game content, and people spoke of their captures in terms of rare-item acquisitions and whether they'd subdued their targets or not.

But this wasn't *Elder Tales.* Even if they'd failed to subjugate the

Black Dragon, even if they hadn't gotten any rare items, even if KR and Leonardo had collapsed in the middle of it— As long as they'd managed to halt the monster invasion, the heroes had won.

Now that village won't take any damage... Right?

That was how Leonardo summed up his thoughts, which the blood loss had left weirdly clear.

He didn't think the people of that village would ever know about this fight. Not only that, it was doubtful whether Leonardo's group would ever visit the village again.

Still, that's fine, isn't it? he thought.

That was what heroes were like.

Those four, the ones Leonardo idolized, fought without bothering themselves about that stuff. If there was somebody they wanted to save, and they saved them and took down injustice, then it was all good.

Even so...

Leonardo thought about the golden-haired girl he'd fought in mortal combat. Her existence had been much too graphic. She'd oozed an outsized lunacy.

Even among the Puerto Rican pushers that hung out in the ghettos, there was nobody that crazy. He remembered Rasfia's superficially calm and pretty speech and her feverish gaze.

It was true that New York didn't have the world's best public order. As he walked its streets, he'd heard gunshots more than a couple of times. There were a ton of crazies living there, too.

Still, to him, those people and that girl seemed different.

All-knowing... Privy to the secrets of the cycle of transmigration.

Considered in the ordinary way, Rasfia's words were probably some sort of quest-related hint, but Leonardo just couldn't think of them like that. He sensed trouble much nastier than that in them.

The idea of his having grasped the secrets of destiny was ridiculous. Only a god could do that sort of thing. Gods just sat up there in heaven and smiled. That was all.

That crazy-eyed woman, and Coppélia...

According to Leonardo's understanding of everything up to this point, neither of those two was human.

Rasfia was a monster, and Coppélia was a bot.

Still, in this world, that was probably wrong. Even if it was a logically accurate conclusion, his hero's soul insisted that something was off. In that case, Leonardo believed in his soul. Skill might be what reviewed code, but the desire to review it came from the soul. His soul was what made Leonardo himself.

"Heeeey, Croooakanaaardooooo!"

At the sound of the carefree hailing, he sat up. His three companions were approaching from downstream, with Kanami in the lead. Apparently, they'd managed to drive the gnolls away.

Kanami was waving at him energetically, and at the sight of her expression, the tension rapidly drained out of Leonardo's mood. He sensed that trouble was on its way, but at the moment, from the bottom of his heart, he truly didn't care.

At any rate, in this world, there wasn't much besides trouble to begin with. Heroes' lives consisted of detecting incoming trouble, dealing with trouble, and cleaning up after trouble. Peace was just an intermission, an interlude.

Leonardo smiled a little. *I'll have to get a lot tougher.* For a guy, toughness was a condition of survival. That was true both in good old Big Apple and here in Aorsoi.

He didn't see KR, but they'd already said their good-byes.

They'd probably meet again. Leonardo no longer had any doubt that he'd reach the Japanese server. He wouldn't forget that sarcastic Summoner, the guy who'd saved him from danger. He swore that, if KR got himself into a tight corner someday, he'd be the one to rescue him.

Noisy Kanami seemed to be arguing about something with the Ancient. The words "not grateful enough" and "I am grateful" reached Leonardo's ears. Then, before more than a few words had been said, there was a big splash. Elias had been kicked into the river, and Kanami was laughing merrily. They really couldn't have been louder.

A shadow fell over Leonardo, and Coppélia peeked in at him. Behind her, the sun was beginning to travel down the western sky. As always, the girl's inorganic, beautiful face looked indifferent. She tilted her head slightly and spoke to Leonardo:

"Coppélia would like to point out that your HP has been greatly reduced. Do you wish to be healed?"

"Coppélia."

"Yes?"

Lying stretched out on the ground, Leonardo looked deep into the young woman's eyes for the first time. In those eyes, he felt as if he'd found what he was searching for, and his heart grew warm. There was something he needed to say.

"I'm sorry."

"Coppélia failed to detect the context for that apology."

"That's fine."

Leonardo searched for just the right words for the perplexed young woman.

"I'm Leonardo."

"Yes. Sir Leonardo."

"And yeah, I want to be healed."

"Understood."

She said his name for the first time, and he had asked for healing for the first time. The healing light was white with a faint crimson mixed into it, a color that reminded him of innocence. Coppélia's recovery spell enfolded Leonardo like a warm cocoon, taking away the pain and fatigue.

Wordlessly, the young woman examined Leonardo's wounds closely. Her face was terribly serious. That expression was so careful that Leonardo finally managed to find the right words.

"Coppélia."

"Yes?"

"You do have a soul."

"?"

"You've got one, all right. I can see it. The color of your soul is—"

The healing pale pink that flowed from her slim fingertips.

Leonardo said it with conviction.

<Log Horizon 9—Go East, Kanami! The End>

LIST OF MEMBERS

【DEBAUCHERY】

Tea Party Members List

Introducing the members of the legendary group to which Shiroe and Kanami belonged, the band that conquered raids like Hades' Breath and Nine Great Gaols of Halos!

※ Members shaded in gray weren't logged in at the time of the Catastrophe.

NAME	SUIKAZURA	NAOTSUGU	GOROUHACHIROU
SEX	FEMALE	MALE	MALE
TRIBE	WOLF-FANG	HUMAN	ELF
CLASS	GUARDIAN	GUARDIAN	SAMURAI
SUB CLASS	SURVIVOR	FRONTIER INSPECTOR	MASTER-LESS SAMURAI
	Normally kind, but merciless in battle; the mightiest housewife. Nickname: Big Sis Suika.	Of the members of this group, he's relatively sensible, but the guy has unique opinions about panties.	A master-less samurai from the PvP fields. Even during combat, if he spots an opening, he does piecework for his side job.

NAME	SEX	TRIBE	CLASS	SUB CLASS	
SOUJIROU SETA	MALE	HUMAN	SAMURAI	MASTER SWORDSMAN	Even in the Tea Party, lots of people wanted him. A popular guy who shows faint signs of being a harem samurai.
HAYATO	MALE	HUMAN	MONK	SEAMAN	Likes training on his own, is serious to a fault, and talks like a soldier. Considers himself Suikazura's underling.
NURUKAN	MALE	FELINOID	MONK	BREWER	A rugged guy who prefers action to talking. Crazy about liquor.
AIHIE	MALE	HALF ALV	ASSASSIN	POISONER	A bad-mouthed tsundere pseudo-villain who runs hot and cold with the people he likes. A good event player.
KAZUHIKO	MALE	HUMAN	ASSASSIN	KNIGHT	A man of the world and an uncommonly able guy who always has wrinkles in his forehead because of the outrageous group members.
TULI	MALE	WOLF-FANG	ASSASSIN	GUNNER	A gruff sniper who thinks like a kid. In the Tea Party, he holds the position of pet dog.
KANAMI	FEMALE	HUMAN	SWASHBUCKLER	UNKNOWN	A human typhoon who constantly hits everything at full power and is crazy about anything that looks fun.
NYANTA	MALE	FELINOID	SWASHBUCKLER	CHEF	A wise advisor who's considered the Tea Party's oldest member. His calm words and actions have earned him solid trust from the rest.

NAME	SEX	TRIBE	CLASS	SUB CLASS	
SUZUNA	FEMALE	FOXTAIL	BARD	SONG-STRESS	An elegant girl whose use of old Kyoto dialect is striking. Loves lively things, festivals, and mischief.
WHISTLER	MALE	HUMAN	BARD	ANGLER	A carefree guy who isn't comfort-able unless he's constantly humming, whistling, or chatting.
SAKI	FEMALE	DWARF	CLERIC	ARTIFICER	A fast-talking, sharp-tongued, mini-tank healer. Always takes Soujirou's side.
STALLBOURNE	MALE	DWARF	CLERIC	MINER	A front-line healer who teams up with Sui-kazura so often that he's almost exclusively hers. Not good at talking.
CALM.H.DALE	MALE	ELF	DRUID	SCHOLAR	Loves bugs, and when he sees insectoid monsters, he'll tell you everything he knows about them.
GINGAMI	MALE	WOLF-FANG	DRUID	UNKNOWN	A middle-aged guy who calls himself a firepower fiend even though he's a healer. He's apparently a heavy smoker.
NAZUNA	FEMALE	FOXTAIL	KANNAGI	GAMBLER	A dependable busybody and big-sister type with a big weakness for gambling.
TSUKINE	FEMALE	FELINOID	KANNAGI	FORTUNE-TELLER	The queen bee of the younger female members. Her special-ties are fortune-telling, fashion, and love advice. In real life, she's a voice actress.

NAME	★KURAMA☆	INDICUS	YUUKO	YOMI	KR	TIGERMARU	SHIROE	LAMBMUTTON
SEX	MALE	FEMALE	FEMALE	FEMALE	MALE	MALE	MALE	MALE
TRIBE	HUMAN	ELF	HUMAN	HUMAN	ELF	RITIAN	HALF ALV	RITIAN
CLASS	KANNAGI	SORCERER	SORCERER	SUMMONER	SUMMONER	SUMMONER	ENCHANTER	ENCHANTER
SUB CLASS	TALIS-MANCER	ELDER MAID	CHILD	WRAITH-USER	PUBLICITY BAND MEMBER	CHEF	SCRIBE	CHEMIST
	A hot-blooded guy from Kyushu, although he doesn't look like it. Looks up to Soujirou as his teacher in love.	A talented woman who works hard every day to get to the top of the server with Kanami (and the Tea Party).	A serious girl who loves flashy magic and adores Soujirou. Actually in elementary school.	A shy and reserved user who often logs out at midnight. Nicknamed "Cinderella."	A hedonist and self-described "bystander." His latest hobby is messing with Indicus.	Mild-tempered and loves to eat, but is also extremely gifted at block-ing other members' escape routes.	A skilled bus guide who's constantly getting yanked around by Kanami's reckless actions and impossible demands.	A laid-back guy with a drawl. In a comedy duo, he'd be the funny half, but when he works, he does it properly.

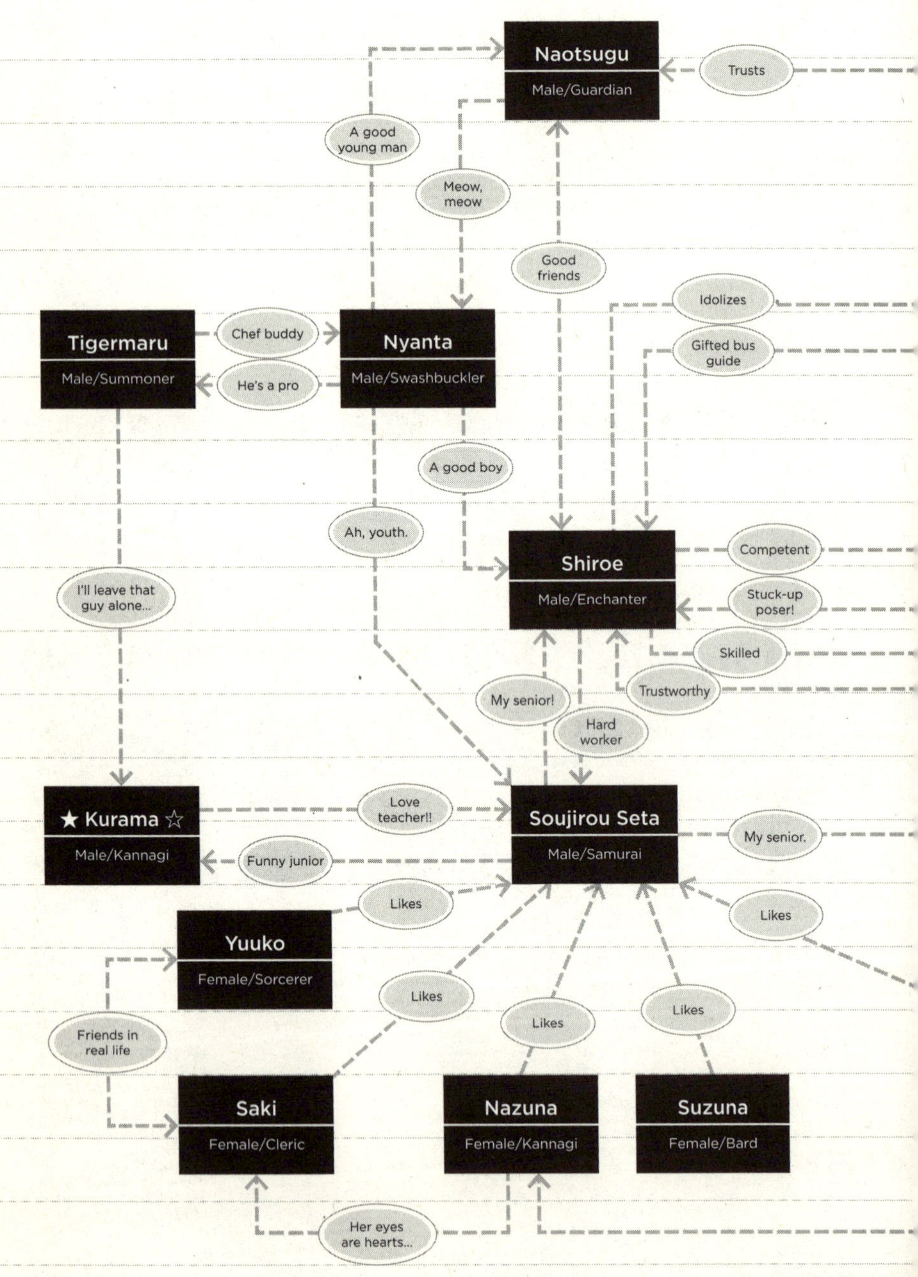

Naotsugu
Male/Guardian
Trusts
A good young man
Meow, meow
Good friends
Idolizes
Gifted bus guide
Tigermaru
Male/Summoner
Chef buddy
He's a pro
Nyanta
Male/Swashbuckler
A good boy
Ah, youth.
Shiroe
Male/Enchanter
Competent
Stuck-up poser!
Skilled
Trustworthy
I'll leave that guy alone...
My senior!
Hard worker
★ Kurama ☆
Male/Kannagi
Love teacher!!
Funny junior
Soujirou Seta
Male/Samurai
My senior.
Likes
Yuuko
Female/Sorcerer
Likes
Likes
Likes
Likes
Friends in real life
Saki
Female/Cleric
Nazuna
Female/Kannagi
Suzuna
Female/Bard
Her eyes are hearts...

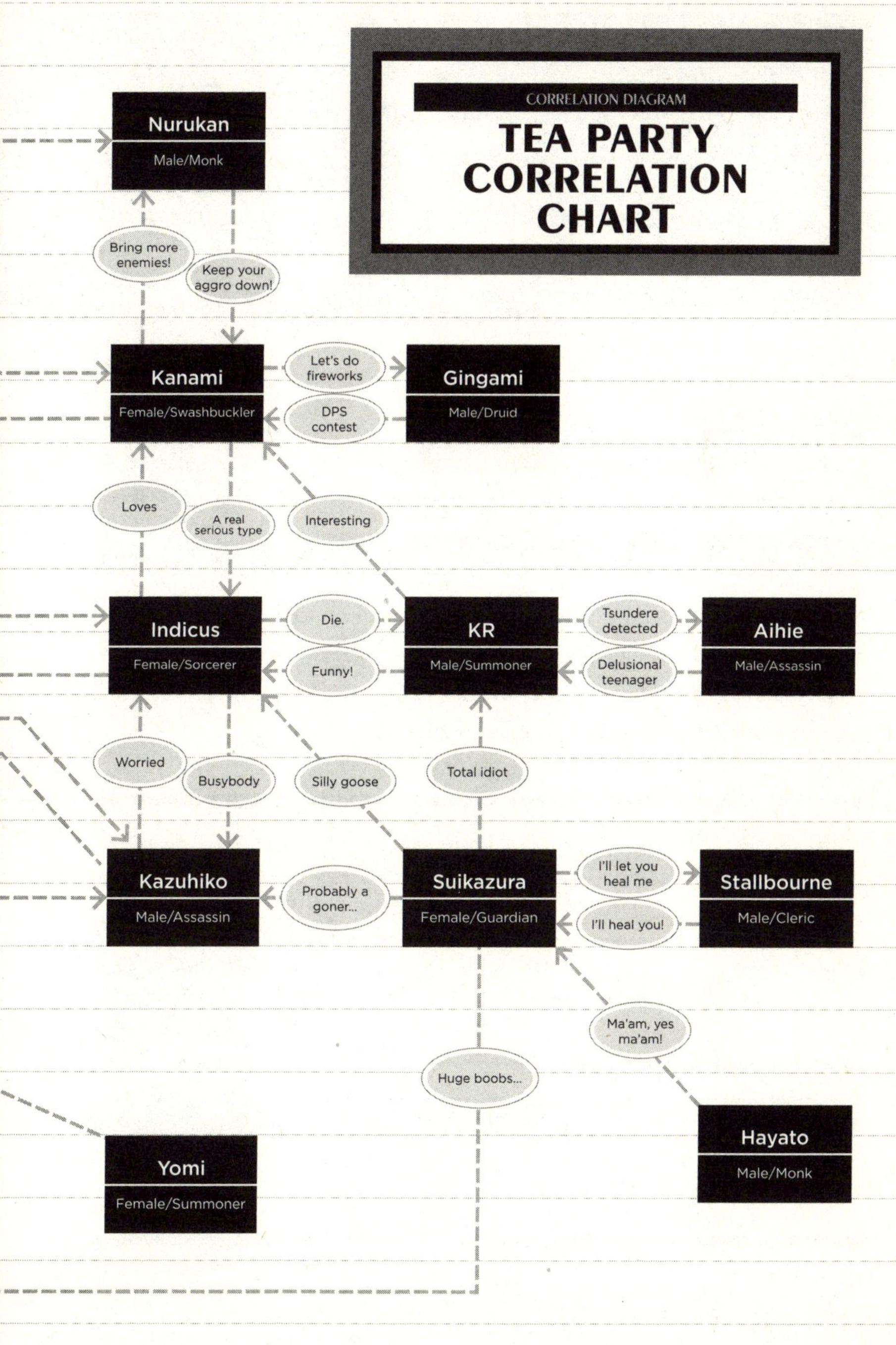

CORRELATION DIAGRAM
TEA PARTY CORRELATION CHART
Nurukan
Male/Monk
Bring more enemies!
Keep your aggro down!
Kanami
Female/Swashbuckler
Let's do fireworks
DPS contest
Gingami
Male/Druid
Loves
A real serious type
Interesting
Indicus
Female/Sorcerer
Die.
Funny!
KR
Male/Summoner
Tsundere detected
Delusional teenager
Aihie
Male/Assassin
Worried
Busybody
Silly goose
Total idiot
Kazuhiko
Male/Assassin
Probably a goner...
Suikazura
Female/Guardian
I'll let you heal me
I'll heal you!
Stallbourne
Male/Cleric
Ma'am, yes ma'am!
Huge boobs...
Hayato
Male/Monk
Yomi
Female/Summoner

ELDER TALES OVERSEAS SERVER ORIGINAL CLASS INTRODUCTIONS PART 1

On New Year's in 2014, the official site (tounomamare.com) put out a call for original classes for the overseas servers! Beginning on the next page, we'll introduce the classes we selected from among the many submissions. (On our end, we've edited and added to the introduction text.)

WHAT ARE THE OVERSEAS SERVER ORIGINAL CLASSES?

▶ WHAT ARE THE OVERSEAS SERVER ORIGINAL CLASSES?

Elder Tales is an MMORPG with players all over the world, and it has thirteen servers, which are tailored to the separate play regions. Each server has a few original main classes that players can choose from. For example, Samurai and Kannagi are the Yamato server's original "regional classes."

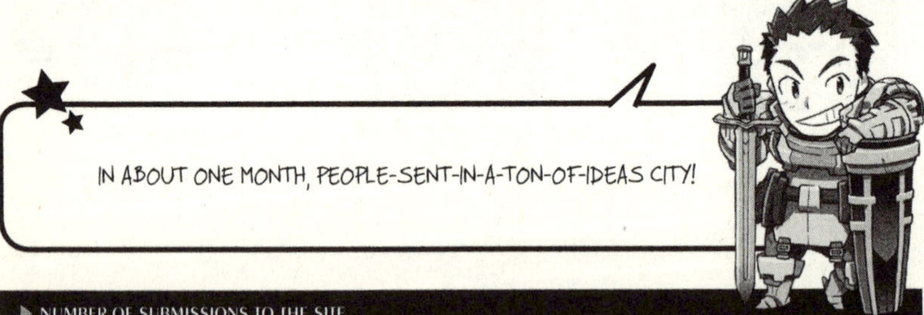

IN ABOUT ONE MONTH, PEOPLE-SENT-IN-A-TON-OF-IDEAS CITY!

▶ NUMBER OF SUBMISSIONS TO THE SITE

2400

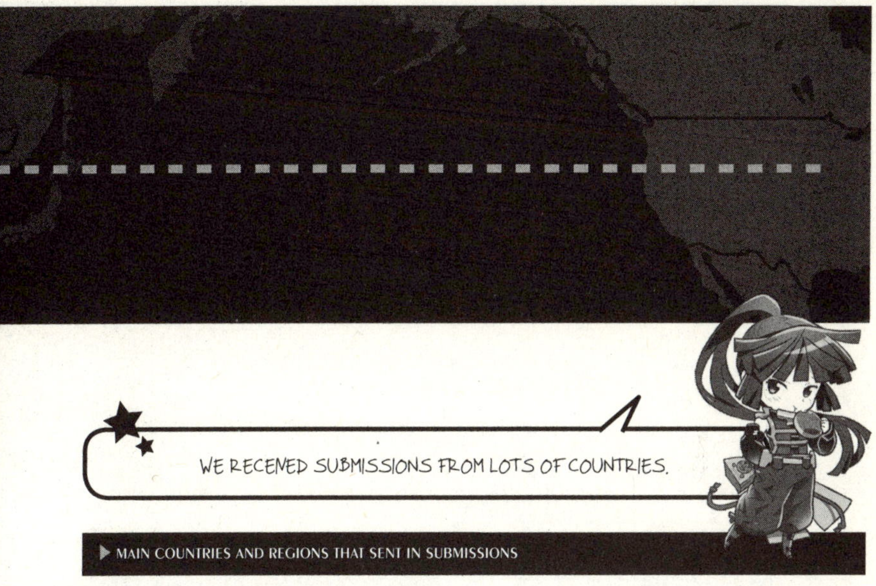
WE RECEIVED SUBMISSIONS FROM LOTS OF COUNTRIES.

▶ MAIN COUNTRIES AND REGIONS THAT SENT IN SUBMISSIONS

Argentina, Australia, Austria, the Bahamas, Brazil, Canada, Chile, Colombia, the Czech Republic, Denmark, England, Finland, France, Germany, Ghana, Greece, Hong Kong, Hungary, India, Indonesia, Iran, Ireland, Israel, Italy, Japan, Kazakhstan, Korea, Lebanon, Lithuania, Malaysia, Malta, Mexico, Morocco, the Netherlands, New Zealand, Nigeria, Norway, Panama, the People's Republic of China, Peru, the Philippines, Poland, Portugal, Puerto Rico, Qatar, Russia, Saudi Arabia, Singapore, Slovenia, Spain, Sweden, Switzerland, Taiwan, Thailand, Turkey, the United Arab Emirates, the United States, Venezuela, Vietnam, and more.

▶ COMMENT FROM MAMARE

This project began on a whim, but when we launched it, we got an absolute ton of submissions and ideas from all over the world. Thanks to the anime, the world of *Log Horizon* has expanded dramatically. When I asked the anime's director, Director Ishihira—even though I knew I was asking way too much—he actually gave me image sketches for the overseas classes! (See the pages at the beginning of the volume!) Now we're introducing those overseas classes to you, too. I hope they reach the people who made submissions. (They're all over the world, though...) I'd like to keep expanding the spheres of activity for the classes that appear here.

JUST LOOKING AT THEM IS THRILLING.
THERE ARE DRAWINGS OF THE OVERSEAS CLASSES BY LOG HORIZON ANIME DIRECTOR ISHIHIRA ON THE COLOR PAGES!

NORTH AMERICA

PIRATE

(Substitute for Samurai)

A Warrior class based on pirates. They fight using sabers and other swords, but their defensive gear is severely restricted. Like Samurai, this class holds the battle lines by using special skills to compensate for its low endurance. The sense of balance Pirates develop in shipboard battles gives them resistance to move-obstruction effects, and they have tricky attack methods that use things like hooks and ropes. They're well suited to the sea-related quests implemented on the North, Central, and South American servers, and there were lots of players who shuttled between the servers on the American continent as they played.

MEDICINE MAN

(Substitute for Kannagi)

A Recovery class known for using their own body as a medium, drawing power from the various totems that live on land and using that energy to work spells of healing and protection. They're able to use Ghost Walk, a unique spell that lets them evade damage by temporarily turning into spirit beings. In addition, their ability to use the Ritual of God-Channeling (which Kannagi can use as well) is greatly expanded, and many self-reinforcement skills can be implemented. Sacred Eagle and the many other special skills that are linked to local totem legends have a rich variety of special effects, and this made them popular on video submission sites.

ORIGINAL CLASS

SOUTH AND CENTRAL AMERICA

PAJÉ

(Substitute for Druid)

A Recovery class that's also known as "Witch Doctor." In addition to being able to summon various spirits and use them as servants, they can amplify the effects of their recovery spells by using medicinal herbs, consumable items unique to this class. The medicinal herbs that overflow from their bags are practically a synonym for Pajé. SPEEE, the development company in charge of the South and Central American server, didn't have a sizable budget, and it often purchased secondary usage rights for additional graphics and effects from other servers. As a result, Pajé equipment is sometimes different-colored versions of things from other servers.

CAPOERISTA

(Substitute for Monk)

A Warrior class that excels at bare-handed fighting and places particular emphasis on kicks. It has various stances that are based on capoeira skills, and it's possible to pay out powerful kicks from handstands or while falling. The magnificent acrobatic movements were incorporated through motion capture, and they were incredibly popular on video sites as well. As a substitute class for Monk, they're tough to handle, and the performance of their combos is about two rungs lower, but in exchange, their power has been adjusted toward the high end with a focus on kicks, the class's trademark symbol.

KOREA

A Warrior class that bears the name of a legendary martial arts group. They're particularly good at wielding one-handed weapons, such as straight, uncurved swords and large-bladed swords known as *hwando*. Although they aren't able to equip shields, they have high damage reduction abilities built around parrying. However, their goading motions to fan opponents' aggro and their special taunting skills—which are powerful but unwieldy, with overlong recast times—make using them as tanks rather tricky. Many exclusive pieces of equipment were implemented for them, such as scabbards with beautiful graphics and magnificent pieces of jewel-studded defensive gear, and they were a bit of a local attraction.

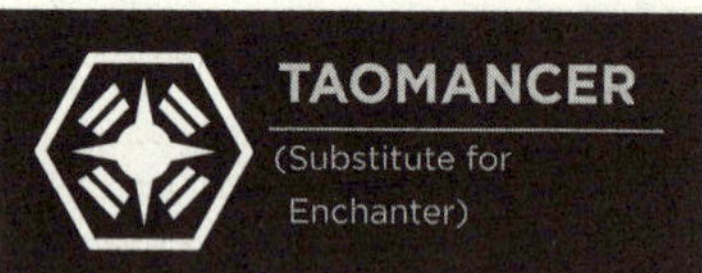

A Magic Attack class said to have acquired supernatural powers by training to become immortal mountain wizards. They can invoke good and bad luck at will and are outstanding at weakening their enemies or strengthening their companions. This substitute class was added with the expansion pack *Cendrillon's Legacy*, and some of the veteran players on the Korean server are Enchanters with the same specifications as those on the North American server. (It currently isn't possible to create them.) Since its development resources were shared with Hwarang, Taomancer is rather drab when it comes to additional items and effects, and its popularity is apparently stagnant.

ORIGINAL CLASS

CHINA

DAOSHI

(Substitute for Sorcerer)

A Magic Attack class well versed in the powers of nature. It fundamentally echoes the Sorcerer class: Daoshi wield elemental power freely and excel at defeating their enemies with lightning, flame, snow, and ice. A portion of the special skills with long recast times have been weakened, but to compensate for that, system items known as "treasure items" have been implemented as class-exclusive equipment. Since treasure items dramatically boost the effects of special skills of any attribute, the Daoshi on the Chinese server tackle raids in search of a variety of such items. The battles of Daoshi who have a full range of treasure items are adorned with elaborate, dazzling VFX.

YOUXIA

(Substitute for Samurai)

A Warrior class that uses finely honed martial arts in order to repay its obligations. Although, like Samurai, it has some restrictions on equipment, the class is able to use a variety of weapons, including swords, katanas, spears, axes, halberds, and more. The motions for each special skill and stance are extremely elaborate, and it's said that the Youxia "seem to be playing a different game." Because they have a lot of exclusive weapons and defensive gear, they have many fans. In addition, because rankers on the Chinese server were able to register their own aliases on the system, crowds of domestic and foreign players gathered and competed to defeat them.

→ Part 2 will appear in the next "overseas" edition! Keep an eye out for it.

Adventurer, you whose weight is borne by your winged soul! The mystical world of Theldesia is home to dragons and giants, magical beasts, and demihumans. Fragrant green winds blow across this new yet ancient land that opens before you like a blank page. Fill it with your life.
LOG HORIZON

【GLOSSARY】

▶*ELDER TALES*

A "SWORD AND SORCERY"—THEMED ONLINE GAME AND ONE OF THE LARGEST IN THE WORLD. AN MMORPG FAVORED BY SERIOUS GAMERS, IT BOASTS A TWENTY-YEAR HISTORY.

▶THE CATASTROPHE

A TERM FOR THE INCIDENT IN WHICH USERS WERE TRAPPED INSIDE THE *ELDER TALES* GAME WORLD. IT AFFECTED THE THIRTY THOUSAND JAPANESE USERS WHO WERE ONLINE WHEN *HOMESTEADING THE NOOSPHERE*, THE GAME'S TWELFTH EXPANSION PACK, WAS INTRODUCED.

▶ADVENTURER

THE GENERAL TERM FOR A GAMER WHO IS PLAYING *ELDER TALES*. WHEN BEGINNING THE GAME, PLAYERS SELECT HEIGHT, CLASS, AND RACE FOR THESE IN-GAME DOUBLES. THE TERM IS MAINLY USED BY NON-PLAYER CHARACTERS TO REFER TO PLAYERS.

▶PEOPLE OF THE EARTH

THE NAME NON-PLAYER CHARACTERS USE FOR THEMSELVES. THE CATASTROPHE DRASTICALLY INCREASED THEIR NUMBERS FROM WHAT THEY WERE IN THE GAME. THEY NEED TO SLEEP AND EAT LIKE REGULAR PEOPLE, SO IT'S HARD TO TELL THEM APART FROM PLAYERS WITHOUT CHECKING THE STATUS SCREEN.

▶THE HALF-GAIA PROJECT

A PROJECT TO CREATE A HALF-SIZED EARTH INSIDE *ELDER TALES*. ALTHOUGH IT'S NEARLY THE SAME SHAPE AS EARTH, THE DISTANCES ARE HALVED, AND IT HAS ONLY ONE-FOURTH THE AREA.

▶AGE OF MYTH

A GENERAL TERM FOR THE ERA SAID TO HAVE BEEN DESTROYED IN THE OFFICIAL BACKSTORY OF THE *ELDER TALES* ONLINE GAME. IT WAS BASED ON THE CULTURE AND CIVILIZATION OF THE REAL WORLD. SUBWAYS AND BUILDINGS ARE THE RUINED RELICS OF THIS ERA.

▶THE OLD WORLD

THE WORLD WHERE SHIROE AND THE OTHERS LIVED BEFORE *ELDER TALES* BECAME ANOTHER WORLD AND TRAPPED THEM. A TERM FOR EARTH, THE REAL WORLD, ETC.

▶GUILDS

TEAMS COMPOSED OF MULTIPLE PLAYERS. MANY PLAYERS BELONG TO THEM, BOTH BECAUSE IT'S EASIER TO CONTACT AFFILIATED MEMBERS AND INVITE THEM ON ADVENTURES AND ALSO BECAUSE GUILDS PROVIDE CONVENIENT SERVICES (SUCH AS MAKING IT EASIER TO RECEIVE AND SEND ITEMS).

▶THE ROUND TABLE COUNCIL

THE TOWN OF AKIBA'S SELF-GOVERNMENT ORGANIZATION, FORMED AT SHIROE'S PROPOSAL. COMPOSED OF ELEVEN GUILDS, INCLUDING MAJOR COMBAT AND PRODUCTION GUILDS AND GUILDS THAT COLLECTIVELY REPRESENT SMALL AND MIDSIZED GUILDS, IT'S IN A POSITION TO LEAD THE REFORMATION IN AKIBA.

▶LOG HORIZON

THE NAME OF THE GUILD SHIROE FORMED AFTER THE CATASTROPHE. ITS FOUNDING MEMBERS—AKATSUKI, NAOTSUGU, AND NYANTA—HAVE BEEN JOINED BY THE TWINS MINORI AND TOUYA. THEIR HEADQUARTERS IS IN A RUINED BUILDING PIERCED BY A GIANT ANCIENT TREE ON THE OUTSKIRTS OF AKIBA.

▶THE CRESCENT MOON LEAGUE

THE NAME OF THE GUILD MARI LEADS. ITS PRIMARY PURPOSE IS TO SUPPORT MIDLEVEL PLAYERS. HENRIETTA, MARI'S FRIEND SINCE THEIR DAYS AT A GIRLS' HIGH SCHOOL, ACTS AS ITS ACCOUNTANT.

▶THE DEBAUCHERY TEA PARTY

THE NAME OF A GROUP OF PLAYERS THAT SHIROE, NAOTSUGU, AND NYANTA BELONGED TO AT ONE TIME. IT WAS ACTIVE FOR ABOUT TWO YEARS, AND ALTHOUGH IT WASN'T A GUILD, IT'S STILL REMEMBERED IN *ELDER TALES* AS A LEGENDARY BAND OF PLAYERS.

▶FAIRY RINGS

TRANSPORTATION DEVICES LOCATED IN FIELDS. THE DESTINATIONS ARE TIED TO THE PHASES OF THE MOON, AND IF PLAYERS USE THEM AT THE WRONG TIME, THERE'S NO TELLING WHERE THEY'LL END UP. AFTER THE CATASTROPHE, SINCE STRATEGY WEBSITES ARE INACCESSIBLE, ALMOST NO ONE USES THEM.

▶ZONE

A UNIT THAT DESCRIBES RANGE AND AREA IN *ELDER TALES*. IN ADDITION TO FIELDS, DUNGEONS, AND TOWNS, THERE ARE ZONES AS SMALL AS SINGLE HOTEL ROOMS. DEPENDING ON THE PRICE, IT'S SOMETIMES POSSIBLE TO BUY THEM.

▶THELDESIA

THE NAME FOR THE GAME WORLD CREATED BY THE HALF-GAIA PROJECT. A WORD THAT'S EQUIVALENT TO "EARTH" IN THE REAL WORLD.

▶SPECIAL SKILL

VARIOUS SKILLS USED BY ADVENTURERS. ACQUIRED BY LEVELING UP YOUR MAIN CLASS OR SUBCLASS. EVEN WITHIN THE SAME SKILL, THERE ARE FOUR RANKS—ELEMENTARY, INTERMEDIATE, ESOTERIC, AND SECRET—AND IT'S POSSIBLE TO MAKE SKILLS GROW BY INCREASING YOUR PROFICIENCY.

▶MAIN CLASS

THESE GOVERN COMBAT ABILITIES IN *ELDER TALES*, AND PLAYERS CHOOSE ONE WHEN BEGINNING THE GAME. THERE ARE TWELVE TYPES, THREE EACH IN FOUR CATEGORIES: WARRIOR, WEAPON ATTACK, RECOVERY, AND MAGIC ATTACK. SEE THE SECTION BELOW FOR DETAILS.

▶SUBCLASS

ABILITIES THAT AREN'T DIRECTLY INVOLVED IN COMBAT BUT COME IN HANDY DURING GAME PLAY. ALTHOUGH THERE ARE ONLY TWELVE MAIN CLASSES, THERE ARE OVER FIFTY SUBCLASSES, AND THEY'RE A JUMBLED MIX OF EVERYTHING FROM CONVENIENT SKILL SETS TO JOKE ELEMENTS.

▶MYSTERY

ALSO CALLED OVERSKILL BY SOME PLAYERS. UNIQUE, POWERFUL TECHNIQUES THAT ARE UNLIKE CONVENTIONAL SPECIAL SKILLS. CREATED WHEN INDIVIDUAL PLAYERS EVOLVE AND EXPAND ABILITIES FROM THE DAYS OF THE GAME.

▶ARC-SHAPED ARCHIPELAGO YAMATO

THE WORLD OF THELDESIA IS DESIGNED BASED ON REAL-WORLD EARTH. THE ARC-SHAPED ARCHIPELAGO YAMATO IS THE REGION THAT MAPS TO JAPAN, AND IT'S DIVIDED INTO FIVE AREAS: THE EZZO EMPIRE; THE DUCHY OF FOURLAND; THE NINE-TAILS DOMINION; EASTAL, THE LEAGUE OF FREE CITIES; AND THE HOLY EMPIRE OF WESTLANDE.

▶CAST TIME

THE PREPARATION TIME NEEDED WHEN USING A SPECIAL SKILL. THESE ARE SET FOR EACH SEPARATE SKILL, AND MORE POWERFUL SKILLS TEND TO HAVE LONGER CAST TIMES. WITH COMBAT-TYPE SPECIAL SKILLS, IT'S POSSIBLE TO MOVE DURING CAST TIME, BUT WITH MAGIC-BASED SKILLS, SIMPLY MOVING INTERRUPTS CASTING.

▶ MAIN CLASSES
[WARRIOR CLASSES]
[WEAPON ATTACK CLASSES]
GUARDIAN
BOASTS THE HIGHEST DEFENSE. ABLE TO ATTRACT ENEMIES WITH TAUNTS.
ASSASSIN
A FOCUSED ATTACKER. SKILLED WITH A WIDE VARIETY OF WEAPONS.
SAMURAI
USES JAPANESE EQUIPMENT AND TECHNIQUES WITH POWERFUL EFFECTS.
SWASHBUCKLER
A VERSATILE, MOBILE FIGHTER. USES TWO SWORDS.
MONK
A BALANCED TYPE. SHORT ON WEAPONRY, BUT HAS FANTASTIC EVASIVE SKILLS.
BARD
A LIGHTLY EQUIPPED WARRIOR. USES A WIDE RANGE OF "SONGS" WITH MAGICAL EFFECTS.

▶MOTION BIND

REFERS TO THE WAY YOUR BODY FREEZES UP AFTER YOU'VE USED A SPECIAL SKILL. DURING MOTION BIND, ALL ACTIONS ARE IMPOSSIBLE, INCLUDING MOVEMENT.

▶RECAST TIME

THE AMOUNT OF TIME YOU HAVE TO WAIT AFTER YOU'VE USED A SPECIAL SKILL BEFORE YOU CAN USE IT AGAIN. THIS RESTRICTION MAKES IT VERY DIFFICULT TO USE A SPECIFIC SPECIAL SKILL SEVERAL TIMES IN A ROW. SOME SPECIAL SKILLS HAVE SUCH LONG RECAST TIMES THAT THEY CAN BE USED ONLY ONCE PER DAY.

▶CALL OF HOME

A BASIC TYPE OF SPECIAL SKILL THAT ALL ADVENTURERS LEARN. IT INSTANTLY RETURNS YOU TO THE LAST SAFE AREA WITH A TEMPLE THAT YOU VISITED, BUT ONCE YOU USE IT, YOU CAN'T USE IT AGAIN FOR TWENTY-FOUR HOURS.

▶RAID

THE TERM FOR A BATTLE FOUGHT WITH NUMBERS LARGER THAN THE NORMAL SIX-MEMBER PARTIES THAT ADVENTURERS USUALLY FORM. IT CAN ALSO BE USED TO REFER TO A UNIT MADE UP OF MANY PEOPLE. FAMOUS EXAMPLES INCLUDE TWENTY-FOUR-MEMBER FULL RAIDS AND NINETY-SIX-MEMBER LEGION RAIDS.

▶RACE

THERE ARE A VARIETY OF HUMANOID RACES IN THE WORLD OF THELDESIA. ADVENTURERS MAY CHOOSE TO PLAY AS ONE OF EIGHT RACES: HUMAN, ELF, DWARF, HALF ALV, FELINOID, WOLF-FANG, FOXTAIL, AND RITIAN. THESE ARE SOMETIMES CALLED BY THE GENERAL TERM "THE 'GOOD' HUMAN RACES."

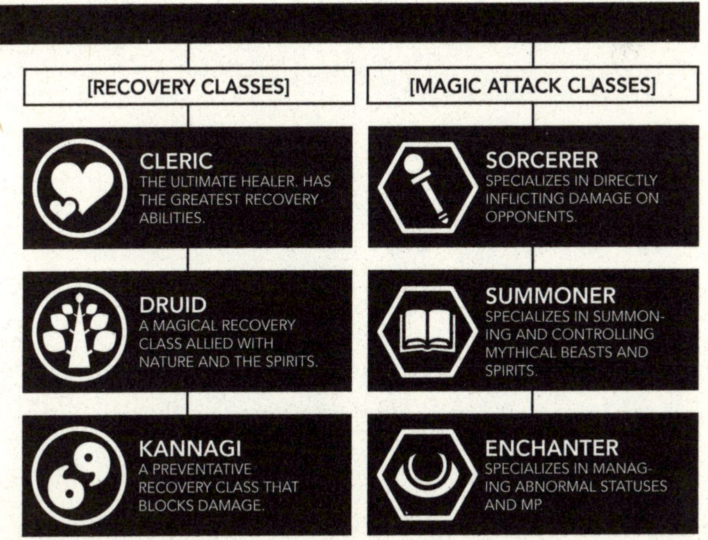

[RECOVERY CLASSES]
[MAGIC ATTACK CLASSES]
CLERIC
THE ULTIMATE HEALER. HAS THE GREATEST RECOVERY ABILITIES.
SORCERER
SPECIALIZES IN DIRECTLY INFLICTING DAMAGE ON OPPONENTS.
DRUID
A MAGICAL RECOVERY CLASS ALLIED WITH NATURE AND THE SPIRITS.
SUMMONER
SPECIALIZES IN SUMMONING AND CONTROLLING MYTHICAL BEASTS AND SPIRITS.
KANNAGI
A PREVENTATIVE RECOVERY CLASS THAT BLOCKS DAMAGE.
ENCHANTER
SPECIALIZES IN MANAGING ABNORMAL STATUSES AND MP.

AFTERWORD

I wrote something in an afterword about "wanting to put out one more volume before the year was over," didn't I? This is Mamare Touno. I was going to ask Ms. F——ta if we could take that bit out of the previous afterword when we published reprints, but I didn't. It wouldn't have solved anything. On the contrary, I realized that it would be more constructive to claim that March is still 2014. Saying this stuff is making me feel really ineffective.

It's currently a certain day after (cough, cough) Valentine's. The second season of the *Log Horizon* anime is broadcasting its second half. The younger group's adventure is over, and new trouble is bearing down on Akiba.

Thank you very much for buying this volume, *Log Horizon, Volume 9: Go East, Kanami!* This time, for a change, the protagonist is the American geek Leonardo. The heroine is the elegant maid girl Coppélia. She's accompanied by (how mean!) Elias and KR. And our hero, Kanami, finally makes her appearance. The stage is Aorsoi, in Central Asia. I've been there once; I remember the blue of the sky really was perfectly clear, and there was a steel-like darkness to it. It wasn't a vague, soft "sky blue." It was sharper, like cobalt.

What with this and that, at the end of March, a book called *Log Horizon TRPG Replay 3—Goat-Slime Tank and the Endless Journey—Part 1* will be released at the same time as this volume. What's that "Part 1" bit about?! What a disaster. Anyway, I'd love it if you'd pick that one up, too.

Moving on, let's talk about the second-term heroine.

In other words, about Ms. F——ta, my supervising editor.

We've been holding preparatory meetings for a little while now (and this is an open secret, but the world is moving forward on a terrifying schedule. The cause-and-effect relationship between writing and printing has gone off-kilter, and the order of the universe is crumbling), and Ms. F——ta abruptly said, "You know, I'm starting to see light!"

I'm in the same painful predicament as she is, so it was hard for me to bring it up, but I thought the "light" she'd started to see now, right as we were finishing the proofreading, might be some kind of intracerebral narcotic substance… But I couldn't ask her that. I wondered if she was okay.

"Are you okay?"

"I'm fine!" *Bounce.*

"You weren't energetic before, you know."

"I didn't have any energy before."

What's that supposed to mean?

"Because I was hungry…"

Had she disappeared from the meeting because she'd been eating? Apparently.

For a little while, I thought we'd cleared that up, but then:

"I had *dandan* noodles, so my head works better now!"

So she eats things besides meat. I thought spicy noodles were probably energy efficient.

"I'm super-energetic now! At this point, I think I can make it!" *Bounce, ba-bounce.*

"Uh-oh. It says 'Go West' here!"

"You're right! That's a shock! Seriously not good!"

And so we fixed it.

The book you hold in your hands was made from meat, marmalade sandwiches, and *dandan* noodles.

* * *

With that report on super-close-range current events, this has been *Log Horizon 9*.

As we live out our lives in our own ways, being aware of standards is pretty important. However, it's hard to internalize the boundaries between good and evil by learning them as rules. Or actually, just reading rules is rough to begin with.

For that reason, most boys (girls probably do this, too, by a different route) foster their ideas of "standards" through stories, instead of through the rules themselves. I don't mean difficult stories or anything like that. I'm talking about tales of heroes.

I happen to be male myself, so I have solid knowledge about that. Courage, tackling difficulties, the spirit of chivalry, self-restraint, nobility—you really can't have a hero story without those things. The same goes for friendship, humanity, and sympathy. We learn these rule-precursors, these role models, from anime, special effect–driven programs, manga, and novels.

What am I talking about, you ask? I'm making excuses for the fact that I only consume things like that at my age.

This volume, *Log Horizon 9*, was a story that revolved around "hero memories" like those.

It's true that almost all little boys idolize heroes, and they try to live by their example. However, in many cases, when those heroes hold on to their innate goodness through everything, there are separate abilities in the background. It takes ability to hold fast to your own will, even if it's in the cause of justice, and on top of that, you also need to put in a lot of effort. The vast majority of ordinary people don't have abilities on that level. In other words, at some point, that adoration breaks down.

Leonardo, who appears in this volume, is old enough to be living as a full-fledged member of society. However, his longing for heroes still smolders in his heart. What do we need in order to make those resolutions we'd given up on? *Log Horizon 9* is a rather old-school story.

This time as well, the items listed on the character status screens at the beginning of each chapter were collected on Twitter in November

2014. I used items from @4u49971475, @MZ_pipe, @NEO_hakukou, @chysophylax, @dharma0430, @drooop_ura, @highgetter, @hpsuke, @kazamasa504, @log_mousou, @mimitabu_sub, @nakigaeru, @nyaru kamini, @sig_cat, @suiga_mk_2, @tatara26, and @tk_leana. Thank you very much!! I can't list all your names here, but I'm grateful to everyone who submitted entries. It was hard to make selections this time. Everyone thought up great items, and there were a ton of them!

For details, and for the latest news, visit http://tounomamare.com/. You'll find information about Mamare Touno that isn't *Log Horizon*–related there as well. By the time this book is released, the remodel should be all finished, too.

They're also launching an SNS game. The details are on the book band of the Japanese edition. (I had them put Elias's medal in the game!)

And now for the acknowledgments! Shoji Masuda, the producer, and Kazuhiro Hara, the illustrator (please take care of your health). Tsubakiya Design, the designer, and little F——ta and Sakakibara of the editorial department! Oha, I'm in your debt this time, too! Tosho Printing, thank you very much! This time, in addition to those, I got lots of help from Ishihira, who directed the anime; Studio DEEN, the anime production company; Nemoto, who handled the series composition; and the rest of the script team, plus everyone at NHK and NEP. With regard to the SNS game *Log Horizon—Land of a New Adventure*, thank you GREE and AZITO. (There are a ton of elements.)

Since this book was (I think you'll have noticed already, but) an overseas volume, it has illustrations and background info for the region-limited main classes from servers other than Yamato! Get this: Director Ishihira of the anime designed them. They're really cool, and very cute. This was festival data that we chose from submissions sent in from all over the world, so I'm especially thrilled.

Volume 9 turned out to be really substantial. Now all that's left is for you to savor this book. Bon appétit!

Mamare "I seem to be living like a mole person" Touno

EXCELLENT WORK. (KAZUHIRO HARA)

▶LOG HORIZON, VOLUME 9
MAMARE TOUNO
ILLUSTRATION BY KAZUHIRO HARA

▶TRANSLATION BY TAYLOR ENGEL
COVER ART BY KAZUHIRO HARA

▶LOG HORIZON, VOLUME 9
GO EAST, KANAMI!

▶FIRST PUBLISHED IN JAPAN IN 2015 BY KADOKAWA CORPORATION ENTERBRAIN. ENGLISH TRANSLATION RIGHTS ARRANGED WITH KADOKAWA CORPORATION ENTERBRAIN THROUGH TUTTLE-MORI AGENCY, INC., TOKYO.

▶YEN ON
1290 AVENUE OF THE AMERICAS
NEW YORK, NY 10104

▶VISIT US AT YENPRESS.COM
FACEBOOK.COM/YENPRESS
TWITTER.COM/YENPRESS
YENPRESS.TUMBLR.COM
INSTAGRAM.COM/YENPRESS

▶FIRST YEN ON EDITION: OCTOBER 2017

▶YEN ON IS AN IMPRINT OF YEN PRESS, LLC.
THE YEN ON NAME AND LOGO ARE TRADEMARKS OF YEN PRESS, LLC.

▶LIBRARY OF CONGRESS CATALOGING-IN-PUBLICATION DATA
NAMES: TOUNO, MAMARE, AUTHOR. | HARA, KAZUHIRO, ILLUSTRATOR. | ENGEL, TAYLOR, TRANSLATOR.
TITLE: LOG HORIZON / MAMARE TOUNO ; ILLUSTRATION BY KAZUHIRO HARA ; TRANSLATION BY TAYLOR ENGEL.
DESCRIPTION: FIRST YEN ON EDITION. | NEW YORK, NY : YEN ON, 2017–
IDENTIFIERS: LCCN 2015038410 | ISBN 9780316383059 (V. 1 : PBK.) | ISBN 9780316263818 (V. 2 : PBK.) | ISBN 9780316263849 (V. 3 : PBK.) | ISBN 9780316263856 (V. 4 : PBK.) | ISBN 9780316263863 (V. 5 : PBK.) | ISBN 9780316263870 (V. 6 : PBK.) | ISBN 9780316263887 (V. 7 : PBK.) | ISBN 9780316470957 (V. 8 : PBK.) | ISBN 9780316470971 (V. 9 : PBK.)
SUBJECTS: | CYAC: SCIENCE FICTION. | BISAC: FICTION / SCIENCE FICTION / ADVENTURE.
CLASSIFICATION: LCC PZ7.1.T67 LOJ 2016 | DDC [FIC]—DC23
LC RECORD AVAILABLE AT HTTPS://LCCN.LOC.GOV/2015038410

ISBN: 978-0-316-47097-1

10 9 8 7 6 5 4 3 2 1

▶LSC-C

▶PRINTED IN THE UNITED STATES OF AMERICA

▶AUTHOR: **MAMARE TOUNO**

▶SUPERVISION: **SHOJI MASUDA**

▶ILLUSTRATION: **KAZUHIRO HARA**

▶AUTHOR: MAMARE TOUNO

A STRANGE LIFE-FORM THAT INHABITS THE TOKYO BOKUTOU SHITAMACHI AREA. IT'S BEEN TOSSING HALF-BAKED TEXT INTO A CORNER OF THE INTERNET SINCE THE YEAR 2000 OR SO. IT'S A FULLY AUTOMATIC, TEXT-LOVING MACRO THAT EATS AND DISCHARGES TEXT. IT DEBUTED AT THE END OF 2010 WITH *MAOYUU: MAOU YUUSHA* (*MAOYUU: DEMON KING AND HERO*). *LOG HORIZON* IS A RESTRUCTURED VERSION OF A NOVEL THAT RAN ON THE WEBSITE *SHOUSETSUKA NI NAROU* (*SO YOU WANT TO BE A NOVELIST*).

WEBSITE: HTTP://WWW.MAMARE.NET

▶SUPERVISION: SHOJI MASUDA

AS A GAME DESIGNER, HE'S WORKED ON *RINDA KYUUBU* (*RINDA CUBE*) AND *ORE NO SHIKABANE WO KOETE YUKE* (*STEP OVER MY DEAD BODY*), AMONG OTHERS. ALSO ACTIVE AS A NOVELIST, HE'S RELEASED THE *ONIGIRI NUEKO* (*ONI KILLER NUEKO*) SERIES, THE *HARUKA* SERIES, *JOHN & MARY: FUTARI HA SHOUKIN KASEGI* (*JOHN & MARY: BOUNTY HUNTERS*), *KIZUDARAKE NO BIINA* (*BEENA, COVERED IN WOUNDS*), AND MORE. HIS LATEST EFFORT IS HIS FIRST CHILDREN'S BOOK, *TOUMEI NO NEKO TO TOSHI UE NO IMOUTO* (*THE TRANSPARENT CAT AND THE OLDER LITTLE SISTER*). HE HAS ALSO WRITTEN *GEEMU DEZAIN NOU MASUDA SHINJI NO HASSOU TO WAZA* (*GAME DESIGN BRAIN: SHINJI MASUDA'S IDEAS AND TECHNIQUES*).

TWITTER ACCOUNT: SHOJIMASUDA

▶ILLUSTRATION: KAZUHIRO HARA

AN ILLUSTRATOR WHO LIVES IN ZUSHI. ORIGINALLY A HOME GAME DEVELOPER. IN ADDITION TO ILLUSTRATING BOOKS, HE'S ALSO ACTIVE IN MANGA AND DESIGN. LATELY, HE'S BEEN HAVING FUN FLYING A BIOKITE WHEN HE GOES ON WALKS. HE'S BEEN WORKING ON THE *LOG HORIZON* COMICALIZATION PROJECT WITH COMIC CLEAR SINCE 2012.

WEBSITE: HTTP://WWW.NINEFIVE95.COM/IG/